# Silver in the Blood

ALSO BY JESSICA DAY GEORGE

*Dragon Slippers*
*Dragon Flight*
*Dragon Spear*

*Tuesdays at the Castle*
*Wednesdays in the Tower*
*Thursdays with the Crown*

*Sun and Moon, Ice and Snow*

*Princess of the Midnight Ball*
*Princess of Glass*
*Princess of the Silver Woods*

# SILVER IN THE BLOOD

## JESSICA DAY GEORGE

BLOOMSBURY

NEW YORK   LONDON   NEW DELHI   SYDNEY

First published in the United States of America in July 2015
by Bloomsbury Children's Books
www.bloomsbury.com

Bloomsbury is a registered trademark of Bloomsbury Publishing Plc

For information about permission to reproduce selections from this book, write to
Permissions, Bloomsbury Children's Books, 1385 Broadway, New York, New York 10018
Bloomsbury books may be purchased for business or promotional use. For information on
bulk purchases please contact Macmillan Corporate and Premium Sales Department at
specialmarkets@macmillan.com

Library of Congress Cataloging-in-Publication Data
George, Jessica Day.
Silver in the blood / by Jessica Day George.
pages    cm
ISBN 978-1-61963-431-2 (hardcover) • ISBN 978-1-61963-432-9 (e-book)
[1. Shapeshifters—Fiction. 2. Supernatural—Fiction. 3. Cousins—Fiction. 4. Family
life—Romania—Fiction. 5. Romania—History—19th century—Fiction.] I. Title.
PZ7.G293317Sil 2015          [Fic]—dc23          2014027934

Book design by Donna Mark
Typeset by Westchester Book Composition
Printed and bound in the U.S.A. by Thomson-Shore Inc., Dexter, Michigan
2 4 6 8 10 9 7 5 3 1

All papers used by Bloomsbury Publishing, Inc., are natural, recyclable products
made from wood grown in well-managed forests. The manufacturing processes
conform to the environmental regulations of the country of origin.

*Once again for my husband*

# SILVER
## IN THE
# BLOOD

26 April 1897

Dearest Lou,

    Whoever said that travel was exotic and full of adventure clearly has not sailed on the <u>White Lady</u>. Before you worry yourself sick that I am sitting in some squalid cabin, suffering from seasickness, fear not! Of course it is all that is respectable and luxurious, and I would never do something so horribly undignified as become seasick. Fear, rather, that I, your dearest cousin and bosom companion since infancy, shall die of boredom before the trip is even halfway through! I do not know why Papa would not allow me to take the train from London. I could have stopped in Paris and waited for you, and we could have made our way to Bucharest together. The Orient Express is all that is fashionable.

    But my mother was adamant that I avoid Paris at all costs. I am to be punished until the end of time for one moment of frivolity! Or do you think it was some fancy brought on by her delicate condition? She couldn't possibly know that William Carver is spending the summer in Paris, could she? I certainly didn't tell her! I have been dying to see Paris, and I could have gone shopping with you besides!

Aunt Kate reminds me endlessly that Bucharest is the Little Paris, and that should be good enough for me, but I disagree! Why limit myself to the "Little Paris" when I could have seen the larger one? And thus far there is nothing to see but ocean, and no shopping, and no Will Carver or any reasonable substitute. I am becoming most disagreeable. Aunt Kate is threatening to lock me in my cabin if I do not shake off my "mood," as she calls it. She has yet to see me in a true "mood," dare I say. Much more of this and I shall descend into a despair so black that no amount of elegant dinners in the dining room or walks along the ship's promenade to take the air will bring me out of it.

Unless, of course, we are attacked by pirates. Young, dashing pirates. Will Carver would look very handsome in pirate costume, don't you think, Lou? Oh, you are too far away to ask!

Dear Lou, the other thing that is missing is _you_! If you were here this would be far more bearable. I shall console myself that one of us shall see Paris—the real Paris—and that soon we will be reunited! Even if it is in a strange place! And I shan't even be able to send this letter until we reach land, which I pray is soon.

Much, much love,

D

# ROMANIA

Dacia picked up her book and put it down again. It was good, but rather lurid, with a ghost haunting some young woman trapped in a castle in Yorkshire. She'd bought it on her last day in England, and just couldn't summon the energy to finish it. Aunt Kate kept accusing her of pouting, but pouting was the furthest thing from her mind. She hated to admit it, even to Lou, but Dacia was worried.

Worrying was not something that she did a great deal. Dacia was who she was, and she made no apologies for it. One didn't get to be the most widely admired young lady in fashionable New York by apologizing or worrying. She knew the boundaries of good taste, and she never crossed them.

Or at least, she had never crossed them before she went to London, met Lord Johnny, and nearly ruined everything. And now she was restless and worried. Restlessness was something she knew well. She had felt this same restlessness all her life.

But worried was a different matter.

She knew that her mother would scream and shout and confine her to her room when she got home, but she didn't know when that would be. What Dacia feared more was that her mother would make Dacia stay in Romania for years, cut off from real society as punishment. Romania was hardly a backwater, nor would Dacia be living alone in some hut. Bucharest was indeed fashionable, and her mother's family was extremely wealthy. Dacia had scores of aunts, uncles, and cousins there, so she would hardly pine for company. But to be trapped there for years? It could not be contemplated.

And how much trouble was she in, really? Would her parents see temporary exile as punishment enough, or would they take stronger measures when she returned to New York? They knew everything, of course. Aunt Kate had sent a telegram immediately, and her mother's answering telegram had resulted in Dacia being hustled onto that dreadful ship. It was only by the sheerest luck that she had managed to break away from Aunt Kate to duck into a bookstore and buy the first two novels that she laid eyes on. Aunt Kate had decided not to add this to Dacia's list of crimes, however, when she came to the realization that a bored Dacia with nothing to do or read on a long journey would make life hell for her aunt.

Or, more of a hell than her aunt was already suffering. And that was the other thing that worried Dacia.

She had looked forward to visiting Romania all her life. The journey had been dangled before her like a treat for "when she was old enough" as long as she could remember. It had never been clear when that would be—until gossip indicated that Will Carver had asked his grandmother for her sapphire engagement ring. There was no other young lady in New York he might offer it to but Dacia. But before he even had the chance, Aunt Kate whisked her away to England to "acquire some polish" before meeting Lou and Lou's parents in Bucharest. To travel the world with Aunt Kate had been even more appealing to Dacia than receiving Will Carver's proposal. But now that Dacia was in disgrace, Aunt Kate was talking of their journey as though it were a punishment instead of a reward. Three months had become six, so that they could stay for Christmas, and Aunt Kate had begun to hint that even six months might not be long enough to mend Dacia's wild ways.

—⚬—

Not knowing how long that alleged treat would last was a bit alarming, but not half as alarming as Aunt Kate's behavior. Her aunt, a fixture in Dacia's life since the day she was born, was quite simply not herself, and Dacia had decided that she couldn't take the blame for all of Aunt Kate's behavior. Her chilliness on the ship was certainly because of her disappointment in Dacia, but once they boarded the train? No. That was something else. The closer they got to Bucharest, the more tension radiated from her aunt.

Romania was Kate's home—her childhood home, anyway. Her mother was here, her brothers, cousins, her dozens of nephews. Yet to Dacia's knowledge her aunt had not been back since moving to New York at age twenty with her two sisters.

And even now, as their train lurched through the countryside, her aunt was smoothing the lapels of her traveling suit with her gloved hands. Smoothing them over and over. Adjusting the belt of her skirt. Repinning her hat. Adjusting her gloves. Dacia had never seen her aunt fidget before. The book Aunt Kate was supposedly reading had long ago slid down her skirts and onto the floor of their compartment, and Kate appeared not to have noticed.

What was waiting for them in Bucharest that could make *Aunt Kate* nervous?

The train lurched to a stop, and now Dacia's book slithered down her skirts to the floor. When she picked it up, she picked up Aunt Kate's as well and gave it to her. Her aunt made no comment, but opened the book to the middle and made the appearance of reading. Dacia watched her aunt over the top of her own novel and saw that Kate didn't turn the page or move her eyes at all, just stared blindly at the words until the train started up again. When several men strode down the corridor outside their compartment, Aunt Kate put the book aside and didn't even pretend not to listen.

"Quite repulsive. And they've no idea how it got there." The man spoke Romanian, with aristocratic accents, and the scent of cigar smoke wafted into the compartment.

"Some animal dragged it onto the tracks and had to run off without its kill when the train came, most likely," another man said.

"What sort of animal can kill something that large?" The first man sounded almost admiring. "That's a whole cow out there!"

"Wolves, perhaps," his companion supplied. "They hunt in packs, you know . . ."

Dacia wrinkled her nose, but quickly unwrinkled it when she saw Aunt Kate's face. Rather than being mildly disgusted, her aunt had gone quite white.

The train had just reached its normal speed when it slowed again. The only good news was that this time it didn't stop, but continued crawling along as though it might have to call a halt at any moment. Dacia sighed. This was the longest journey of her life, and the combination of boredom and tension was about to send her screaming down the corridor for air or excitement or *something*. How did one write a travel journal that would be even remotely interesting to readers? The only thing of note that Dacia had to look at was Aunt Kate's taut mouth, and it was only notable to her, not to mention extremely worrisome.

The shade was down over the window to the corridor, but it didn't quite meet the window frame. Through that crack Dacia saw the red-and-gold livery of a train conductor, and made an abrupt decision. Without asking permission, she tossed aside her book, leaped up, and opened the door into the corridor.

"Hello there," she practically shouted in English, momentarily forgetting her Romanian.

The conductor jumped, startled by her sudden greeting.

"Good evening, miss," he said in Romanian, tipping his cap.

Dacia gathered herself to answer in that language. "What seems to be the problem, if I may ask? We are going dreadfully slowly. Not something wrong with the train, is there?" Dacia knew she was babbling and forced herself to stop.

"Not at all, miss," he said. He gave her a rueful smile. "Just some pests bothering the train."

"Some pests?" She looked down. She could not abide mice. She had had a spirited argument with Lord Johnny back in London that this was neither a sign of squeamishness nor cowardice, but merely practicality on the part of one who had to wear a great many long skirts and petticoats.

"A pack of wolves, miss. They're running alongside the tracks, and sometimes they dart across, like they're daring each other to play with the train. The driver slowed down so he wouldn't hit any of them, thinks it's bad luck. I say, that's one less dumb animal in the world, and who cares?" He shrugged. "Now they've gone and left something . . . unpleasant on the tracks, the filthy beasts."

"What a completely appalling attitude," Aunt Kate said coldly. She had risen and was looming over Dacia's shoulder.

The conductor stared past Dacia at Aunt Kate as if he'd seen a ghost. He made a weird little noise in his throat that might have been a whimper.

"Wolves are not only far smarter than you think; they are far smarter than *you*," Aunt Kate snapped at the man. Then she latched on to Dacia's elbow and pulled her niece inside the compartment, locking the door behind them.

Aunt Kate settled herself back in her seat with a small huffing noise and picked up her book again. "Don't fraternize with the staff, Dacia; it's common."

"Asking after problems with the train isn't fraternizing with the staff; it's merely being cautious," Dacia countered, but her heart wasn't really in the argument.

Nor was Aunt Kate's. She ignored Dacia for the next hour, staring out the window with what seemed to be a very real absorption. Aunt Kate's eyesight was excellent (Dacia and Lou had many times bemoaned both her keen eyesight and hearing as children), but Dacia was quite as sharp-eyed and she couldn't see anything out of the darkened glass at all. Clearly her aunt was just trying to keep her from talking. Although this wasn't unusual with Aunt Kate, it was unnerving now the way she kept her eyes glued to the window, and Dacia could actually smell the tension rolling off her aunt.

The silence went on for so long that Dacia stopped herself twice from asking her aunt what on earth was the matter with her. She decided instead to break the quiet with an innocuous comment about British fashions, when the creeping train came to a complete halt and the night air was shattered by gunshots. Aunt Kate leaped up as though she had been struck by lightning and went to the door of the compartment. Dacia half rose, and her aunt gave her a Look.

"Stay here. Don't move. Don't speak to anyone."

Kate went out, slamming the door behind her.

Dacia waited for ten minutes, which she felt showed herculean forbearance on her part.

What finally drove her from the compartment was the sound of running in the corridor, followed by more gunshots and shouts from outside the train. Her heart was pounding and her legs shook when she stood, but if bandits were attacking them, she certainly wasn't going to sit in her compartment and wait for someone to attack her. And where in heaven's name was Aunt Kate?

The corridor was eerily silent. The shades of every other compartment were closed, and the train seemed almost abandoned. She wanted to go to the front of the train and demand to know what was happening, but the gunshots were coming from that direction and Aunt Kate had gone to the rear. Dacia was certain that her aunt knew more than she was letting on, so she decided that following Aunt Kate was the better idea.

But by the time she had reached the second-to-last car there was no sign of her aunt, and she worried that she had passed her in one of the compartments. Dacia hoped that she hadn't been foolish enough to get off the train entirely! The last car was a smoking car for the gentlemen, and Dacia could not imagine her aunt setting foot in there. Not only would it be highly improper, but Kate was very sensitive to strong odors. She often claimed that she had never married because she couldn't find a man who didn't reek of cigars.

Still, Dacia was sure that her aunt had gone this way. And she could see a dim figure through the back window, standing on the deck in front of the smoking car. Taking a deep breath, because she also had a sensitive nose, Dacia opened the back door.

To her utmost shock, she discovered Aunt Kate wrapped in the arms of a tall man in a long cloak. Dacia nearly choked on her own breath. She had never seen two people kiss so passionately, and had certainly never suspected *her* Aunt Kate of being capable of such . . . scandalous intimacy.

"Aunt *Kate!*" She found her voice.

The couple broke apart, and Aunt Kate turned toward her as though there were nothing out of the ordinary, despite her red lips and disheveled hair. The man bowed as elegantly as if they were in a ballroom. Then he gathered up his cloak and leaped off the train, disappearing into the darkness.

"I told you to stay in the compartment," Aunt Kate said coolly.

She went past Dacia into the train and started down the corridor without looking back. Not knowing what else to do, Dacia followed her in silence. At the door of their compartment, the conductor was waiting for them, wringing his hands. His face went white again when Aunt Kate looked at him, but he gathered himself to speak.

"You have to put a stop to this, *doamna mea*," the man said with respect and even a little fear. Dacia could hardly blame him, but she did think it was a bit much to address her aunt as "my lady."

"They were only paying tribute," Aunt Kate said, her tone even icier than before. "They have our attention, and are done now."

The man began to babble his thanks, but Aunt Kate ignored him as she went into the compartment. As they sat down and took up their books again, Aunt Kate leveled one of her sternest Looks at Dacia.

"Don't ever disobey me again," she said.

Dacia was dying to ask who that man was, and who was trying to pay tribute to them, and to get out her stationery and write down the whole incident for Lou, but she did nothing. Instead she found the marker in her book, opened it up, and from behind this barrier announced softly, "*I* haven't done anything wrong."

26 April 1897

To my dear Dacia,

I am writing to you even though this letter will probably reach you long after I arrive in Bucharest and we are together again. Even so, I must confide this strange thing that has happened to me, and I know that Mama and Papa would be very upset if I were to tell them. I have no desire to be mewed up in my cabin for the remainder of the journey, and I am sure that would be the consequence of my confidence.

There, enough teasing (you know I didn't mean to)! I will tell you that yesterday as I took the air upon the west deck, a strange young man approached me. There was no one else nearby, and I was watching the waves by myself. (They are quite mesmerizing, and I am often drawn to the promenade.) Quite suddenly there was a man at my elbow! I did not see him approach, he was simply there. He was very tan, or perhaps naturally swarthy, with very dark hair that had a reddish tint because of the setting sun. I had ample time to note all this, you see, as he also looked me over in the most blatant fashion! I became quite flushed and turned to walk away, when he began speaking to me.

"Are you the wing?" he said.

I stopped because it was such an odd question, and I did not understand it. I could not help myself: I turned and looked at him inquiringly. He had very dark eyes, almost black, and he was staring at me so intently I felt quite... well, quite naked, if you must know!

"Are you the wing?" He said it again, and looked me up and down yet again! "You are not the claw, and there is never a smoke anymore."

Complete gibberish, Dacia! What was I to do? I simply goggled at him for a moment. When I gathered myself, I started to turn away again, when he said, "You are the wing; I see it now."

Whatever that meant, I decided that it was outside of enough, and I gave him one of Aunt Kate's patented Looks. I'm sure you can guess which one, and many of New York's freshest young men would recognize it as well!

"Sir," I said, "the sun has gone to your head, I'm afraid. First you address me without an introduction, and now you are speaking in riddles. Good day!"

I marched away and went to my cabin as quickly as I could, but I was quite shaken, and not the least by my own boldness. It was all I could do to dress for dinner, and Mama and Papa were afraid that I had taken too much sun myself. I felt so queer that I almost confided in them, but I could not bring myself to do so in the end. And so I confide to you, Dacia, to unburden my heart and imagine your indignation, even though I cannot witness it firsthand.

I know that you are jealous of our stop in Paris, and would

love to spend days looking in all the shops and seeing all the sights, so I know that my reluctance will be a shock to you, for I would much rather we stopped not at all, and hastened onward to Romania. For even one such as I, ever chided for not being much in conversation, longs to have my bosom friend nearby so that you and I may speak face-to-face again. Please do not think me a goose for this, if you get this letter before I arrive!

Yours,
LouLou


P.S. Rather thought you'd like this clipping I found upon our arrival! I don't know who Mr. Arkady is, but look at the next paragraph!

# LA GAZETTE DE PARIS
## SOCIETY NOTES

ALL OF PARIS is agog at two new bachelors from foreign lands who have chosen to grace our fair city with their presence. The first eligible gentleman is Mr. Theophilus Arkady of Istanbul, lately arrived in our city on business. But despite his refusal to explain what this business might be, Mr. Arkady (the son of a prominent Turkish family) has been seen strolling the many parks and boulevards of Paris, quite sadly alone. We hope that Mr. Arkady finds someone to share his walks with soon. A noted opera lover, Mr. Arkady has also taken a box at the Paris Opera. Will he be staying the entire season? Certain young ladies breathlessly await the answer to that question!

And American society is surely the poorer for having lost Mr. William Carver, son of Mr. and Mrs. Henry Carver of New York City, who has been seen in our many parks and public gardens with his sketchbook in hand. Mr. Carver is a noted amateur artist, and we are sure that he has found ample inspiration in our Parisian beauties to occupy his brush for some time.

Monsieur and Madame Duchosne have been gadding about, despite her delicate cond—

# RUE DES BLANCHES

Lou had once had a governess who recommended she have a cold bath daily followed by two large spoonfuls of cod liver oil, to cure her of her nerves. She was very lucky in that, rather than taking the governess's advice, her father had simply dismissed the woman.

"My Louisa doesn't suffer from nerves," Mr. Neulander had insisted. "She is a tender child, and shy. I refuse to have her dunked in ice water every morning. It's more torture than cure!"

Lou's mother had protested at first. The governess's references had been impeccable: one of the Vanderbilt children had been in her care previously. But since Lou had never struck her as being nervous, either, she let the matter drop. In the end, Lou and Dacia had shared a governess: a kindly, rather horse-faced woman who spoke impeccable French as well as Romanian, having had a Romanian mother just like Lou and Dacia. Though this didn't improve Lou's shyness one whit, it was markedly better than being tipped into cold water like a Puritan accused of witchcraft.

Now that they were in Paris, however, Lou was feeling decidedly nervy, and wondered if she should order a cold bath the next morning. Of course, that would mean requesting such a thing from Vivienne, the frightening maid the hotel had assigned to Lou. Lou was doing everything possible for herself in an effort to avoid Vivienne. She missed Millie, her maid back home in New York, with great ferocity. Millie had a cheerful face and a snub nose covered with freckles, and brought Lou hot chocolate when she woke, without being asked. She knew just how Lou liked her room and her clothes and her food, and she never seemed to be judging any of her preferences.

Lou had actually dared argue with her mother about bringing Millie, but Maria had been adamant that they not bring any of their servants, including her own lady's maid and Lou's father's valet, which displeased Mr. Neulander a great deal. Maria had insisted that her family's properties in Romania were well staffed and so were the hotels, and thus there was no need. Now that Lou had encountered a real French maid, however, her mother's foible had gone beyond oddity to causing her outright distress.

Added to the strain of travel, of being in a strange place and meeting strange people every day, having snobbish maids who pretended they didn't understand you even though you had been told for years that your French was perfect, there was also That Awful Man to deal with.

That Awful Man, as Lou had dubbed him, was the man from the ship who had approached her without invitation and spoken so strangely. He was here, in Paris, and he seemed to appear out of nowhere whenever Lou left the house. She saw him watching her as she strolled the boulevards with her family, saw him sitting alone a few tables away at restaurants, even saw him on the bank of the Seine as they took a riverboat cruise. He was tall and dark, and perhaps twenty years old. His clothes were good, without being exceptional, and he was always watching her. Every time he was near, Lou felt the most uncomfortable tingle up her spine, and she was coming to dread leaving the hotel.

What if he approached her again? What if he spoke to her? His words were meaningless, truly, but there was something upsetting about them all the same. He didn't appear mad, and yet he spoke nonsense with the greatest air of conviction! She wished Dacia were there, and not only so they could discuss the strange events that her cousin had witnessed. Lou had gotten a letter from Dacia that very morning, describing Aunt Kate's scandalous tryst on the train and her enigmatic words about someone (or something) paying tribute.

Full of questions about this, Lou didn't even notice as That Awful Man sidled up to her outside a milliner's shop. Her mother was still inside, trying on hats, and had asked Lou to step out on the sidewalk and wait for her father, who was meeting them for lunch.

The day was beautiful: the spring sunshine sparkling off the glass windows of the shops, and the Parisians out in their finest pastels. Lou tried to put the scandal with Aunt Kate and the man on the train out of her mind and enjoy the weather and the glory of being in Paris, when she felt that sensation travel up her spine.

"You are the Wing, I see it clearly," said a voice behind her.

She whirled to see That Awful Man standing no more than a pace away.

"And you are more than that," he said. "You are a houri, taunting me with your gray eyes and your delectable form!"

Once again, his words did not make sense, although that bit about her delectable form sounded quite vulgar, and Lou was absolutely at the end of her tether. Without thinking, she raised her still-furled parasol and struck him about the head and shoulders with a violence that surprised both of them.

He shouted an oath in some unknown language and ran off. Lou looked after him for a moment, panting, and screamed when someone came up behind her and asked if she was all right. She spun around to see her father standing there with a concerned look, and promptly burst into tears. Mr. Neulander quickly hailed a hansom and took her back to the hotel, where she lay on her bed with a cool cloth over her eyes until evening. Her mother insisted that she take supper on a tray in her room, and Lou did not object, but while everyone else was dining she pulled on a dress and went downstairs to the hotel library, to look up the word *houri*.

Then she rather wished she hadn't.

## THE DIARY OF MISS DACIA VREEHOLT

*4 May 1897*

The ship from London to Greece was deathly boring. The train from Greece to Romania (Bucharest, to be exact) was grimy yet interesting. But the last few days shut in this house with no callers and no one to talk to but the servants were truly awful! I thought that I was brought here to get close to my mother's family, yet the only member in evidence is Aunt Kate. I have known Aunt Kate all my life, and she is therefore not all that interesting to me. (Unless she continues to have secret trysts with strange men, in which case she becomes very interesting, but not much of a role model for a young lady of my tender years.)

My disgraceful behavior in England was only a ruse, after all, and Lord Johnny explained it all very well. It wasn't as though a marriage announcement appeared in the papers, or any such thing! Must I be exiled because of it?

I say no!

I shall now test the bonds of my captivity. More later, if there's time.

# CALEA VICTORIEI

Dacia, where do you think you are going?"

Looking down at her lavender-and-white-striped walking gown with its eyelet lace trim, and then back at her aunt with an assumed expression of utmost innocence, Dacia shrugged her shoulders. "Why, out shopping, of course, Aunt Kate. Do you need anything? Some ribbons, perhaps?"

Aunt Kate didn't even bother to argue with her, just stood in the hallway looking impeccable as always in a morning gown of dove gray. She didn't sigh, didn't speak, just Looked.

Dacia knew that the best way to prove to her aunt that she was mature and in control was to remain silent and simply look back, but she never could. She stayed still for all of two seconds before she began her one-sided argument.

"I can hardly get into trouble; I don't know anyone here! And I'll take a footman with me. A large, burly footman. I have my own pin money, and I'll be back by lunchtime. Just please let me go, Aunt Kate! I haven't been anywhere by myself in weeks and weeks and I just can't stay in this house another minute!"

Steely-eyed, Aunt Kate just Looked.

Irritated, restless, and several other emotions she could not accurately describe, Dacia looked back. She was just moments away from tearing off her walking gown and sliding down the banisters in her underthings, whooping like a savage, but she fought that urge with an effort. Instead, she played dirty.

"Very well, Aunt Kate. I suppose I shall just go up to my room and write a letter to my mother. Perhaps she will be able to tell me who it was that you were embracing on the back of our train that night." She turned slowly and put her hand on the doorknob of her bedroom.

"Oh, take two footmen and get me some blue ribbons for my striped poplin, you terrible child," Aunt Kate said, then she disappeared back into her own room.

Dacia couldn't believe that her ploy had worked, and simply stared at her aunt's door for half a minute. Then she really did whoop like a savage and ran down the stairs so fast that she might as well have slid on the banister.

She already had her hat on and her purse dangling from her wrist. All that remained was to find a pair of footmen to accompany her, and that was easily done. There was one right there in the entrance hall, staring at her. She quickly told him to find a friend and come along, and went out on the front steps to wait while she put on her gloves.

The sun was shining and it was pleasantly warm. She smoothed her gloves a final time and then unfurled her parasol. An entire city awaited her, and she could hardly wait to walk its streets. Even the view from her bedroom window had been enticing: the Calea Victoriei, where her family's townhouse was located, was the most prosperous street in Bucharest. Every house, including their own, was enormous and gorgeously appointed with carved cornices and elegantly draped windows, manicured lawns, and lush gardens.

All her life it had been the same routine: New York City society, with its same old families in their old houses having their old parties, enlivened only slightly in the summer with a trip to Newport, where one stayed at the same hotel with the same families and the same parties once again, but at least there was sunshine and the shore to walk along. Lou never seemed to understand, but to Dacia the old routine was not remotely comforting. Instead it was becoming more and more stifling, and Dacia perpetually felt as though there was something fighting within her chest, ready to burst out. She wanted to run and leap and scream and do a thousand forbidden things all at once.

Aunt Kate; Dacia's mother, Ileana; and Lou's mother, Maria, had traveled to America from Romania as young women and ended up staying when Ileana and Maria fell in love with two of New York's most eligible bachelors. They had not been back to Romania since, but all her life Dacia had heard stories about glorious Bucharest, with its elegant boulevards and magnificent homes. She had been taught Romanian from birth, she knew the country's history backward and forward, and she knew the details of each uncle and cousin still living there, even though she had met only a handful of them on their infrequent trips to New York.

And now that she was in Bucharest at last, Aunt Kate

seemed determined to keep Dacia away from it all. Dacia had practically been a prisoner for a week, and Aunt Kate would only give her a quelling look when she asked why. She knew why, but she wanted to make Aunt Kate say it aloud. If she was to be punished by being kept in a beautifully furnished prison, she wanted someone to have the humanity to tell her outright. Dacia was sure things would be better once Lou arrived with Uncle Cyrus and Aunt Maria, but she wasn't sure she could wait that long.

So she had played her final card, dangerous as it was. The footmen stepped out of the house to join her, and Dacia strolled forth at last.

The weather was very fine. The streets were lined with beech trees, and giant lilac bushes bloomed in every garden. The purple flowers filled the air with scent, and Dacia drank it all in. She knew New York so well that none of it excited her anymore, and she had spent the last few months in London, which was like New York only older and dirtier, in her opinion. But Bucharest was magnificent. Exotic without being off-putting, she decided. She recognized the French influence of the architecture, mixed in with some decidedly Eastern styles that pleased her a great deal, like houses painted bold colors, colonnades with striped and pointed arches, and exotic plants that stretched toward the sunlight. Dacia beamed at them and stretched herself, standing even taller.

She had studied a map and a guidebook assiduously back at the house so that she could make her way to the best shops without having to ask the footmen to lead her. They seemed almost nervous, and she could see them out of the corners of her eyes, scowling at anyone who dared to look at her. Was the city really that dangerous? She was not the only young woman out and about, and the streets were full of carriages bearing wealthy men and women who seemed not in the least bit anxious for their pearls. She herself wore only a small gold locket, and carried just enough money to buy some trinkets, so she was hardly a target for pickpockets, and even if she were robbed, it would be no great loss.

Dacia glared over her shoulder at one of the footmen when he moved in too close, and that's when she knew they were being followed.

Just as she had looked over her shoulder, someone behind them had moved a little too quickly for this lazy spring afternoon, though no one else seemed to notice.

Telling herself that it was a silly fancy, she kept on going. But the feeling that they were being watched—that she, in particular, was being watched—would not leave her. It prickled down her back, little hot pinpoints beneath her dress. She straightened her shoulders and lifted her chin, but the feeling persisted. She adjusted her parasol over her shoulder so that it concealed more of her, but still something was not right.

The city began to feel less and less welcoming. The lines of the buildings were foreign, and she took a sudden dislike to the mixture of French and Eastern architecture. Couldn't they find their own style, rather than copy from everyone else? There was a rococo-fronted hotel just next to a restaurant with striped Byzantine arches over the doors, and she shook her head. She glared at a bank and, consequently, a banker coming down the stone steps, and he looked startled.

When she saw a shop selling ribbons and lace, she let out a little huff of breath and almost ran to the door, telling the footmen tersely to stay outside. In the dim coolness of the interior, she relaxed, and the shopkeeper had to ask her three times if he could help her before she came to herself.

"Ah, yes!" She remembered to speak Romanian. "I am looking for blue ribbons, dark blue, and perhaps something the color of the lilacs outside."

The man smiled at her indulgently and agreed that the lilacs were very beautiful, and very suited to her coloring as well. Dacia thanked him, though she knew that it was merely the empty flattery of someone trying to sell his wares. She was very tall, and too slim for true beauty, and added to that she appeared to be the only woman in Bucharest who didn't have masses of beautiful dark hair. Her hair was blond with ashy streaks that she secretly contemplated dyeing some brighter shade.

The shopkeeper brought out bolts of ribbons, but Dacia was distracted again. There was a scent in the air, not of dust and silk, but something else. It was familiar and strange at the same time. Dacia resisted the urge to raise her head and sniff, and focused on the shopkeeper and his wares.

At last Dacia selected wide dark blue satin for Aunt Kate, who had bought a straw hat in London that Dacia thought needed some ribbon to really make something special of it. And some narrower ribbon to go with her aunt's poplin walking gown. Then Dacia bought herself some lilac silk ribbons in different widths.

As she was handing the man the correct amount of lei, the

prickling returned. She turned her head slightly and saw a tall figure blocking the glass in the upper half of the shop door. She knew it was the person who had been following her before, knew it deeply and without a doubt.

Thanking the shopkeeper, Dacia tucked the packet of ribbon firmly under her arm and stalked to the door. She whipped it open, staring up at the man on the step. He was taller than she was, with great broad shoulders that strained the seams of his dark coat, and offensively bright red hair. The footmen were just standing there like simpletons, so Dacia jabbed the tip of her parasol firmly into his breast.

"Who are you, and why are you following me?"

"Hmm, and why do you think I am following you? Perhaps I am merely shopping for ribbons like any young man on a fine day? Do you perhaps think too much of yourself, Miss Dacia of New York?"

He spoke English! And he knew her name! Dacia squinted at him, and then she drew back and whacked him on the shoulder with her parasol as hard as she could.

"Radu! You bad thing," she berated him. "Did you try to frighten me on purpose?"

The young man laughed and blocked her next blow with his forearm. "Ouch! I'm a bad thing? You are the terrible cousin; you didn't even recognize me!"

"It's been eight years since you visited New York," Dacia protested. "And none of your letters mentioned that you'd turned into a giant!" She turned her face up to him. "You may kiss the royal cheek."

Radu sighed and shook his head, but leaned down and kissed

her on one cheek and then the other. Then he wrapped his arms around her and squeezed for good measure. The footmen pretended to look elsewhere, but the shopkeeper was staring out the window without shame.

"Now you may take the royal arm, and buy Her Highness lemonade," Dacia instructed.

She unfurled her parasol and then waited while Radu clutched at his heart and pretended to be honored beyond words. She finally slapped him lightly on the elbow, and he held it out for her. Radu was the only one of her Romanian cousins whom she had met. He had come with his father, Uncle Horia, to visit New York when Radu and Dacia were both ten. His father had called Dacia and Lou "the little princesses," and it had become a game between the cousins. They had exchanged many letters over the years from "Their Highnesses to the lowly servant Radu" and from "the humble Radu to the royal ladies."

"Why haven't you come to see me before?" Dacia demanded as Radu led her up the Calea Victoriei to a café. "I've been here for days and days, dying of boredom. Aunt Kate won't let me go anywhere, and we've had not one single visitor!"

"We've all been traveling," Radu said, looking around vaguely.

"Traveling? Where?"

"Nowhere important," he replied, but the tips of his ears were pink. "Just getting things ready for your visit. Ah, here is a good place."

"Radu, are you being evasive?"

"I? Never!"

He seated her on the terrace of a café, and the footmen sat

down on a bench across the way, looking relieved to be in the shade. And to have turned over her care to Radu, as well, Dacia thought, settling her bustled skirts carefully on the tiny café chair.

She scowled at her cousin as he ordered them lemonade, and when he turned back from the waitress, he saw Dacia's expression with great surprise. He was clearly baffled by her dour look and the way she was impatiently tapping her gloved fingers on the tabletop.

"Radu, I need to have one person here I can trust," Dacia said, very serious now.

"What are you talking about? Whom *can't* you trust? You have Aunt Katarina, my father, the other cousins and uncles and aunts . . ." He trailed off, fussing with his napkin.

"Radu." Dacia stopped and fiddled with her gloves while she put her thoughts in order. "Radu, I know that you've probably heard about the Incident in London."

He snickered, indicating that he had, but wisely did not comment as she went on.

"But even before that, it seemed that Mother and Aunt Maria and Aunt Kate were keeping secrets. Lou and I were supposed to come later, in the autumn, and then go back to New York after Christmas. But suddenly we're being sent here now, months ahead of schedule, and not told when we will return to New York. They're behaving as though I did something truly disgraceful when you know it wasn't that bad! Not bad enough to permanently ruin my reputation, anyway.

"I asked Aunt Kate if we could wait in Paris for Lou and her parents," Dacia went on, struggling to keep her voice under control now. "But she insisted on coming around the coast as fast as we could travel. I thought she was simply eager for us to reach Bucharest. Yet now that we're here, as I've said, she won't leave the house, nor do we have any visitors.

"It's terribly strange, and I don't like it," Dacia finished. "I need to have one person I can confide in, until Lou gets here, at least." She frowned. "And Lou is having a difficult time as well. In her last letter she said that a strange young man approached her on the ship, and was very impertinent." She toyed with her gloves. "In all honesty I thought that's who you were just now, and I was prepared to have you arrested!"

Radu was clearly baffled by this last item. "Someone being fresh with LouLou is hardly a crisis, Dacia, unfortunate as it is."

"Well," Dacia said, refusing to let this insult to her beloved Lou get tossed aside. "He said some odd things to her, things that made her uneasy. And they're making me uneasy as well. It's a shame that Uncle Cyrus wasn't there to chase that cad away!"

Radu patted her hand. "From now on, she'll be under the protection of her Florescu family," he said. "She will not need to worry about anyone bothering her again!"

The waitress brought their lemonade, and Dacia sipped at hers. It was far too sweet, but she didn't care. The day was really quite warm, and she didn't want Radu to see how discomfited she was by all that had happened, and most especially what he had just said, and the rude way he had dismissed Lou's father. Dacia worked very hard to appear like a sophisticated young woman, and it didn't help that she had outbursts of scandalous mischief that she couldn't seem to control, like the Incident in London. She was hardly going to start weeping in an outdoor café because she'd had an emotionally trying day.

"Dacia," Radu said, once more covering her hand with one of his enormous paws. "I promise you, no one is keeping you locked up to hurt you. We are merely . . . planning many things. There is to be a big celebration for you and LouLou, when she arrives, which is why I haven't been to see you. We were at the estate planning the celebration.

"But the family . . . business . . . has also suffered some upsets recently, and many of the uncles and older cousins are working on that. I am very sorry that you feel neglected." He gave her a one-sided smile. The waitress nearly dropped her tray, and even Dacia found herself smiling back. Even with the impossible hair, Radu was quite the charmer and he looked like he knew it, too.

"The princess must never be neglected!" he cried. "So we must find a way to entertain her at once! What is your will, Princess?" He tried to bow despite the fact that he was sitting at a table, and knocked over his glass of lemonade.

Dacia shrieked and jumped to her feet before the wave could reach her, throwing her napkin at it to try and stop its progress as it ran over the side of the little marble-topped table. Radu swore in Romanian, leaped up, knocked over his chair, and nearly unseated the man behind him, who also swore. Dacia started laughing helplessly. Radu turned bright red, handed far too much money to the waitress, and then hurried Dacia off the terrace and onto the street.

"Oh, my parasol!" She started to turn back.

"I'll buy you a new one," Radu said, still blushing.

"That parasol was a gift from Lou," Dacia said. "Bring it to me right now, silly boy!"

"Allow me, miss," said a smooth voice in perfect English.

Dacia turned and saw the most handsome young man she had ever seen in her life. He was holding out her parasol and smiling at her. His teeth were white and perfect, and he had black eyes, lashes Dacia would have killed for, and curling dark hair that brushed the collar of his impeccably tailored Savile Row suit. He smelled like money and masculinity.

The waitress, on the other side of the little terrace fence, was no longer looking at Radu, but gazing at the young man as though she were about to fall into a swoon, a reaction that Dacia understood completely.

Dacia reached out a shaking hand and took her parasol from him. As she did, her fingers brushed against his. Despite the gloves they both wore, a charge of electricity ran through Dacia and she nearly did swoon.

But strangely enough Radu growled, and the hair on the back of Dacia's neck stood on end. She was about to look at her cousin, sensing the tension radiating from him, but the beautiful young man laughed and Dacia's whole attention returned to him.

"What a pleasure to meet you at last, Miss Dacia," he said. "I am Prince Mihai, and I know precisely how to entertain you here in Bucharest."

*20 May 1897*

*I never have been much for keeping a diary. I know that Dacia is faithful in her recording of each day's events, but then, Dacia's life has always been much more exciting than mine, even though we are always together. Perhaps it is in how she views the world? I often fear that someone will find my diary, read it, and then I shall be humiliated. But no matter. I must tell someone, and I have already sent a letter to Dacia, but who knows when it shall reach her?*

*Perhaps I shouldn't have written to Dacia, for now I begin to think that I was mistaken, and she will think that I am the silliest person on earth. But if I am not mistaken, does this mean that I am going mad? First I am repeatedly hounded by That Awful Man, no matter where I am, though no one else seems to ever see him. Then I am surrounded by the smell of lilacs, when there are no lilacs in sight. Perhaps it is a popular perfume here in Paris? Yet I smell it when I am alone, or out on the street, and never in company. And then there is the face that I keep seeing in my mind: a man, perhaps twenty years old, with dark hair and beautiful eyes, but every word he speaks is red, as though it bleeds. What a horrible fancy this is that has struck me! And why? I am not certain how much* longer I can bear these secrets on my own. I am nervous about the trip to Bucharest, and about staying there—so far from New York and home!—for so long, but at the same time, I am filled with anticipation at seeing Dacia again, and Radu, and meeting the rest of our family.

But what if That Awful Man follows me to Bucharest?

And what if the dark-eyed young man of my dreams is real? What does he want of me?

Too many questions, but it is breakfast and I must go.

# THE TUILERIES

Are you feeling better, LouLou?" Lou's father sat down at the breakfast table opposite her and smiled.

Lou smiled back, a genuine smile for the first time in days. She *was* feeling better. Writing in her diary had relieved some of her tension, and she had gotten a letter from Dacia, always a treat. Traveling by sea from New York had not made her ill, precisely, but the food on board the ship had not been as delicious as their cook's at home, and so she had lost a little weight, which made shopping with her mother all the more pleasant.

Dacia ate like a starving bear (although with considerably better manners) and was almost unfashionably slender, but Lou, no matter how many sweets she passed up, always felt a little too plump. Her parents told her that she was beautiful, and Dacia was frankly envious of her figure, since Lou had a very trim waist and curvy bust and hips. Lou had never been quite happy with it. But now that she'd even had Parisian dressmakers compliment her figure, she suddenly felt light as a bird.

"I'm very well, Papa," she said, smiling as she looked up at her father in the golden light of the hotel suite's dining room. "And how are you this morning?" She took a slice of toast and a boiled egg, but ignored the quince jelly and croissants. She disliked quince, and croissants were too messy.

"I am well, because my girl is well," her father said, and opened the paper. "And perhaps, if she has done enough shopping, she will condescend to tour the Tuileries with me today?" He lowered one corner of the paper and eyed her over it.

"I would be honored, sir!" Lou blew her father a kiss.

"Excellent!"

"Where are you going, dear?" Lou's mother bustled into the room. She was a small, stout woman, vastly different from her two tall, slim sisters. "Take the boys with you, wherever it is." She put two croissants on her plate and got a cup of coffee from the urn.

Lou felt a red flush rise up her cheeks. She wanted to go to the Tuileries with her father, just the two of them, just this once. Her twin brothers were ten and extremely rambunctious. They would probably run amok in the gardens and get the entire family arrested.

The need to protest rose in her chest, and she fought it down. She wanted to argue, to shout that it wasn't fair and that the boys should stay home until they learned to behave like civilized human beings and less like heathens, but she didn't. She never did. Dacia would have, but Lou just couldn't.

"Maria," Lou's father said coolly from behind the paper, "I am taking LouLou to the Tuileries. Just LouLou. Then we shall go to lunch. The boys may stay here with their tutor and learn to speak French. And attempt to sit still for five minutes without starting something on fire."

Lou made an unladylike noise, trying not to giggle at that. Or to shout with triumph.

"But boys need their father—" Maria began.

"Those boys need a good whipping," their father observed. "But since you will not let me do so, they will have to live with being confined to the house until they can show that they are fit to be seen in society. Yesterday I tried to take them to the Louvre, but David took it into his head to have a swim, climbed a railing, and nearly leaped into the Seine before I stopped him."

"He's very high-strung, and you must be gentle with him," Maria scolded her husband.

"He's an awful little brat, and so is Adam," her husband said in his mild voice. "And I am resolved to stop being gentle, because gentle is getting us nowhere. Meanwhile," he went on, "our daughter has turned out to be a beautiful and charming young woman, and it will be my pleasure to reward her always delightful behavior with a treat today."

Lou glowed with pride.

"Our daughter I am not worried about," Maria said sharply. "Louisa's place in this world is secure. Our sons, on the other hand . . ." She trailed off, muttering darkly into her coffee.

Her father lowered the corner of his paper again, winked at Lou, and then raised it.

Lou winked back, but her father couldn't see it. She felt a surge of elation that he had refused to let the twins spoil their day together. She felt guilty about it, but she just couldn't enjoy having her brothers around. They seemed to multiply, as though they were quadruplets, and they made enough noise for a whole herd of small boys.

Although at night when they were scrubbed and sleepy and tucked into bed, they could be very sweet. Occasionally.

After breakfast, she put on her hat and walking boots and got her gloves, purse, and parasol. Her father, in a straw hat and a smart new spring jacket, looked very dapper as he took her arm. He had been very young when he married her mother, only eighteen, and Maria herself had been only seventeen. A handsome and still-young man, from one of the best families in New York, which showed in his clothes and bearing, he drew many admiring glances from women as they walked through Paris. The confidence that came from knowing That Awful Man would not dare to approach her with her father so near made Lou smile, her cheeks flushed with color and her eyes sparkling.

The Tuileries were magnificent. The early-summer flowers were blooming, the grass was very green, and the sky above them very blue. Lou wanted to gather the flowers and the sky together into her arms and simply dissolve into the crystal air. Dacia had confided to her of that feeling of restlessness she sometimes had, a feeling that came on so strong at times that Dacia wanted to run and run and never stop. She had tried to prod Lou into feeling the same way, but Lou never did. Instead, in moments of great happiness, or even in moments of distress, she simply wanted to break apart and float onto the breeze, something that Dacia understood even less than Lou herself.

As she was bending down to admire some pansies, Lou heard a familiar voice behind her, a strange thing so far from home.

"Don't move, fair one, for I shall paint you just as you are!"

Blushing, she disobeyed, and straightened to face a young acquaintance from New York, William Carver. Dacia fancied herself to be madly in love with him, and everyone expected them to become engaged soon. Seeing him now, Lou thought of Dacia's letters from London, filled with stories of a handsome young lord named Johnny Harcastle, and she blushed even more. She felt inexplicably guilty, though she was sure not a flicker of guilt would cross Dacia's mind if she were here.

"No, really, Miss Neulander, I would like to paint you," he said, frowning, but not as though he were angry. He was holding a large drawing board and a handful of pencils. "Perhaps if you stand just there, and I sit here?" He backed up until he reached a small bench, and then sat on it. "Turn your head to the left, and then don't move," he instructed.

Lou sighed. William Carver was determined to be an artist, and he was always trying to get people to hold still so that he could sketch them. It was quite tedious, but she would never admit that to Dacia. Nor would she admit that she didn't think his paintings were very good, because she admired his need to do something with his life. He would never have to work a single day to earn a living, so he had tried to find himself a vocation to take up his time. Lou rather wished he would do something more useful, like study medicine, but art was apparently more suited to his temperament, if not to his talents.

She turned her head to the left, scanning the area for her father while she posed. He had just stepped over to look at something, and should be back any moment. Ah! There he was! She tried to signal to him with her eyes.

"LouLou, are you all right? Are you hurt?" Her father hurried toward her.

"She's just fine," William Carver said testily. "But you're blocking the light."

"Mr. Carver is an artist," Lou said as best she could without moving her head.

"Is he now?" Her father's eyebrows rose. "I had no idea that you wanted your portrait painted, LouLou. You should have told me!"

"I—well—" Lou didn't know what to say.

"It's not a portrait," William Carver said, even more cross. "I'm not some hack portrait painter, flattering old ladies by painting out their chins! I am a true artist, like the Pre-Raphaelite Brotherhood!" He struck his breast with one fist, leaving a smear of charcoal on his lapel. "Miss Neulander shall be a nymph, standing before her oak tree." He gestured at the tree just behind Lou and went back to his work.

"That is a linden," Lou's father said. "And also a very strange angle for my daughter's head to be tilted at for very long."

"The tree hardly matters," William said vaguely, returning to his picture. He stuck his tongue in his cheek as he shaded something with the side of his pencil.

Her father gently moved her head over by pushing her chin with one finger, and Lou felt a rush of blood to her neck, making it tingle. She gave her father a grateful look. He smiled at her and then went over to William.

"Are you Henry Carver's boy?"

"Yes, sir," William said, looking up at her father with an expression that said he was suddenly aware of how rude he had been. He dropped his charcoal pencil into a little case and held out a smudged hand to Mr. Neulander.

Lou's father smiled and handed him a handkerchief instead of shaking hands. "Son, I'm not here to scold you," he said. "I know your parents have done a fine job of educating you as a young man should be educated. But I would like to give you two pieces of advice. Will you listen?"

Will Carver gulped. "Yes, sir."

"First of all: treat all ladies, even young ladies you've known for years, as if they were princesses and you merely a servant. Understand?" Mr. Neulander cocked his head.

"Yes, sir," said Will Carver in an abashed voice.

"And second . . ." Mr. Neulander stopped for a moment and looked at Will's drawing. "You don't need a model in front of you, just paint from the heart." He held out his own hand then, and Will, looking rather dazed, shook it, stammering his thanks. He offered Mr. Neulander his handkerchief back, gray with charcoal, but Lou's father just waved it away with another smile and shake of his head. "You keep it, my boy. Good day to you." He held out his arm to Lou. "Shall we, my dear?"

Lou took her father's arm and they strolled out of the Tuileries in search of lunch. She sighed happily, drinking in the sights and sounds of Paris.

"You're a good girl, LouLou," her father said, putting his other hand on top of hers where it rested in the crook of one elbow. "Perhaps too good," he said in a low voice.

"Whatever do you mean, Papa?"

"Just a moment, my dear; I did want to talk to you, but let's get comfortable first."

He took her into a hotel that was quite as grand as the one they were staying in, if not grander. There were ladies in fanciful hats and elegant gowns going in and out, servants bearing luggage or boxes from fine shops, struggling along in their wake. Lou instantly felt very young and rather grubby, and tried to adjust her hat and straighten her gown as best she could as they went into the restaurant, which had a chandelier the size of a small carriage hanging from the ceiling.

"Papa, I don't think I'm dressed properly," Lou whispered as they followed the maître d' to a table.

"Nonsense," her father said, squeezing her hand again. "My LouLou is beautiful enough for any restaurant in Paris."

Lou reminded herself sternly that while New York may not have been as elegant as Paris, it was hardly Robinson Crusoe's desert island. And she was from one of the oldest families in New York on her father's side, Romanian gentry on her mother's. She straightened her shoulders and gracefully sat down in the chair offered to her.

Her father ordered lunch for them in his impeccable French, learned from private tutors and polished with a grand tour of Europe. They ate and chatted about the food and the enormous chandelier and the other diners, but all the while Lou was wondering what her father wanted to tell her, and could see that whatever it was occupied his thoughts as well.

When their plates had been cleared and they were eating

sorbets garnished with fresh berries, her father at last looked her in the eyes and began to speak very seriously.

"LouLou, I know that you don't always feel like you are beautiful, but you are."

"Thank you, Papa," she murmured, looking down at her dish.

"No, look at me."

She looked up at her father, a little puzzled. His expression was so grave: quite unlike his usually sunny countenance.

"You struggle to be tall and slender like Dacia, but you aren't, and that doesn't matter. Everywhere we have gone today, the young men haven't been able to take their eyes off you."

She blushed and wished she dared look down. She had a feeling that her father wasn't simply going to warn her about speaking to strange young men in public gardens. She met her father's gaze as frankly as she could and nodded a little to urge him to go on.

"And you are also a very intelligent young lady. I'm proud of how well you did with your studies, and if you wanted to continue at a young ladies' college, I would be happy to support you in that."

Her mouth opened slightly in surprise, and she put some sorbet into it hurriedly. College? She really had not thought of such a thing ... well, that wasn't true. She had, in fact, toyed with the idea of studying to be a nurse, but had mentioned it just once to her mother.

"Mama said ... it's just foolishness," she said when she had swallowed her sorbet. "Young ladies with my upbringing ... don't do such things." She was a little surprised by how much that still stung. She remembered sobbing into Dacia's lap that young ladies of their upbringing never got to do anything, startling them both with her vehemence.

"That's precisely what I wanted to talk about," Mr. Neulander said, putting down his spoon. "Your mother." He grimaced. "And her sisters. And the whole damn family—pardon my language."

Lou's eyes widened and she set aside her own spoon.

"You've always been a sweet and obedient daughter," her father continued. "And I know I should be grateful, but just at present this worries me. Your mother and her family are . . . different. More different than you think, and it has everything and nothing to do with where they come from."

Lou stared at her father. "I don't understand."

"I know you don't." Her father scowled. "And I'm sorry, but I promised to let your mother and her kin tell you more about the family once we arrive in Bucharest. Why I agreed to such a thing I'll never know. But I have always tried to honor my promises . . . and I know you have, too. Which is why I need you to promise me something now, Maria Louisa." He reached across the table and took her hand.

"All right, Papa." Her voice was shaking. She was bewildered and frightened by her father's words, and the unusual pallor that had come over his face.

"I want you to swear to me that you will listen to your own heart. If your mother's family asks you to do something that . . . that sounds too strange, or that you don't want to do, I want you to listen to your heart and follow it instead. You and Dacia both. You can come to me, and I will do my best to help you. Both of you."

Lou was very frightened now.

"Can you promise me, darling?" her father said. "If you are ever scared, you can come to me, and I will take you and Dacia home to New York at a moment's notice. I will send you to college, or whatever you like. That is my promise to you, if you will just listen to your heart, and refuse if you are asked to do something that . . . that feels wrong."

"I promise, Papa," she said, her voice little more than a whisper.

"Thank you." He squeezed her hand and sat back. "I'm sorry to darken our day like this. I'm sure it will all be nothing but a silly fancy of mine, and in a few months we shall return to New York with a song in our hearts!" He signaled the waiter and ordered a plate of crepes with strawberries and chocolate sauce. "To cheer ourselves up," he told Lou.

She smiled automatically in reply, but she was too shaken to enjoy the rest of the day.

22 May 1897

Oooh la-la! Whatever shall I do? There are far too many beautiful young men in the world, and I am just one girl! First there was Will Carver in New York, then Lord Johnny in London, and now I have just met the most delicious of them all! And it seems that he is a prince! Prince Mihai of Wallachia, if you please! It's an old title, and one that (sadly) does not mean much anymore. Still. A prince! A prince with beautiful long lashes and thick curling hair. A prince who wears perfectly tailored suits and speaks seven languages, who likes to go to plays and concerts and read popular novels!

If anything, I would say that he is too perfect for words! Yes, yes, diary, I can hear Lou's voice in my head right now, asking me about Will Carver and Lord Johnny. Well, I'm sorry, but neither of them are here at present. Surely it can't hurt to amuse myself a bit in Romania? When I return to New York, dear Lord Johnny will be but a memory, and Will Carver will be back from France, eager to dance with me once more. Until that day, however, Prince Mihai and his beautiful eyes are here to entertain me. That is, if Aunt Kate will let him!

# STRADA SILVESTRU

I don't like it!"

"I don't care! I say yes!"

"You have been gone too long; this is not a matter that you can decide alone!"

Dacia pretended that she wasn't listening to the shouting across the hall and took a card, looked at it, and discarded it with a sigh. Radu looked at his own cards, frowned at the one she had discarded, and raised his bid by a penny.

"Thank you for telling me what I can and cannot do," Aunt Kate screamed at her brother. "May I remind you of *who I am?*"

"You know," Dacia said, drawing another card, "I think that I should be the one who gets to scream."

They had been listening to Aunt Kate arguing with Radu's father, Horia, for nearly an hour now. It was because of Dacia, naturally, but this time it wasn't something disgraceful that she had done. Instead the argument was about whether she should be allowed to do something: specifically, to go to the opera with Prince Mihai. Uncle Horia and Aunt Kate wouldn't dream of talking it over with Dacia, and Radu seemed to despise the prince, so Dacia was sitting in the parlor playing cards with her cousin and trying to avoid the topic altogether.

As well as anyone can avoid a topic that is being discussed in the next room by two irate and shouting adults.

"I really don't see what all the fuss is about," she murmured.

"You don't know Mihai," was all Radu would say. "Call."

She threw down her cards, which were completely useless anyway, and watched with a sour expression as Radu gathered up the pennies they had been bidding with.

"And you do?" She studied Radu, but his expression was closed as he pocketed the coins and then began to shuffle the cards. "What can you tell me about him?"

"You should stay away from him, that's what I can tell you about him," Radu said, sounding more like his father than usual.

"It's just the opera," Dacia said. "I don't understand why your father objects."

"Nothing is ever 'just' anything with Mihai," Radu muttered.

"Have I been gone long enough for you all to run mad?" Aunt Kate's voice pierced the walls. "This is an opportunity we cannot pass up!"

"It is an opportunity *you* think we cannot pass up," Uncle Horia countered. "But those of us who remained here—"

"You know why I left, and what I've given up," Aunt Kate shouted. "Now I'm back, with *her*. It's time! It's long *past* time! The rest of the family—"

"The rest of the family spends too much time in the country, pretending it is still the twelfth century," Uncle Horia shouted back. "I who know the Draculas all too well—"

"I not know the Draculas? *I?* Don't make me laugh!" Aunt Kate's voice was so enraged that Dacia cringed.

"Who are the Draculas?" Dacia forced herself to nonchalantly pick up the cards Radu had just dealt her. "That can't possibly be their real name. Who would call themselves *Dragon?* Or want to be associated with Vlad Tepes?" She wrinkled her nose.

"Mihai's family name is Dracula," Radu said, arranging his own hand. He glanced up and caught her expression. "No, really. He's descended from Vlad the Impaler too. Which just proves that you don't know him well enough to see him."

Dacia tossed aside the information that the elegant Mihai was related to the twelfth-century butcher known as Vlad the Impaler. It was impossible. She and Lou both had nightmares for a week after their governess had regaled them with stories about that monstrous warlord.

"How can I know Prince Mihai if no one will let me see him?" she asked reasonably.

Radu just snorted, but Dacia thought that she had scored a point. It had been three days since she had met the prince on the Calea Victoriei. They had walked and talked for an hour, with Radu trailing sullenly behind them. The day after their meeting, Prince Mihai had sent flowers and a note. The day after that, an invitation to dinner and the theater, which she'd been made to turn down, and today he had sent her a beautiful black velvet cape lined with lilac silk to wear to the opera, with a plea that she join him for just one night. Aunt Kate had agreed that Dacia had been punished for the Incident in England long enough, and had given Dacia permission to attend the opera with the prince.

But Uncle Horia and Radu had arrived after breakfast that morning and Dacia had made the mistake of telling them about her upcoming outing with Mihai. The shouting match in the library had commenced not ten minutes later.

"It's your bid." Radu jingled the coins in his pocket.

"I don't think my head is in the game," Dacia said drily. "Actually, I want a book from the library." She rolled her eyes at his skeptical look. "No, I really do! I want a dictionary. Lou sent me a letter, and I wanted to look up one of the words."

"Her vocabulary *is* more expansive than yours," Radu said with a smirk. "It seems that one of you was paying attention to that fancy American governess."

"Ha-ha!" Dacia flicked him with a finger. "No, a strange man in the street called her an insulting name, and I can't believe it means what she said it means."

"Another man has insulted LouLou?" Radu was instantly outraged. "Tell her to describe him for me, and I will hunt him down!" He made a fist.

"As long as you let me help," Dacia said, gingerly curling her own hand into a fist. She'd always wanted to punch someone. But only if she could knock them out with one blow. And only if they truly deserved it, which this man did. "And, of all things, it's the same man from the ship. Apparently he's following her through Paris."

"The bas—" Radu bit back the insult. "Something must be done! What did he call her?"

"He called her a houri, and he kept— What on earth is so funny?"

"A *houri?*" Radu was still laughing. "Is she certain?"

"Yes, of course she is! This man has been following her, Radu! First the ship, then in Paris. It's very serious!"

"Oh, he certainly must be discouraged, but it's not . . ." Radu laughed again.

"Explain yourself, or I shall get my parasol and smack you," Dacia ordered.

"A houri is a sort of temptress," Radu said. "A creature so beautiful that she drives men mad. An unearthly being, magical and alluring." He started laughing again. "If Lou doesn't like it, we must certainly take steps, but some women would be flattered."

"But that's not flattering, it's atrocious," Dacia insisted. "It's vulgar, it's forward, it's—"

"If he does it again, I will take care of him for her, since her father certainly won't," Radu said, casually dismissing Uncle Cyrus, but Dacia didn't know what to say about that. Radu gathered up the cards and shuffled them again, though they hadn't played a hand.

"We might as well play one more time," he said as the fight in the library continued.

Dacia subsided, not entirely mollified. As Radu dealt the cards, she strained to hear more of the argument in the library. It wasn't exactly difficult.

"This is the reason I brought her here!" Aunt Kate shouted.

"Don't play obedient daughter now," Uncle Horia retorted. "You came back for your own sake, not hers!"

"This is the reason she was even born!"

Radu froze with one hand on the cards he was about to deal. His eyes were enormous. Dacia stiffened, but only for an instant, then she was on her feet. She crept through the parlor door and across the hall to the library. She pressed her ear against the door, holding her breath to make sure she heard her uncle's answer.

"Not for this," Horia said, his voice so quiet that if Dacia hadn't had her ear to the door, she never would have heard him. "Not for him."

"Have you forgotten? My task? Your task? Our part in all this?" Aunt Kate was no longer shouting, either. In fact, she was quiet and icy calm.

"I never forget," her brother said calmly. "How could I? But I do not approve."

"You do not approve?" Aunt Kate's voice was cold. "It is not for you to approve. It is for you to uphold the honor of the family—or are those words only flung in *my* face?"

"Do not remind me," Horia said. Dacia heard him sigh heavily, even through the door. "You have been gone too long, Katarina, to truly understand. Gone too long, and returned with nothing to show for it." A heavy pause. "And your own sins are tainting your thoughts, even now."

Heavy steps approached the door, and Dacia sprang away. Or she tried, anyway. Radu had come up behind her so silently she hadn't even noticed him there, and now she ran right into him. He jumped back and then to the side, trying to move out of her way, and stepped on her foot instead. She let out a cry and lurched sideways, Radu tried to catch her, and they both fell to the floor in a heap.

The library door opened.

"Radu, what is this?"

"Dacia, behave yourself!"

Aunt Kate and Uncle Horia were standing above them wearing matching annoyed looks. Radu and Dacia looked at each other, and then at the adults standing over them, and just shrugged. Normally Dacia would have laughed, but not after hearing what she had just heard.

"Ana Katarina, what is going on here?"

The new voice was sharp, the Romanian very formal. And very angry.

Dacia, who was facing away from the speaker and looking up at her aunt, saw Kate go pale. Swallowing, Dacia pushed her skirts down so that they covered her legs and feet, and then twisted around slowly to face whoever it was who had frightened Aunt Kate.

She found herself looking at a very old and rather stout woman wearing a traditional embroidered dress and a headscarf. She looked like the matron of some goat-herding clan, and the top of her head would not have reached Dacia's chin, yet somehow she seemed to dominate the hall. Dacia goggled at her while the old woman stared back with great disdain, then struck the floor with the tip of her carved walking stick.

"Get up," the old woman ordered.

Dacia scrambled to her feet, cheeks burning, and made a little curtsy to the old woman, who in point of fact barely came up to Dacia's shoulder. She was shaped like a barrel: hard and strong without a hint of softness. Her white blouse was thickly embroidered with gold thread and tiny red beads, and her apron was so stiff with more beads and embroidery that Dacia didn't think the woman could sit down.

"*Doamna,*" Dacia murmured.

"Do you know who I am?" The old woman's black eyes raked Dacia from head to toe.

"No, *doamna,*" she said meekly.

"I am Lady Ioana Florescu. Your grandmother," the old woman said, neither offended by Dacia's ignorance nor noticeably appeased by her humility now.

Her grandmother? Dacia gaped unbecomingly. This was a grandmother of a different stripe than she was used to. Clearly this grandmother didn't invite confidences, or hold little tea parties in the back garden, the way her grandmother Vreeholt did. And Dacia was relatively sure that there were no small dogs playing about on the rug in front of the fire at this grandmother's house, either.

"It's very nice to meet you, Grandmother," Dacia said.

"You will call me Lady Ioana," the old woman snapped. "I am the head of this family, not some daft old woman who keeps biscuits in a jar for sticky little children!"

"My apologies, Lady Ioana," Dacia said.

She found herself missing Grandmother Vreeholt with a

sharp stab of longing. This frightening old woman was just one more trial in a long list of horrors since she had started on this journey.

"Perhaps you'll do," Lady Ioana said, but not with any real approval. "Come with me into the library; I have words to say to you." She looked down at Radu, who was still crouched on the floor. "Get up, you stupid boy! You're the worst of the lot."

"I'm sorry, Lady Ioana," Radu mumbled, and scrambled to his feet, bowing.

"Radu, why don't you come with us?" Dacia did not want to be alone with this nasty old woman. Even having Radu standing in the corner looking awkward would be better than nothing.

"I don't wish to speak to Radu," Lady Ioana barked, striding across the hall toward the library door. "I've spoken to him enough, and yet he never improves. Now is the time to see if there is any hope for *you*, girl."

Dacia stiffened her spine and followed the old lady into the library, shutting the door behind them without being asked. Lady Ioana sat in the largest chair, an enormous wing-backed affair of heavy leather and brass studs. Dacia refused to stand on the rug in front of her as though she were a schoolgirl being called to task. She sat down opposite her grandmother in a velvet-upholstered chair and idly picked up the book on the small table at her elbow, flipping through it and smoothing the pages to hide her nerves.

"Yes, Lady Ioana?" She looked up at the old woman through her lashes, as though only mildly interested in what she had to say.

"You are bold," Lady Ioana observed. "But is it only for show, or is it backed with a real spine?"

Dacia had no answer for that, or at least none that didn't sound like childish protesting, so she simply didn't answer.

"You cause a great deal of trouble, that is for certain. First the boy in New York, then another in England, and now you have caught the eye of Prince Mihai."

"Aunt Kate doesn't seem to mind that," Dacia said tartly.

"Ana Katarina has her own opinions," Lady Ioana said flatly. "But she should keep them to herself in this matter. If she'd been a good judge of proper behavior, she wouldn't have been sent away to begin with."

Dacia felt the floor drop out from under her feet. Aunt Kate had been *sent away*? She always made it sound as if she and her sisters had gone to New York out of sheer boredom! Did this have something to do with the man on the train? Dacia leaned forward eagerly as her grandmother went on.

"The princely family is not like your New York society," Lady Ioana said. "It is not a great conquest for you to have caught his eye this soon. These things have taken oceans of time to prepare for, and cannot be rushed."

As her grandmother's words sank in, Dacia felt her ire with the old woman rising again. She'd been hoping for juicy secrets about her mother and aunts and their past, not to be scolded and told . . .

"Are you saying that I'm not good enough for Mihai?" She drew her head back, putting on her most haughty expression. "I assure you, he does not seem to think so."

"If he chooses to amuse himself with you so quickly, we are not to tell him no."

"Just because he's a prince . . . My father is descended from the oldest families in New York . . ." Dacia faltered. "I don't understand," she confessed at last, swallowing her pride.

"Of course not," her grandmother snorted. "But you will soon enough. Once the other one arrives, we'll take you both to the estate, and then you'll learn what it means to be a Florescu!"

Crashing her stick on the floor again, Lady Ioana got to her feet. Dacia also stood, but much more slowly. She was even more confused and upset than before, but at least she understood some of what had just been said: Lou should have left Paris that very morning.

"You're tall and skinny," the old woman observed as she looked up at Dacia. "You'll be the Claw. Ana Katarina says the other is the Wing, like me." Lady Ioana gave a pleased smile, creasing her already wrinkled face.

Dacia looked at her, stunned. "Did you just say that Lou is the *Wing*? And I'm the . . . What does that mean, exactly?"

"Soon you will know," her grandmother said. "Very soon." She went stumping out, leaving Dacia standing in the middle of the rug.

Someone knocked on the open door a minute later and then came in. It was Radu. He only nodded when he saw Dacia standing there, shaken. He pushed her shoulder, and she slumped into a chair.

"She has that effect on people," Radu said.

"She said what that man said," Dacia said, aware that she

wasn't making any sense. But then, she didn't think that anyone else was, either. "She said that I am the Claw, and Lou is the Wing."

Radu's face went white. *"She told you?"*

"What does it mean, Radu?" Dacia felt feverish. "What does all this mean? Why did that man ask Lou what she was, the Wing or the Claw . . . and what on earth is *the Smoke?"*

Impossibly, Radu's face went even paler, and Dacia noticed for the first time that he had a few freckles on his nose. *"Who said this?"* His voice came out strangled.

"The man, the one who called Lou a houri. He asked which of those things she was." She pulled his face closer to hers, still gripping his lapels. "You know, Radu Florescu, and you're going to tell me. Now."

"I can't," Radu choked out. "If I do, they'll kill me!"

"They'll kill you?" Dacia let go of him, suddenly weak in the face of his sheer terror. He really believed what he was saying. "Who will kill you?"

"The family!"

"Our family?" Dacia didn't believe him. "Nonsense! And Lady Ioana just—"

"Lady Ioana can say such things," he said. "Of course she can! But I'm not Lady Ioana! If *I* say anything, they'll kill me! Now give me Lou's letter. I have to show my father so that he can find that man."

"Find him?" Dacia felt like there were too many thoughts in her brain, and if one more was added, she would go mad. "Why do they need to find him?"

"So that they can kill him," Radu said as if the answer should have been obvious. "He shouldn't know such things! He will need to be removed."

"If you don't need me, then I'll indulge in some hysterics," Dacia announced calmly. "I believe I'm due. Now back away, I'm going to scream."

But the sound that came out of her throat was more like a sob.

*22 May 1897*

*Dear Dacia,*

*We are leaving Paris at last, but I am not sure that is a good thing. How is Bucharest? Does it feel safe? I know that this is a strange question, yet I cannot shake the feeling that I am traveling into danger. I have not seen That Awful Man, as I call him, since that day I hit him with my parasol. Yet my dreams are troubled, and I cannot be easy. I am sure that I will feel better once we are reunited.*

*I have enjoyed your letters a great deal, though I am sorry that you were bored on the ship from London. Sea travel is not all that exciting, I am quite agreed. And Aunt Kate's tryst on the train (though I hardly dare to write the words, they are so scandalous) is quite the most amazing piece of news! I want to hear all about it in person when I get there. I am not sure if I am too shocked to find it romantic or not. Who was he? Do you suppose he has been waiting for her return all these years she has been in New York? Is he the reason that she has turned down so many offers of marriage? And did he put the nasty thing on the tracks so that the train would stop, and they could steal a*

moment together? There now, that sounds romantic, if
slightly deranged.

*All my love,*
*Louisa (Lou)*

P.S. I could have sworn that I saw Lord John Harcastle getting
into a hired carriage the other day outside the Louvre. I
recognized him from your clippings. But I have searched and
searched the papers for a notice of a visiting British lord, and
there were none. They have documented Will Carver's every
move... and even mine, I blush to say! So perhaps I was
mistaken.

# THE ORIENT EXPRESS

The train moved through forests and mountains, steaming, smoking, clanking, and whistling, and Lou hated every minute of it. What was wrong with human beings, she wondered, that they needed to declare themselves so loudly everywhere they went? Must there really be so much noise, and smell, and . . . weight . . . pressing down on the earth?

There were thin clouds in the sky, and Lou longed to float up and wind them around her like a scarf. She lifted one hand, wondering what a cloud would feel like. Would it be cold? Or warm and soft like the feathers of a bird?

"Will we ever learn to fly?" she murmured to herself as she gazed out the window.

Even the houses they passed, the train stations, the barns, seemed to press on the ground, crowding out the trees, sneering at the world. She hated it all. Everything seemed to be too rough, even her beautiful new traveling suit of corded blue silk.

"You will learn to fly soon enough," her mother said.

Lou's head jerked up. She had forgotten that her mother was not asleep, and Maria Neulander had always had incredibly sharp ears. Lou had sometimes wondered if it was compensation for her mother's poor eyesight.

Lou looked at her mother, who had her spectacles perched on her nose and was knitting a little white bonnet out of soft wool she had bought in Paris. Dacia's mother was expecting, which was why her cousin had traveled with Aunt Kate. Lou had been trying her best to knit some booties, and though the first one had gone well, the second was turning out twice as large, so she'd put it aside. She knew Aunt Ileana would despise anything that wasn't perfect, no matter how heartfelt the sentiment behind the gift, and had decided she'd better buy her gift instead.

"I was just— I didn't mean—" Lou was flustered, and not entirely certain what she had meant.

"You will learn to fly soon enough," her mother repeated with a secretive smile. She looked as though she was going to say something else, paused, and then changed the subject. "Did you write to Dacia before we left?"

"Yes, but the letter is probably on the train with us," Lou pointed out.

"Oh, they have faster trains for that sort of thing, I believe," her mother said vaguely. "Did you tell her about the gowns we're bringing for her?"

"Yes, of course."

Lou's mother had gotten several telegrams from Aunt Kate before they left Paris. Maria was very excited about something, and had gone to the dressmakers and ordered a number of things for Dacia using measurements she had on hand. Maria loved to shop, and she carried the measurements for her sisters, daughter, and nieces in a little notebook in case she saw something that she thought would suit them.

So it transpired that, even though she hadn't been able to stop in Paris herself, Dacia now also had a Parisian wardrobe consisting of a corded blue silk traveling suit identical to Lou's, an evening gown of white satin with lavender embroidery on the bodice, and several morning dresses, not to mention stockings, gloves, and hats, all in the latest mode. Maria had already ordered the evening gown as a surprise for her oldest niece but picked out the other things ready-made, saying they would have them altered in Bucharest if they needed to. Maria and Kate were clearly plotting something, and with Aunt Ileana's full permission, Lou was sure. Her mother had sent telegrams to New York almost daily so that Aunt Ileana wouldn't be left out, despite her delicate condition.

"My mother will want you to wear traditional gowns for the family parties, but for social calls, Dacia will look like a fashion plate." Maria paused. "And so will you, of course."

Maria returned to her knitting, humming happily under her breath. The twins were asleep, and so was Lou's father. Lou needed air, or she thought she might have the vapors or something worse. Muttering something that her mother could hear but wouldn't understand, she got to her feet and left their compartment.

"Maria Louisa, you are not chaperoned," her mother called after her.

For once in her life Lou ignored her mother and kept going. She walked down the length of their car, into the next car, and then the one after that. It was the last car on the train, and she'd hoped it would be empty, since it was only small and not reserved by any particular families that she knew of.

But it turned out to be the gentlemen's smoking car, and Lou walked into a cloud of blue cigar smoke that made her cough. All conversation stopped, and several of the gentlemen also coughed, and someone asked if she needed help.

"I just want . . . air," Lou gasped, and thought for a moment that she really was choking.

"You won't find it in here," said a gentle voice behind her.

A hand took hold of her elbow and steered her out of that car and into the one just before it. She was still blinking smoke out of her eyes when she was guided into a compartment, and her rescuer opened all the windows so that she could breathe. She plopped down on a plush seat and stuck her head out a window.

"Oof! Vile!" Lou gasped.

"Well, that's what I get for hopping on this train last minute," said her rescuer. "Every time the wind gusts, I get clouds of smoke in here unless I keep the windows shut tight—so be careful! And the passageway is constantly traveled by men with big cigars already in hand."

Lou giggled in sympathy, and also a bit in embarrassment, and pulled her head back inside to look at her companion. He was British, she could tell by the accent, but she hadn't thought she would recognize him.

"You're Lord John Harcastle!" A red flush stole up her neck and into her cheeks.

"Ah. Yes. I suppose I am." He fiddled with his cuffs and smiled awkwardly.

"But you're so young! The photograph made you look . . . and the papers made it sound like . . ." She trailed off, and blushed even darker.

"Saw that, did you?" Lord John made a face. "That was not the best day I've ever had, I must confess."

"I—I imagine not," she said, and then giggled a little before she could help herself.

To her relief, he joined her, laughing easily and hiding his eyes with one hand in an endearingly bashful way. He was probably no more than a pair of years older than her, nineteen at the most. He had brown hair that looked mussed as though he'd been sleeping, and his blue suit was rumpled as well. His collar was open and he wasn't wearing a tie, but Lou saw something with red stripes crammed between two seat cushions that she thought might be the missing item of clothing.

Dacia had sent the newspaper clippings to Lou, just a few months ago. Lord Johnny, as everyone called him, had gotten into an altercation with a member of the House of Lords on the steps of Parliament and had punched the other lord, knocking him unconscious. When police had tried to restrain him, Lord Johnny had fought them as well, and accidentally kicked a newspaper reporter who had arrived on the scene. The newspapers, protecting one of their own, had revealed that Lord Johnny had incurred enormous debts (gambling was implied) and his father was on the verge of cutting him off before he squandered their entire fortune. The papers had made him sound like a hardened criminal, and the photograph that had run with the articles had made him look older, decidedly unkempt, and downright devilish.

And this was all before Aunt Kate had saved Dacia from a scandalous adventure with Lord Johnny, which made Lou blush to think about even now. Dacia gaily referred to it as the Incident in London, but Lou had no idea how her cousin could be so cavalier about it.

Furthermore, Lou was amazed that she had recognized him at all, since in person he was so much nicer, with a bright smile and twinkling blue eyes that made him look even more boyish. She could see why Dacia found him so irresistible.

She was also certain that he was the young man she'd seen at the Louvre just before leaving Paris. So strange that the society pages hadn't uncovered his whereabouts. According to the last clipping from London that Lou had received, Lord Johnny was hiding from his debts at his family estate in Suffolk.

"You have met my cousin," Lou said to the young lord tentatively. "Miss Dacia Vreeholt of New York."

Lord Johnny's entire face lit up. If Lou had thought him handsome before, if in a mischievous way, it was nothing to how he looked at the mention of her cousin's name. He even sat up straighter, and dazzled her with his smile.

"Dacia is your cousin? Marvelous! Is she here?" He peered out into the corridor.

"No," Lou said, and was a bit disappointed. She rather wished that someday a young man might light up like that at the mention of *her* name. Dacia had young men falling at her feet no matter where she went. "But I'm on my way to meet her," she admitted. "In Romania. Bucharest."

"Why are you going *there?*"

Now Lord Johnny was on the edge of his seat, his spine ramrod straight, but the glow was gone, along with the smile. His blue eyes searched her face, and he moved a shock of brown hair off his forehead with an impatient hand.

"Are you traveling alone?" he asked, but then answered himself. "No! Surely not! And Dacia? She's already there? Who is with her?"

"I'm with my parents," Lou said, taken aback by his reaction. "And my brothers. They are at the other end of the car, in our compartment. Dacia is at one of our family's houses. With our aunt Kate. We own a lot of houses . . . our mothers are Romanian."

She was babbling, she knew, and it was obvious that she was edging toward the door of the compartment, but he really was alarming her now. Also, it had occurred to her that she herself didn't know this young man, who had nearly been sent to jail this very year for his crimes. Even worse: he had enticed Dacia to . . . to . . . well to nearly disgrace herself! Lou moved back to the door of the compartment.

"You're Romanian? I didn't know that." He screwed up his face, thinking. "Then I think you'll be all right. Romania can be dangerous, though, if you don't know what you're doing. I'm sure your mother's family will look out for you."

Ignoring that, Lou asked him a question. "What are *you* doing here?" She had one hand on the door, but his last sentence caught her attention, and she looked at him with one of her best Aunt Kate expressions. "I mean, why are you on this train?"

"I have business in Bucharest," he said stiffly.

"Well, good luck to you," she said, wishing her voice wasn't coming out so shrill. "Good day, my lord." And she beat a hasty retreat back to her family's compartment.

"LouLou? Are you all right?"

Her father woke up as she slipped in between the sliding mahogany doors. He startled her and she jumped and let out a little scream.

"Oh, goodness! Yes, I'm fine!" She clutched at the lacy fichu at her throat. "I just wanted some air."

Maria sniffed, nose wrinkled in disgust. "Then why did you go to the smoking car?" she demanded. Her sense of smell was almost as keen as Aunt Kate's, as Lou and Dacia had discovered the time they had tried to smoke cigarettes with the coachman behind the stable.

"Having a cigar with the gentlemen, were we?" Her father winked at her.

"I thought perhaps it was just an empty car," she said, trying to sound dignified.

"Well, it isn't, and now you smell like some dreadful gentleman's club," her mother complained. "Open a window, someone. I can't stand the reek."

Lou subsided into her seat, chastened. Why did such things always happen to her? If she wasn't accosted by strange men, then she was wandering into the wrong train car and . . . being accosted by strange men again! She sighed and rubbed at her skirt, hoping that the smell wouldn't stay in the silk permanently.

"Who is that strange man?"

Lou glanced up at her mother's shriek, and let out a small screech of her own. That Awful Man was standing in the passageway, peering into their compartment! She thought she might really have an attack of some sort now, and could only gasp for air. Lord Johnny appeared beside him, and Lou wondered for a fevered moment if she was simply hallucinating all the beaux she didn't have. Lord Johnny spoke to That Awful Man, and then they both went on down the passage toward the young lord's compartment.

"LouLou, are you all right?" Her father knelt in front of her, grabbing her hands. "Just breathe, darling, you're turning quite pale!"

Lou did her best to relax and breathe, but then the twins woke up and demanded something to eat. Maria shouted at them to be silent because she had just had a shock: a strange man had ogled her, and then Adam wanted to know what *ogled* meant. But Lou's father stayed at her side, talking in a soothing voice that she could barely hear above the din, until she was able to catch her breath again.

"I'll be all right," she assured him after a little while.

"Did you know that man? The first one?" Her father pressed her hands.

"N-no," she stammered. "He just startled me." She felt her stomach churn at the lie. "But the younger man was Lord John Harcastle," she admitted. "Dacia's Lord Johnny, you know, from London."

"I see," her father said, looking as if this explained a great deal.

"That horrid boy!" Her mother was even more hysterical now. "Don't ever say his name again! To think what we might have lost if Dacia had . . . if they had . . . I can't even say it!"

"Eloped?" Lou's father suggested.

"Don't say it!" her mother screamed.

"What does *eloped* mean?" David wanted to know. Adam giggled and elbowed his twin in the ribs.

"Never you mind," their father said.

"But they didn't, not really, Dacia thought he . . ." Lou trailed off. Not even her father was listening to her, and she didn't really understand what Dacia had been doing.

The conductor arrived to see what all the screaming was about, and offered Mrs. Neulander wine and smelling salts, both of which she happily accepted. She was less happy that the conductor was unwilling to throw the men who had peeped at her off the train, when he learned that one of them was an English lord.

Lou leaned her face against the cool windowpane, and wished that meeting Lord Johnny had helped her make sense of what was happening with her family. She was just as baffled and frightened as she had been before . . . no, more so. And the train still had more mountains to cross, and more borders, before she reached Bucharest.

Lou could not wait until they arrived in Bucharest and she was reunited with Dacia. Dacia always seemed to have the answers, and if she didn't, she would figure out how to get them.

## THE DIARY OF MISS DACIA VREEHOLT

*22 May 1897*

    I wish that you could somehow help me. I do not know where to turn. There is something very wrong among my mother's family. They are full of secrets, secrets they guard so closely that Radu fears for his life if he tells me. He seems very convinced of this fact: that his life is forfeit if he disobeys that horrible creature that I have the misfortune to be connected to, that awful woman whom fate has cursed me with as a grandmother. Lady Ioana frightens me almost as much as she frightens Radu, and though I find it hard to believe that even she is odious enough to have her own grandson killed, there is still a coldness in her eyes that makes me shudder whenever I see her.

    I long for Lou to join me here, and yet I am frightened for her. What will she make of this situation? How soon can we free ourselves of it? My uncle Cyrus will surely not allow us to be bullied and mistreated by Lady Ioana. Perhaps I can appeal to him to take us straight back to New York. They arrive soon from Paris. I will speak to Lou and Uncle Cyrus as soon as I may, and sound out their feelings. I am not sure I will last another week, let alone months!

I have written to Mother, but it is laughable to think that she would offer consolation, or go against her mother's wishes to tell me the answer to any of my questions. Indeed, she has not answered a single one of my letters since I fell into disgrace in England. Papa writes regularly, but only of general matters: his and Mother's well-being, social events, etc. Besides which, he has never been to Romania, and has never met Lady Ioana.

Will Aunt Maria be of help when she arrives? Who can say? Now that I see Aunt Kate giving in before Lady Ioana, I doubt Aunt Maria will oppose the old woman, either.

Precisely why I am glad that _my_ mother's indisposition kept her at home. Imagine if my own mother were to turn against me!

On second thought, the difference would be imperceptible . . .

# STRADA SILVESTRU

The moment Lou descended from the carriage, Dacia flung herself into her cousin's arms. She was a bit startled at her own vehemence, but just couldn't check her emotion or her flight. It was fortunate that her uncle was right behind Lou, and could catch them both before they crashed to the pavement.

"Oh, Lou!" Dacia caught herself before her words became a sob. "I'm so glad you're here at last!"

Lou muttered something into the lace of Dacia's bodice, and when Dacia stepped back, she realized that Lou had not been able to restrain tears of her own. That prompted more embraces, and Dacia and Lou both sniffled and smiled at each other with watery eyes, while Lou's father handed down her mother and then the twins.

"Dacia, it's been simply awful," Lou said in a low voice, shooting a glance at her parents.

"You, too?" Dacia slumped. Poor Lou! She'd been hoping that at least one of them was enjoying herself. She knew about

That Awful Man, of course, but had hoped that things were going better for her cousin. "Come upstairs at once; we'll talk." She leveled a terrible look at the twins. "And if we're interrupted, I will have the two of you exiled to Turkey, see if I don't!"

They gazed back in the utmost innocence, and Dacia snorted. She put her arm through Lou's and led her up the stairs into the mansion, where Aunt Kate was waiting. Dacia tried to lead Lou past their aunt, but Kate raised one eyebrow and Dacia wilted. The battle of wills with her aunt was becoming increasingly beyond her energy. Though she hated to admit it, Lady Ioana had taken much of the wind out of her sails.

"Aunt Kate, so good to see you," Lou said, and let go of Dacia's arm to hug and kiss their aunt.

Aunt Kate looked like she was going to say something more, but then Lou's parents entered with the twins. In the ensuing babble, Dacia led Lou upstairs. Dacia, seeing Lou's pallor and remembering how grimy she'd felt when she arrived, went past her own room to the adjacent one, which was to be Lou's. Her cousin looked around briefly, set her reticule and hat on the dresser, and then collapsed into a chair.

"I can't speak of it all just now," Lou said. "You had better go first. What has happened since your last letter?"

"It's been awful," Dacia blurted out. "I feel like I've been put in prison, and all because a young man likes me!" She leaped to her feet and paced back and forth. "All Prince Mihai wants to do is take me to the opera one night. But Aunt Kate is acting very strange, and so is Uncle Horia, and you are going to be appalled when you meet Lady Ioana!"

"Who is Lady Ioana?" Lou asked, looking even paler.

"The most unnatural grandmother the world has ever known," Dacia said.

"You mean Grandmother Florescu?" Lou's brow puckered in anxiety.

"Whatever you do, don't call her Grandmother Florescu," Dacia said in a dark voice. "No one warned me, which is beyond rude, but it seems that everyone calls her Lady Ioana, even Aunt Kate—her own daughter! And everyone is terrified of her. Even Aunt Kate! *Especially* Aunt Kate!"

Lou looked shocked, and Dacia made a face. She hadn't meant to terrify her cousin the moment she arrived, but Dacia sensed that it couldn't be helped. Lou was so much more sensitive than Dacia was, and it would do Lou no favors to have her run afoul of Lady Ioana, who was expected for dinner. Dacia looked carefully at Lou's face, to make sure she was ready for the next bit of news. She saw the puckering of her cousin's forehead: a sure sign that Lou was upset. Dacia drew in as deep a breath as her corset would allow. She knew that what she was going to say next would make Lou upset for certain.

"Let me tell you about meeting Lady Ioana," she began, proceeding to tell Lou about her less-than-fortunate introduction to their grandmother, followed by Lady Ioana's strange words.

"The Wing? She said that she was the Wing?" Lou's pallor had gone waxy, and her voice hardly a whisper. "She said that *I* was the Wing?" Her dry lips barely made any sound at all on this last question.

Dacia knelt in front of her cousin and took her hands. "Yes. And that I was the Claw," she said softly. "But I don't know what it means any more than you do. I tried to ask Radu, but he said that Lady Ioana would kill him if he told me before she gave her permission. And Lou, he really meant it. There's something going on here, only I don't know what. Everyone's acting like there's a reason for us to come here, beyond just meeting our cousins.

"The worst part is they make it sound like we're never leaving."

A soft knock came at the door, which made them both jump, but it was only a footman with Lou's luggage. Dacia remained at Lou's feet, both of them frozen in a strange tableau as he brought in her things, trying hard not to gape at them.

"I met your Lord Johnny, Lord John Harcastle that is, on the train," Lou said, changing the subject after the footman had gone. She opened the lid of her trunk and began to remove an array of beautiful new gowns.

Dacia felt a warm flush start up her neck and cheeks. "He's not *my* Lord Johnny," she said, but couldn't keep a faint smile at bay. "What did he say?"

"He—he was very kind," Lou said. "I accidentally wandered into the smoking car, and he offered to let me sit in his compartment for a while and catch my breath."

"Why was he on the Express?" Dacia found that now she was smiling, she couldn't stop, thinking of Lord Johnny. "Did he say? Did he mention me?"

"Of course," Lou told her, laying out her new gowns. Dacia gasped appreciatively at the pale pink satin evening gown. "Well, I brought you up first, because I recognized him from the clippings you had sent me. But he appeared to be very excited to talk about you."

"Did he say where he was going? Istanbul? Or somewhere even more exotic?" Dacia held a blue gown to her shoulders and looked at herself in the long mirror, trying to be nonchalant.

Lou was looking at her with raised eyebrows and a faint smile. Despite being totally guileless herself, she was exceptionally good at reading Dacia. "Bucharest," she said.

"What?" Dacia dropped the gown, then scrambled to pick it up, face burning. "Here? Does he know I'm— Did he say why he's— He's in Bucharest right now?"

Lou laughed her bubbly little laugh, which Dacia had tried to tell her over and over again made every man in the room look at her. Lou just never would believe that any man was paying her notice, which was probably a good thing, since it made her less self-conscious and freer with her smiles and laughter.

"He said that he had business, and he did seem startled that you were here," Lou told her. "But he was blushing almost as badly as you are." Another little laugh.

"Oh, really?" Dacia laid the gown on the bed, trying not to twitter like one of those silly girls who suddenly acts like a flitting, brainless sparrow whenever a young man is in the room. Or even mentioned. "That's . . . nice."

Lou shook her head. "Ah, Dacia, you're going to get into trouble. I've heard about your other suitor as well. Mama has been fussing over it since she got Aunt Kate's telegram. We have trunks of new gowns for you as well."

Dacia goggled. "Your mother . . . she *wants* me to keep company with Prince Mihai?"

"From the sound of things, yes," Lou said, puzzled. "Why wouldn't she? He's Romanian, and a prince!"

"Uncle Horia is firmly against it," Dacia said. "That's why they were fighting when Radu and I listened in and were caught by Lady Ioana. Lady Ioana is supportive, but that makes me highly suspicious. I feel like I'm being 'handled,' you know?" Dacia picked the gown up again, then hung it in the wardrobe before her nervous fingers plucked off all the ornaments.

"And then there's the fact that Lady Ioana and even Aunt Kate act as though an invitation to the opera is a proposal of marriage, which I must accept!"

"But he's some kind of royalty," Lou said, her eyes wide. "They always take their connections very seriously. For him, it might be as good as proposing."

"Oh, hardly!" Dacia threw up her hands. "I mean, to say he's a prince sounds thrilling, but it's one of those older titles that are traditional, not political. He's no relation to the king, you know. It's like the Russians, who have princes simply everywhere."

"Well, your mother doesn't think that it's a lesser title," Lou said. "She and Mama have exchanged a dozen telegrams; they are both so excited about a prince courting you!"

"Mother is?" Dacia tried to keep the squeak out of her voice, and not look too eager to ask her next question. "What did she say?"

Lou put a soft arm around Dacia's waist and gave her a little squeeze. "I don't know the details, only that she wanted you to have the best of everything from Paris," Lou said. "Let's go in your room and you can see what we've brought you."

The cousins went into the next room, neither of them

needing to talk about Dacia's disappointment that her mother hadn't sent *her* a telegram over the matter. Dacia wouldn't want to embarrass herself if tears leaked out or her voice shook, but Lou understood, and nothing needed to be said.

The gowns that the maid was spreading out on her bed took Dacia's mind off her mother completely. They were in the latest mode and utterly gorgeous. Not even the shops in London could deliver that elegant drape to the fabric, that certain something that was so completely French that it could never be mistaken for anything else. Long used to putting her mother out of her mind, Dacia gave herself over to the new clothes: trying on gloves and hats, holding up gowns and posing in the long mirror while Lou laughed and admired them.

But Dacia could still see the faintest traces of a pucker on Lou's forehead, and there was a little twist of sourness in her own stomach that the tea and biscuits the maid brought could not wash away. She picked up her own new evening gown, a white confection with lavender accents, and held it to her shoulders.

Then she nearly dropped that gown, but this time in sheer excitement.

"Lou! I know what we can do!" She whirled around and put the gown on the bed so that she could take her cousin's hands. "We'll *both* go to the opera!"

"What do you mean? Of course we will, Papa said he would—" Lou's eyes widened. "Do you mean with Prince Mihai?" Her voice lifted on the name.

"Yes!" Dacia twirled around, pleased by her solution. "Aunt Kate said I might, but Uncle Horia is being such a bear about it that I've put Mihai off. If we went together—I'm sure Mihai wouldn't mind! He's terribly persistent and he says he'll do anything to make me happy—and if we both went, it wouldn't be quite so serious!" She gave Lou's hands an extra little squeeze, but Lou looked dubious.

"I don't know," Lou said. "What if Prince Mihai doesn't want me there? He's never even met me." She hesitated, looking around the room as though not sure how to go on. "And don't you think it's rather forward of him to keep asking, when you've been putting him off?"

"Not at all! It will be perfect," Dacia announced, brushing both concerns aside. Another idea lit her up. "He really is so eager to please, you know, that I wonder if he'll send you an opera cloak, too!"

This didn't seem to entice Lou, but all the same Dacia immediately went to her desk to write Prince Mihai a note while Lou took a bath. Dacia accepted the prince's invitation to the opera, writing that she had at last brought the family around to her way of thinking. Feeling even more clever, she wrote that now that her cousin was in residence, she was sure Mihai would want to help her show Lou the sights of Bucharest. She summoned a footman at once to deliver the note, watching to make sure that he got out of the house before anyone could intercept him.

"And now if I could just find out where Lord Johnny is staying," Dacia mused, "things would be very exciting indeed!"

*25 May 1897*

Being with Dacia has not assuaged my fears, but rather
added to them. Aunt Kate has become a stranger, and I worry
that Mama will also. Dacia is obsessed with a minor prince
whose interest has polarized the family and caused many
arguments. Papa is busy keeping the twins out from underfoot,
and Mama seems to find excuses for him to take charge of
them, so that he and I never get a chance to speak. I long for
his reassurances, but none are forthcoming.

The afternoon after our arrival in Bucharest was the worst
yet. I met in private with Grandmother Florescu, whom I must
remember is never to be called Grandmother, but to be
addressed always as Lady Ioana, a title I did not know she
held. She is not merely stern, but threatening, and everyone is
afraid of her. She looked me over, gave me a smile that made
me cold inside, and told me that I was the Wing as predicted.
It seems that even my own mother knows this strange thing and
did not say a word to me!

Lady Ioana also told me that I had a less defiant face than
Dacia, which was good, because the Claw always thought too
much of themselves. She joked that she had nearly had Radu
killed three times. At least, I chose to think of it as a joke. Then

she congratulated me on not having a beau, saying that it was for the best, because when the time came, she would find me a suitable mate of my own kind. I felt my face getting redder and redder, and at these words I nearly fainted. So shockingly crass, but she seemed quite unaware of it! I wanted very much to lie, to claim that I had a fiancé waiting for me in New York, but I couldn't do it.

And now I am to attend the opera with Dacia and Prince Mihai. My mother, who would have been shocked by the very idea of Dacia attending the opera with a young man alone in New York, has sided with Aunt Kate and wants Dacia to find every possible chance to be with Prince Mihai!

I just wish that the very idea of meeting this prince didn't fill me with terror.

# LA TRAVIATA

Despite her misgivings, Lou discovered that Prince Mihai did not at all mind taking her to the opera along with Dacia. He seemed delighted, in fact. He had even sent an opera cloak for her, just as Dacia had said he might. It was lined with pink satin that perfectly matched her gown, though how he could have guessed what color her gown was she would never know. She brushed it aside as a lucky guess, pale pink being eminently suitable for a young lady. All the same it gave her a shiver, as though he had been watching her.

She was not quite as intrigued by Mihai as Dacia was. He was polite enough, and very handsome, but there was something about him that Lou did not like, a calculating look that said that he had more planned than simply squiring a pair of young ladies to the opera. By the time they had taken their seats in Prince Mihai's box, Lou found herself siding with Uncle Horia and Radu. This was not a good idea, though her reasons were not as prosaic as theirs. She didn't see Mihai as being above their station, or too old for Dacia (both arguments they had used); she saw him as dangerous, and Lou did not like danger.

Dacia, unfortunately, did.

Dacia loved being at the opera with everyone staring and whispering as they walked by. She loved the way that Prince Mihai raked her with his eyes when she came down the stairs to greet him in her Parisian evening gown. She loved walking with her fingertips just touching his arm, pretending that she was a queen. Dacia didn't have to say anything of the sort to Lou, Lou just knew it was so. She knew it by the lift in her cousin's chin, the sway in her walk as they entered the foyer of the opera house, as they walked down the gilded halls to their box.

Lou knew, too, that Dacia was aware that Lou was nervous about the evening. But it wouldn't occur to Dacia to call it off, because she always thought it was good for Lou to do things despite her nerves. Dacia was convinced that one day she would drag Lou along on some scheme and something in Lou would blossom. Just like that, Lou would become as fearless as Dacia, and they would take on the world together. Lou knew this would never happen, but still she followed where her cousin led. Lou knew deep down that she would always be afraid, and nothing would ever change that, but she followed Dacia for the slim chance that her cousin was right.

Contrary to Lou's fears, Prince Mihai seemed quite amiable. He had arrived on the very stroke of six and complimented them lavishly on their gowns. He had been effusive, too, in greeting the rest of the household, charming Lou's mother and winning a smile from Aunt Kate as well. Lou's father had been wary, though coolly polite to the prince, which said volumes to Lou. Her father had always been quite genial with the young men who had escorted Lou to balls and parties in the past. She took her cue from her father, rather than Dacia, and was polite but as distant as she could manage without feeling rude.

Though even she had to admit that the prince was devastatingly handsome.

Her stomach turned over whenever he smiled at her, and she found herself in a flutter when he first took her arm to go up the steps into the opera house. But then she saw him looking around at the other women in the lobby, and smiling at them when they stared at him, and the flutters stopped. Men who were handsome and knew it all too well did not hold that much of an attraction for Lou.

They took their seats just as the curtain was going up. Lou tried to make herself comfortable in the little gilded chair, wondering why it was that people always needed to cough and rustle their clothing just when everything was going silent. Dacia leaned forward, eager for the music to begin. Dacia loved the opera; it appealed to her sense of drama. Lou preferred lighter music, the kind that tickled you and then soared away.

Still, it was an excellent performance, with marvelous singers and a lavish set. Even Lou quickly became engrossed, and so it wasn't until the intermission that she noticed that Lord Johnny was sitting in a box directly opposite them. He was blatantly watching them, rather than the stage, through his opera glasses.

When Prince Mihai summoned a waiter to bring them lemonade, Lord Johnny stood and made as if to leave his box, his eyes still on Dacia. But someone stepped from the shadows at the back of the box and put a hand on his shoulder, stopping the impulsive young lord and causing him to sink back into his seat with an anxious air.

Lou's every muscle went rigid. She felt a frisson of horror run through her, and her palms began to sweat in their white silk gloves. She wanted to say something to Dacia, but couldn't form any words. She was afraid, too, that if she moved she would draw attention to herself.

Too late. The man with Lord Johnny looked across at their box, and despite the distance, he looked straight into Lou's eyes and made a little bow. Lou leaped to her feet as the frisson of horror turned to an electric shock, and grabbed Dacia's arm, dragging her cousin out of the box and into the corridor. Without speaking a word, Lou pulled Dacia through the crowd of elegantly dressed ladies and gentlemen returning to their boxes, and into the ladies' retiring room, where she at last let go of Dacia's arm.

"Lou! What on earth are you doing? Are you ill?"

Lou put her hands over her face and burst into tears. "He's here," she sobbed. "He's here, and he saw me!"

"Who's here?" Dacia looked alarmed. She backed Lou gently over to a sofa and helped her sit, positioning herself close beside her cousin, but turned so that her narrow back blocked Lou from prying eyes as much as it could.

"That man." Lou hiccupped. "That Awful M-m-man! The one who called me a hou— I can't even say it! The one who called me the Wing," she managed to gasp out.

"What?" Dacia gasped. "Are you certain?"

"Yes," Lou said, finally beginning to recover. She pulled out a handkerchief and hopelessly patted at her face a little. She wasn't wearing any cosmetics, but she wished she were. She knew that her face would be red and blotchy, which the handkerchief could hardly repair.

"Where did you see him?" Dacia had a militant gleam in her eye.

"Directly across from us . . . in a box with your Lord Johnny," Lou said, admitting the last with great reluctance.

Dacia's mouth opened and closed with a little click. "He was with Johnny? You're very certain?"

Lou nodded.

"Well, then," Dacia said. "This changes everything." Dacia rose to her feet.

"What are you going to do?" Lou also got up, with much less grace. "Please don't do anything dramatic, Dacia! Please?" Her cheeks flushed at the thought of what Dacia might do to retaliate on her behalf, and wished she hadn't said anything. A militant Dacia could be amusing or appalling, often at the same time.

"*I* am not going to do a thing, dear," Dacia said, kissing Lou's cheek.

Lou gave her a suspicious look, but Dacia only put on her most innocent smile in return.

"Prince Mihai, on the other hand, is a different matter," Dacia said. "I'm sure if I mention it to him, he would feel honor bound to respond to the insult." She took Lou's arm and led her out of the retiring room and into the deserted corridor. The second half of the opera was well under way, but Dacia did not seem at all bothered by missing it.

"Dacia, please don't tell the prince," Lou whispered as they reached the door to the box. "It would only embarrass me more."

Her cousin had to think about that for a moment, but then she agreed with a nod. "All right, dear. But you must know that I have already told Radu, I was so upset when I received your letter. And I think that it's a good idea to let one of the men of the family know that this boor is in Bucharest. Radu will be with us the most often when we go shopping and the like, so he would be the one to protect you if this cad approaches again."

"Very well," Lou said. "It will be a relief to have Radu there to defend me."

"I agree," Dacia said in her offhand manner that so frequently insulted even while it doled out praise. "Radu may be under Lady Ioana's thumb, but in a brawl I'd still put my money on him."

"A brawl?" Lou shuddered at the very thought, but Dacia had already gone into the box.

Lou could only follow, accept her now warm glass of lemonade, and take her seat with her eyes firmly on the stage. She tried her best not to look at Lord Johnny's box, but during the grand climax of the opera she suddenly could not bear it a moment longer, and quickly peeked in their direction.

Her peek turned into a long look of surprise. The box was not empty, as she'd hoped, but both men were sitting right against the rail, leaning forward and ignoring the action on the stage completely. Their eyes were fixed avidly on someone in the box with Lou, but it wasn't her, and to her even greater surprise, it wasn't Dacia either.

Both Lord Johnny and That Awful Man were staring right at Prince Mihai.

Lou tried to get Dacia's attention without alerting Prince Mihai, but Dacia, after first arranging herself to present her best side to Lord Johnny, was once more caught up in the music. She stared at the stage in unfashionable wonderment, blissfully unaware of the Romanian prince, the British lord, or That Awful Man, until the curtains dropped and she applauded the performers with gusto. Lou applauded as well, but kept watching Lord Johnny and That Awful Man out of the corner of her eye. She saw them talk to each other briefly once the opera was over, but by the end of the curtain call they had slipped out of their box, much to Lou's relief.

Once in the lobby Lou craned her neck but couldn't see either young man. But her attention was soon taken by a number of other young people who came to introduce themselves. They all seemed quite as enthralled by Prince Mihai as Dacia was, approaching him with great deference and only speaking once he acknowledged them. He introduced Lou and Dacia to what must have been every member of young Bucharest society, and the cousins found themselves agreeing to accept calls from a number of people who appeared quite surprised to find that the Florescu family had fashionable young daughters.

Even Lou was glowing with the fun of it all as they got into the carriage. In New York they'd had friends, but they were friends that they'd known for years, and there was hardly a line of new people eager to make their acquaintance. Lou temporarily forgot her nerves and found herself looking forward to being invited to parties and balls. For one thing, it would keep them out of the house and away from Lady Ioana, who had been far more terrifying than That Awful Man, though it felt disloyal to the family to admit such a thing, even in her own head.

"Our carriage, my beauties," Prince Mihai said, and helped them into his elegant barouche. Lou's father had asked for the prince to bring them both home immediately after the opera, and not take them to a ball or dinner, so they waved to their many new friends they passed, and went home considerably earlier than the rest of Bucharest's fashionable population.

"Back so soon?" Lou's mother came to the front hall to greet them, smiling up at Prince Mihai through her lashes. Lou found herself blushing a little at her mother's obvious flirtation with the prince.

"Ah, gentle lady!" The prince kissed her mother's hand, but Lou noticed that Mihai lifted her mother's hand high so that he did not have to bow to her. She realized that all night, throughout all the introductions, he had never once lowered his head to anyone. A bit vain of him, she thought cynically. He was not a *ruling* prince. Wallachia wasn't even a country anymore, just one of the Romanian states. "Your good husband asked me to bring your beautiful daughter and niece home promptly after the opera, and prompt we are! I would never wish to anger your family."

"Of course you wouldn't," Lou's father said, coming out of the library. "That would be a very bad idea."

Lou and Dacia shared puzzled looks, but Lou saw a flash

of rage cross Prince Mihai's fine features, twisting them into something ugly. And her mother was blushing bright red, her mouth set in a thin line.

"No, it would not be at all wise to anger a family that includes so many lovely young ladies," Prince Mihai said, recovering his composure. "Though I am now a bit sorrowful that I might have to share them."

"Share them?" Despite the strain between them, Lou's parents spoke in concert.

"Oh, Uncle Cyrus!" Dacia spoke, her face lighting up. "We've met so many fine young people tonight. Everyone in Bucharest was at the opera, or so it seemed, and Prince Mihai has introduced us all around. We've had many promises of calls, and invitations to parties! We're going to have such fun, aren't we, Lou?" She put her arm through Lou's, and Lou managed to smile.

Something had happened between her parents while she had been out. They were standing on opposite sides of the front hall, her father as tense as a harp string, and her mother's exclamations of delight over this latest news could not hide the tautness around her eyes.

"How lovely," Lou's father said, and she turned a little to look past Dacia at him. A strange smile stretched his mouth, and his eyes were on her mother. "I hope you girls receive many invitations in the next few weeks. They will be a pleasant diversion for you." He inclined his head toward Prince Mihai. "Now if you'll excuse me, I believe I shall retire for the evening."

"I, too, must go," Prince Mihai said. He kissed all their hands, again without bowing to them to any degree, and took his leave.

"Isn't he marvelous?" Lou's mother gave a little sigh. "It's all coming together . . ." Then she straightened and seemed to gather herself. "Well, off to bed with the both of you! If you're going to receive calls tomorrow, you'll want to get plenty of rest!" She flapped her hands at them and they went upstairs.

It wasn't until her mother had gone to bed, and the maid had undressed her and brushed out her hair, that Lou was able to hurry to Dacia's room and talk. Dacia had already dismissed her maid and was braiding her own hair.

"Have you noticed that no one in this family seems to finish their sentences anymore?" Lou asked, flopping down in a chair. "Or if they do, it's because they're not saying what they really mean?"

"It's decidedly odd," Dacia agreed. "But what really worries me more right now is how intensely Lord Johnny and that man who insulted you were staring at Mihai all through the second half of the opera."

28 May 1897

To my dear mother,

I hope that you are well. I am sure that you are very busy getting ready for the journey to Newport for the summer. I must confess that I am jealous, and find that I will miss the old routine. This may come as a great surprise to you, after my protests and complaints of the last few years, but now that I have been gone from home for some time, I do miss it.

In fact, I miss it so much that I truly wish that I could return home, and soon. I have been abroad for three months now, and it is becoming very wearying for me. I know that Lou and I are supposed to stay until after Christmas, but I do not think it will be at all enjoyable for anyone concerned. Lou has only been here two days, and she is already showing signs of nervous strain. Aunt Kate does not seem to be enjoying the visit, either.

I am, of course, pleased to make the acquaintance of my Florescu relations, but I think that a month would be more than sufficient for us to get to know one another. And we could always return in years to come, when you are able to accompany us!

Please consider sending for me. It would be so much better coming from you, I am sure that Aunt Kate would agree completely.

Your loving daughter,
Dacia

# CALEA GRIVITEI

There truly is no rest for the wicked, Dacia thought. Her old nurse had been fond of the phrase, almost too fond, really, trotting it out as an excuse for everything from waking Dacia up at the first light of dawn to making her march bleakly through the park in all weather as a grim form of exercise. But the morning after Dacia had attended the opera with Lou and Prince Mihai, it was all too true.

She and Lou had stayed up late talking, turning over possible reasons for Uncle Cyrus and Aunt Maria's argument, and the scrutiny of Lord Johnny and the man who had insulted Lou. And how did they know each other? Lou had told her about seeing the two men together on the Orient Express as well. It was all too puzzling, and the cousins soon found that they had far too many questions and no answers whatsoever. Finally, exhausted, Dacia had simply climbed into Lou's bed and they had gone to sleep side by side, as they had many times as children. Dacia would never admit how comforting she found it, in this strange house. Even after staying here for weeks, everything about the big mansion still seemed too . . . foreign.

The maid came in and opened the curtains at seven o'clock in the morning, when Dacia and Lou had only been asleep for four hours.

"I'm sorry, young ladies," she had said with an apologetic smile. "But *Doamna* Maria ordered me to wake you now."

"Gnnnh," Dacia replied, and put her pillow over her head.

Lou sat up abruptly, looked blankly at the maid, the open window, then Dacia, and then collapsed back onto the bed. "Gnnnh," she said in agreement.

The maid giggled and went out, but she apparently tattled on the cousins, because Aunt Kate swept into the room a minute later and opened Lou's wardrobe. The doors creaked, and Lou made a noise that was roughly the same pitch.

"Why do we have to get up?" Dacia didn't remove the pillow from her face.

"Because you are being fitted for some traditional clothing this morning. Then we will be making social calls in the afternoon, followed by a dinner with the family this evening. There is no time for you to lie in bed."

Dacia took the pillow off her face and sat up. "Making calls?" She felt her eyebrows approach her hairline and stay there.

She had hardly left the mansion the entire time she had been in Bucharest, other than to do a little shopping with Radu or a pair of burly footmen in tow. Prince Mihai's calls were the only other exception. When she'd asked why they never received any invitations, or went to visit even the next-door neighbors, Aunt Kate had frostily informed her that the Florescu family was above such frivolity.

"Since Prince Mihai has generously introduced you to the young people of Bucharest society," Aunt Kate said, "it now behooves us to introduce you to their parents." She sighed, as though she were not exactly looking forward to this. "We must maintain appearances."

"What appearances?" Dacia asked. "Aren't we just as fashionable here as in New York?"

"Don't be fresh," Aunt Kate snapped, though Dacia hadn't meant to be fresh, and she suspected that Aunt Kate knew that very well.

"Maria Louisa, get out of that bed," Aunt Kate went on. "Put this on, and have the maid help you put your hair up. Breakfast is in half an hour, and the seamstress will be here immediately following."

"Do I really need any more clothes?" Lou's face was still wrinkled with sleep, but she climbed out of the high bed. "We bought so many in Paris."

"Lady Ioana has ordered this clothing for you," Aunt Kate said. "You must thank her at dinner."

"She'll be at dinner again?" Dacia tried to keep the groan out of her voice, without much success. She reflected sourly, again, at how strange it was that the old witch made even her own daughters call her Lady Ioana.

"*Everyone* will be at dinner," Aunt Kate said, her voice suddenly heavy. "I will leave a gown on your bed, Dacia. I suggest you hurry." And she swept back out.

Lou looked at Dacia in a dazed way. "Well, at the very least we'll make some friends," she said, but she didn't sound too certain of that.

"And possibly get some answers," Dacia mused.

Lou wandered over to her washstand, and Dacia forced herself out of the bed. Sauntering into her own room, she found a completely new gown on her bed, one that had been bought in Paris, and decided that the day might not be too bad after all. Also, in the course of their calls, they might run into Prince Mihai, or even Lord Johnny. It struck Dacia that she did not know where he was staying. With that man who had insulted Lou? And who was he?

Dacia washed and dressed, wondering if she would dare to quiz the people they would be calling on. It would be impossible if Aunt Kate hovered, and if she was really planning to have them meet the adults, and only the adults. If, however, she and Lou were left to chat with people their own age, it would be relatively easy to ask if anyone knew the English lord, and to describe the man who had followed Lou around.

The maid who had awakened them came in to help her with her hair. Her name was Nadia, and she had been assigned to assist Dacia and Lou. She was shy, but nice enough, and not that much older than Dacia.

"Nadia," Dacia said as the maid rolled up the back of her hair and pinned it. "Do you think you could do me a favor?"

The girl shot her a wary look in the mirror. "Yes, young miss?"

"Do you know this neighborhood well?" Dacia did her best to sound casual.

"Yes, young miss. I have been with your family since I was

twelve." She drew herself up, though it didn't help much: she was a head shorter than Dacia. "And my family has served the Florescus for many generations."

"How lovely," Dacia purred. "Would you be able to do this one small thing for me?"

Again the wary look. "What small thing, young miss?"

Dacia decided that acting casual would get her nowhere. "There is a young nobleman from England visiting Bucharest. He and I ... became very close when I was in London," Dacia said, which was true. It made her blush, however, which just added to her story. "I would like to find out where he is staying, so that I can send him a message."

"Why can you not ask Mr. Horia?" The maid's eyes were suspicious. "He surely knows everyone in Bucharest. And if he does not know, then he can easily find out, young miss."

"Well," Dacia said, leaning toward the maid in a confidential manner. "My family doesn't exactly approve of—" She stopped, seeing Nadia's face close off.

"If your family does not approve, it is not my place to interfere," Nadia said.

"But surely there's no harm—"

"Lady Ioana would not approve," Nadia said, and would not say another word. She finished arranging Dacia's hair, gathered up her used nightclothes, and left the room.

"Lady Ioana," Dacia muttered, making it sound like a curse.

But she didn't have time to grumble any further about her grandmother. Aunt Kate fetched Dacia, hustling her down the stairs, along with Lou. They ate a hasty breakfast and went back up to Dacia's room. The seamstress was already laying out two nearly finished Romanian costumes. They were thickly embroidered in what Aunt Kate told them was the traditional pattern for their family. They had been begun in advance, and now would only require a bit of alteration to make them ready.

"Are we supposed to wear them tonight at the dinner?" Lou touched the fine linen with a finger.

"If they can be finished in time," Aunt Kate said. "And there will be a special party at the family estate as well."

The seamstress, who until this moment had not said a word, crossed herself and whispered something in a hoarse voice. Aunt Kate gave her a look, which the old woman met with defiance that made Dacia admire her for more than just her skill with a needle.

And the woman's needlework was very skilled indeed. Though she preferred modern fashions, Dacia had to admire the intricacy of the silk embroidery on the smooth linen. The fabric was white, with scarlet embroidery in ranks around the neckline and down the wide sleeves. Aunt Kate helped them out of their dresses—which made Dacia grumble that they could have eaten breakfast in their rooms and avoided some of the dressing and undressing—and into the costumes.

The traditional Romanian costume consisted of a long, pale gown decorated with brightly colored embroidery and gathered at the neck with a drawstring. Over it went a heavy dark-colored apron in the front and back, and a wide sash holding it all together. Though Dacia had seen a rainbow of colors on other women, she and Lou were now dressed alike in white and scarlet. The sashes, aprons, and embroidery were so red they almost hurt the eyes, and made the white stand out just as starkly.

"I always thought I looked better in lighter colors," Lou ventured hesitantly as she took her turn in front of the long mirror.

"Green would suit you. Or blue," the elderly seamstress said, nodding in agreement. Then her eyes squinted at Aunt Kate, whose mouth was decidedly pinched. "But red was ordered."

She fiddled with Lou's gown and pronounced it a good fit, though the hem needed to be taken up just a hair. Dacia's costume needed a bit more work. It was too short, and though the neck and cuffs had a drawstring that should have allowed it to fit almost anyone, Dacia was so slim that there was simply too much fabric bunched around her neck and middle, making her look bulky and feel as though she was being drowned in her own clothes.

"Your cousin is shaped like a proper woman," the seamstress said as she marked the seams of Dacia's shift with sharp steel pins. "But you . . ." Another look at Aunt Kate. "Are a Florescu," she finished with a guttural laugh.

Dacia decided that while she admired the old woman's frankness, she didn't particularly like her for it. "And Florescu women are known to be slender?" she asked tartly.

The old woman didn't answer her. She finished her marking, and helped Dacia to undress so that she wouldn't prick herself on the pins. She wrapped up both costumes and bowed to Aunt Kate. As she was leaving the room, though, she turned as she felt Dacia's eyes on her.

"Florescu women are known to not always be proper women," she said, and crossed herself again.

Aunt Kate just looked as though she'd smelled something foul. She muttered something about superstitions, and then went out with a terse message that they would be going calling as soon as the carriage was brought around.

Lou and Dacia helped each other into their gowns without speaking. There was nothing to say, really. Only more questions to which neither of them had answers.

As soon as they were dressed again, Aunt Kate bundled them into the carriage and they went to make some calls.

"Shouldn't we wait and see who will call on us?" Lou asked timidly. Dacia knew that her cousin had always hated making calls, much preferring to stay home and receive callers, where she could be more comfortable. "Several of the young people we met last night—"

"It is better that we go to them," Aunt Kate interrupted her. "Our family does not often receive callers; they will not expect us to be 'at home.'"

"Oh," Lou said, subsiding against the cushioned seat.

Dacia didn't mind getting out of the house to make calls, even if it wasn't always the most convenient thing to do. There was always the fuss of getting in and out of carriages, standing on the doorstep and giving your card to the butler, only to find that Mrs. So-and-So and her daughter had already gone out themselves to pay calls.

But when they got to the first mansion, it was to find that Mrs. So-and-So and her daughter—or Lady Radescu and Miss

Marcela, as they were actually named—were at home. At home, and both delighted and startled to receive Miss Florescu and her nieces from America. In fact, two other young ladies were there, and they and Marcela were among the young people Prince Mihai had introduced to Dacia and Lou the night before.

Sitting between Marcela and a stately brunette named Flora, Dacia discovered just how startled the Radescus and their guests were, and with good reason. She and Lou exchanged looks, but didn't interrupt the especially chatty Marcela, who actually had a few answers for them.

"We're all so excited to meet you, you know," Marcela said. "The Florescu family is famous, of course, but they never go about in society! And you're from America! It sounds so exotic and thrilling! What is America like?"

Dacia was temporarily at a loss for words. How do you describe an entire country? Not to mention the fact that she'd been born there, and for her it was simply home. Lou, however, had no trouble.

"Big," she said in a wistful voice. "Everything is much bigger. And newer."

Marcela nodded, as though that was just what she had expected. "And then you come here, and of course you spend your time with Prince Mihai. But we didn't expect him to bring you to the opera! Or for you to pay calls on other families!"

"Why is that?" Dacia was quick to ask.

Both Marcela and Flora looked at her in surprise. "Why, because you're Florescus," she said as though that explained everything. "You don't entertain, and the only society you keep is Prince Mihai's family, the Draculas."

Dacia still wasn't used to hearing Prince Mihai's family name, and it sent a cold prickle down her spine. Dracula was such a strange name! In Romanian, it meant either "son of the dragon," or worse, "son of the devil." It seemed insulting.

"We don't know why, do you?" Flora interjected. She smiled at Dacia and Lou. "You're very nice, and your aunt looks like a duchess, or a queen . . . Why do you think your family stays so cloistered all the time?"

"I heard a rumor that it's because they're only supposed to marry into the Dracula family," Marcela told her friend, as though Dacia and Lou weren't sitting right there. "But that can't be true, or why would they have sent Miss Florescu away?" She made a tiny gesture with her fingers to indicate Aunt Kate.

"Wait—who sent Miss Flor—Aunt Kate away?" Dacia leaned in close and whispered the question. Over Elisabeta's shoulder, she could see that her aunt was busy discussing the new motorcars and hadn't heard anything. Yet.

But Marcela recognized that she'd gone too far. "Oh, I hate to bring up old gossip."

"Please do," Dacia urged her. "No one tells us anything." Lou nodded, eyes wide, and Flora moved in closer, an eager expression on her face.

"Well . . ." Marcela shot her own look at her mother and Aunt Kate. "You, I just heard . . . I might be wrong, but . . . the rumor was that Miss Florescu was sent to America with her sisters because she was in love with Prince Mattias Dracula, Prince Mihai's uncle. They wanted to marry, but both families objected, and she was sent away so that they couldn't elope."

Dacia couldn't keep her voice to a whisper. "The man on the train!"

*29 May 1897*

*Dear Grandmother Neulander,*

*I hope that this letter finds you in the best of health. I am myself quite well, and nicely rested now after our long journey. Romania is very beautiful, and it is lovely to meet my Florescu relations and find out all the little details of their lives that weren't included in their letters over the years.*

*I hope that you got my postcard of the Tuileries. You were right: they were simply lovely. I also took a trip on the Seine, as you recommended. I wish that you could have come with us! Perhaps next year your gout will not be as severe and we could make the trip together. I would love to tour the boulevards where you went as a young girl, and hear your stories about the handsome young Frenchmen who wooed you!*

*Give my love to Grandfather, and know that I am missing you both.*

*Your devoted granddaughter,*
*LouLou*

# THE GARDENS AT
# STRADA SILVESTRU

It was plain that Aunt Kate did not want Lou and Dacia to have a chance to talk in private, Lou thought with frustration as they drove back to the house on Rua Silvestre. They had paid two more calls, and during both calls Aunt Kate had sat between the cousins, her demeanor discouraging all conversation.

Then they had accepted an invitation to lunch at a hotel with the last family they had called upon. It had been very nice. The family, the Gradeszys, had sixteen-year-old twin sons who were good fun, and a fifteen-year-old daughter who was equally vivacious. They made a merry party for lunch, and it gave Lou hope that her twin brothers might grow up to be more socially acceptable, though she doubted very much that they would ever be quite *that* nice.

But this gossip that Miss Marcela Radescu had repeated was simply burning its way through Lou's brain, and she wanted to discuss it with someone—anyone!—but most especially Dacia.

Her aunt Kate had been in love, her family had sent her away rather than allow the union, and that man was Prince Mihai's own uncle! If she didn't want Kate and Prince Mattias to marry, why then was Lady Ioana throwing Dacia at Prince Mihai? And did Mihai know? Where was this uncle now? And had he ever married? Or was he truly the man from the train who had been kissing Aunt Kate? That seemed the most likely answer.

Dacia looked positively giddy, and the one thing she'd managed to say to Lou on the subject was, "Some answers at last!" But Lou didn't think they'd gotten answers so much as more questions, which they hardly needed.

But there was no time to even think, because the Gradeszy twins and their sister set out to please Lou and Dacia, whom they had exuberantly declared their new favorite friends. Their family had an estate in the mountains, and they tried to extract a promise that Dacia and Lou would come and visit them when they went there to escape the coming summer heat.

"We shall see," Aunt Kate said in a repressive voice, overhearing the offer. She had been listening to all their conversations since they'd left the Radescus. "We will be retiring to our own estate very soon."

"Oh, but they must come," Mrs. Gradeszy said cheerfully. "It will be our pleasure to have them stay!" Her forehead, smooth and soft despite her age, creased lightly in thought. "Now, where is your estate?" she asked. "Ours is near Bukovina . . ."

"We are near Bran," Aunt Kate said. "Quite some distance, I'm afraid."

"Oooh, have you heard about the new palace?" Miriam, the

Gradeszy daughter, had shining eyes at the very mention of it. "The king's new palace is near Bran! And it's quite, quite modern, with a boiler for heat, and a telephone and electric lights!"

"Truly?" Dacia looked impressed. "Have you seen it?"

"No," Miriam said, sighing. "But I would love to! When the family is not in residence, they allow visitors to tour the palace, even though it's not quite finished, you know."

"We shall go sometime soon, I promise," her mother said indulgently. She turned to Lou and Dacia. "Have you been presented to His Majesty?" They shook their heads and she smiled at them. "Oh, but you must be presented! King Carol is the kindest of men, and his dear queen is like a mother to us all! They do so love to meet the young gentry!"

"I should like that very much," Dacia said.

Lou just smiled weakly. She thought meeting any king, no matter how kind, sounded terrifying. She had a difficult enough time finding conversation among people her own age and status; what on earth would she say to the king?

Lou wanted very badly to invite the Gradeszys to stay at the Florescu estate, and suggest that they all tour the new palace together, but didn't dare. She had, of course, never seen the family's estate near Bran, and it wasn't her place to be inviting friends to visit. It was the kind of impulsive thing that Dacia would do, and she gave her cousin an encouraging look, but Dacia was staring at Aunt Kate. Lou followed her gaze and saw their aunt giving Dacia a look that bespoke horrible, swift retribution if she said a single word. Lou sighed, much like Miriam, and Dacia echoed her.

By the time they parted from the Gradeszys, with many promises to go driving and to the theater together, it was getting late in the day. They rode in the open carriage in silence back to the mansion, and arrived at the same time as two coachloads of their cousins, aunts, and uncles.

There was a great deal of hugging and kissing and loud proclamations about how long it had been, or in the case of Lou and Dacia, what a shame it was that they had not yet met. All their Florescu cousins were boys, so a double line of young men ranging in age from ten to twenty began to form, to greet Dacia and Lou with grave smiles and stiff embraces. Radu appeared, along with Uncle Horia and their other five uncles.

The party filled the entrance hall and spilled into the library, and the aunts kept shrieking with the excitement of it all, which made Lou jumpy. She noticed that the aunts came in two sizes: short and stout or tall and slim. Since she had no hope of ever being tall or slim, it seemed that her lot was to be of the other kind of Florescu woman. She had some hope when an aunt whose name she didn't recognize (she was only recently married to the youngest of the uncles) came forward to embrace her. She was almost as tall as Dacia, but had a beautifully curved figure unlike any of her fellow willowy aunts. But when she hugged Lou, Lou felt the aunt's bust squash and move in a way that told her it was entirely padding.

"There's no hope," Lou said to herself, and Dacia gave her a puzzled look.

Lou did her best to paste on a smile, and tried to extract herself as best she could, ready to sneak away as soon as Dacia gave any sort of signal. But Dacia didn't give a signal. The relations kept arriving, and there seemed to be no way they could leave without raising a hue and cry.

The volume only increased when a footman arrived wearing Prince Mihai's scarlet livery. He had a gift for Dacia, which the entire family gathered around to watch her open. It was a bracelet of carved gold in the shape of a dragon with the head of a lion. The family all gasped in admiration, except for Uncle Horia, who immediately announced that she could not accept such an expensive gift.

Dacia read the note aloud: "The symbol of your ancestry and namesake, this could grace no other wrist, nor find an owner as beautiful. Mihai."

"It is the symbol of the Dacian people, the ancient people of Romania, and your namesake," explained Uncle Daniel. He had a pedantic air, and Lou thought that he was a professor, but couldn't remember. One of her uncles was, anyway.

"Then surely it's all right to keep it," said Dacia airily, and she put it on her wrist. She beamed at the footman, and told him to tell his master that it was lovely, and to expect a letter from her in the morning.

And with that it was time to dress for dinner at last, but their rooms were being used by some of the aunts to change, and so Lou found herself standing with Dacia in Aunt Kate's bedroom, getting dressed in her new Romanian costume alongside Dacia, Aunt Kate, and her own mother.

Hardly the right time for a confidential discussion.

Lou's mother was flushed with excitement, and helped Lou

into her new ensemble without even asking if she wanted any assistance. It was a simple enough style of dress, but her mother pulled the drawstrings with great ceremony. She tied them with fingers that shook, her eyes misty with delight. Lou knew that she should feel the same: this was her family, her heritage . . . but instead she felt suffocated. She wanted to hide, or open the window and somehow fly away. Instead she pasted on a smile and did her best to keep it there.

"Not so big, LouLou, you're looking ghoulish," Dacia whispered, and Lou amended her expression as best she could.

They went down to dinner arm in arm, but without being able to speak. Lou was practically vibrating with the need to talk privately with Dacia, and she could feel the tension in her cousin's arm as well. The gold bangle with its heavy carving trembled on Dacia's slender wrist, making her look like a pagan princess being sent to her doom.

Lou's and Dacia's hair had been put into two braids woven with scarlet ribbons, and Lou's mother wore a white lawn headscarf that floated behind her as she walked. She looked like a bride. When Lou's father saw them, he grinned and kissed his wife despite the crowd of relations watching. He held out one arm to Maria and the other to Aunt Kate. The dining room was not large enough to hold the entire family, so tables had been set up in the gardens, and lanterns were strung from the branches of the trees.

It felt very strange to be outside her bedroom without her corset on. Lou had to fight the urge to fidget and make sure her apron was tied correctly. She felt like she was wearing nothing more than a nightgown, and the breeze blew through her skirt in a most alarming manner as they took their places. On the other hand, with no bustle or demi-train, she could sit far more comfortably on the narrow wooden chair.

They sat down to a long meal with many dishes that Lou had never seen before, like spicy chopped pork wrapped in cabbage leaves, sour cream and chicken soup, and cucumbers in a strange dressing. She had tasted *mamaliga* before, but this time the little cakes of cornmeal soaked in cream had been heavily spiced, and had her reaching for her lemonade several times.

By the time the plates were taken away it was full dark and moths were fluttering around the lanterns. Lady Ioana sat the head of the table in a large chair not unlike a throne. Lou had been watching her carefully all evening, waiting for the old woman to do something. Thus far she had only eaten with hearty appetite, making a little conversation with Uncle Horia on her right hand and Uncle Daniel on her left. But when the footmen had filled everyone's glass with rich red wine, including Lou's and Dacia's, Lady Ioana dismissed the servants with a sharp word and rose to her feet.

The family also stood, waiting in eerie silence until the maids had scuttled indoors. Lady Ioana raised her glass and they all copied her. Across the table, Lou could see Dacia's eyes shining in the dimness, clearly delighted to be included in the toasts.

But they quickly turned their attention to Lady Ioana, who was almost swelling with her impending toast, or speech, or whatever it was. Lou felt her ears straining, she was so determined not to miss a single word.

"We are the Wing and the Claw," Lady Ioana announced, her shoulders back and her chest puffed out. "We guard the greatest treasure of the Romanian people!"

Lou dared not take her gaze off Lady Ioana, not even to get a glimpse of Dacia's reaction. Lady Ioana was peering down the table at them, and Lou was afraid to move without the old woman's permission.

"The time is coming," Lady Ioana went on, "when that treasure must be revealed, and we must have every Florescu with us, ready to fight and defend! The daughters we sent to America, and their daughters, have returned to us, and we must initiate them into the family's great power. For now the time has come! Now the signs are clear! We must depose the false king, and put the true king on the throne of Romania, that he may rise to rule all of Europe!"

A cheer went up from the family, and Lou felt her jaw slipping downward. Lady Ioana raised her glass as high as she could, and cried out.

"Down with Carol the Usurper! Long live King Mihai! Long live House Dracul!"

"Long live House Dracul!" The family chanted it together, and then they drank deeply from the glasses.

All except for Lou and Dacia, who were standing there with shocked expressions on their faces. Dacia let her glass fall to the table, spilling the red, red wine on the white cloth. Lou felt her father put a hand under her elbow. "Steady, LouLou," he whispered to her. He sounded concerned . . .

. . . but not surprised.

5 June 1897

    Arrived in Bran late in the night, after an uneventful journey. Rather hoped that Aunt Kate's "true love" would stop us along the way. Perhaps stage an abduction dressed as a highwayman and carry her off.

    We will be touring Castelul Bran tomorrow, Peles the day after, to be presented to the king and queen. I find it odd, considering that my family is apparently plotting treason. I suppose these are Aunt Kate's "appearances" that must be kept.

    Note: Remain calm. Take mental stock of new Parisian gowns to prevent hysteria. Stay away from any plots to overthrow the current, beloved monarchy. (Surely Uncle Cyrus will take Lou and me home if Lady Ioana is serious . . . ?)

    Note, second: find out if Mihai really _does_ have better claim to throne.

# CASA DRAGOSLOVEAN

The Florescu country estate was a few miles from Bran, hidden in the rolling, forested slopes of the Carpathians. It was a long, low house, whitewashed, and with a red tile roof in the style of the local farmhouses, just on a much grander scale. In addition they owned much of the surrounding mountain, with a beautiful stream and a small farm where the maids' husbands grew vegetables for the table and kept chickens and cows for the eggs and milk and cheeses.

Standing in front of the traveling carriage, Dacia looked at the long house and suddenly felt tears spring to her eyes as the inexplicable feeling that she had come home swept over her. She had never been here before, had never even seen a picture of this house, but yet she knew it. Everything about it was foreign to her, far more foreign than the mansion in Bucharest, but she had never felt at home there. Here, the smell of the earth and the trees, the bleating of the goats in a nearby field, everything reached out to embrace her.

She looked at Lou, and saw her cousin staring at the house with a shocked expression. Dacia could tell that Lou felt the same way. Radu stepped between them, taking Dacia's hand and then Lou's.

"You can feel it, can't you?" His voice was subdued.

Dacia only nodded, embarrassed by how emotional she felt. It was as though she recognized each tile and beam and window, and they were as dear to her as her own family members.

Lou answered aloud. "Oh, yes," she said quietly, fervently. "We're home. Home at last."

"Then I'm both glad and sorry," Radu said, maddeningly. "Come inside."

They paused before the front door, which was low and wide and had the Dacian dragon carved on the lintel. Radu was tall enough to reach up and touch his hands reverently to the carving, which was smooth and black from age. Dacia adjusted the gold dragon bracelet on her wrist, then reached up and found that she was just tall enough to brush it lightly with her fingers. She expected to feel something: the prick of teeth, the dryness of scales, but it was just carved wood. Beside her Lou gave a little shiver and walked in without trying to touch the carving.

Silent servants in traditional dress showed them to a pair of bedrooms. The rooms were small but clean and bright, with white walls and dark wood floors, and beautiful blue coverlets on the beds. Most importantly, Dacia's and Lou's rooms were side by side, opening onto a shared balcony, sadly also shared with Aunt Kate's room. Dacia still couldn't believe the change that had come over Aunt Kate, their onetime supporter and confidante. Would she act this strange and grim forever?

"Still," Dacia whispered to Lou, "she can't watch us every minute. We'll be able to speak privately soon!"

They would need to make plans, sooner rather than later. No matter how at home they felt here, Dacia was determined not to let herself or Lou be caught up in some mad plot to murder the king!

Lou gave her a knowing nod, while Radu looked on from the doorway of Lou's new room. The maids slipped away to see to the luggage, and Dacia realized that the three of them were alone for once.

"I know it's hard—" Radu began.

Dacia pounced on him. She pulled him into her room, slapping his hand when he tried to cling to the doorjamb. "You can either give us some answers to what is going on, or you can . . . go away!" She didn't want to say anything too threatening, since she knew that Radu meant well. He was simply too terrified of Lady Ioana to be much help.

He heaved an enormous sigh. "I don't know what I can say that won't get us all in trouble," he said.

"Is the family really planning to overthrow King Carol?" Lou's voice was soft, but it didn't mar any of the urgency in her voice. "And then take over the rest of Europe?"

"The *family* isn't planning to, no," Radu said carefully, after a small pause. "Because that's not our decision to make."

"Then whose decision is it?"

Dacia had to admire Lou's astute line of questions. She herself was so bubbling over with the many tangles around them that now she didn't even know where to begin.

"Prince Mihai's," Radu said reluctantly.

Dacia managed to sort out one question she'd been meaning to ask. "Does he really have the better claim to the throne?"

Radu's broad, handsome face twisted into an oddly scrunched expression. For a moment, Dacia couldn't tell if he was thinking, or in pain. It seemed, though, that he was thinking. "It's hard to say," he answered finally.

"No, it's not," Lou retorted.

She waved one hand as though the question didn't matter, and Dacia felt a little stung. Mihai was courting Dacia; his royal status was very important to her, at least!

"Mihai is a prince of *Wallachia*," Lou reminded them. "Carol is the king of *all Romania*, united. Why would Mihai have any claim to the throne of Romania?"

"There's . . . it's complicated," Radu said, wincing. "Very complicated."

"Clearly," Dacia said, grabbing at another vital question. "Then tell us this: What are the Claw and the Wing? And the Smoke?"

The squished expression fled Radu's face entirely, to be replaced by something akin to sorrow. He looked them both up and down. "I can't believe it," he said, almost as though talking to himself. "I don't want to believe that you're going to . . . join us . . ."

"Radu! Stop dithering and tell us!" Dacia moved toward him menacingly, even though he was twice her size.

He actually cowered, eyes cast down. "It's just . . . not something I imagined my beautiful little cousins being a part of. And I cannot tell you what it all means! I promise that I would if I could. But you'll find out soon. In two or three nights, I hear."

"Why not now? Why can't anyone tell us anything?" Lou twisted her hands together in frustration.

"It's not something you can simply *tell* someone," Radu said. Dacia was about to take him to task, but she realized that he wasn't trying to be evasive. He truly did not know how to tell them. "It's something that you have to . . . see . . ." He looked over his shoulder into the corridor for a moment, then leaned forward conspiratorially. "Promise me something?"

Dacia looked at Lou, and Lou pressed her lips together for a moment before nodding. Dacia looked back at Radu and answered for them both. "All right."

"I would take you away right now if I could," Radu said, his face very grim.

Dacia was about to say something scathing, but Radu's words sank in and she stopped. He would take them away? From their family? There was a coldness in her chest, and she suddenly didn't want to know what the Claw or the Wing or the Smoke was.

"But I can't," Radu said. "I'm too much a coward, I suppose. But when you find out . . . when it all happens . . . if you can't bear it, please leave. Tell your father, LouLou, to take you both away. He has to take you both away. I'm afraid if he tries it right now, Lady Ioana will have you brought back by force."

"I'd like to see her try," Dacia said, trying to sound strong.

"No," Radu said, shaking his head. "You really wouldn't."

"Radu," Dacia said, chilled and exasperated in equal measure. "Please don't give us more questions to—"

"The bathroom is at the end of the corridor," Aunt Kate said, appearing out of nowhere. Dacia's heart banged against her breastbone, and she took an involuntary step backward. Kate moved Radu out of her way with a single finger on his sleeve. "Did Radu tell you already? Though the house is quite old, it has all modern fittings. My room is just there, next to Lou's. Dinner is at eight o'clock, we dress for it in our traditional clothing." She looked at them with her head cocked. "Any other questions?"

Dacia went from cold to hot, her anger boiling over. How *dare* Aunt Kate? She knew very well they weren't asking where the bathroom was! Aunt Kate had been as close as a mother to Dacia and Lou (closer, in Dacia's case). How could she turn on them, treat them like strangers, now when they needed her?

"Yes," Dacia said, speaking as clearly as she could with her teeth gritted. "What is the Wing, the Claw, or the Smoke? Does Prince Mihai have a better claim to the throne than King Carol? Are you really asking us to take part in treason? Was that man you were kissing on the train to Bucharest Prince Mihai's uncle?"

"What delights me," Aunt Kate said in a voice so icy that Dacia took a step backward and Lou let out a small whimper, "is that very soon you two will finally know your place."

Dacia had never responded well to fear. Whenever she was afraid, she lashed out instead of retreating, which frequently resulted in her saying and doing things that she normally never would have. The Incident in London had been a result of that, in a roundabout way.

"Just like you've learned *your* place?" Now Dacia cocked her own head to the side. "We can all see how happy that's made you, all these years." She took Lou's arm, pulling her cousin around, and did her best to stroll casually out to the balcony with Lou in tow. "We shall see you at dinner, then."

Aunt Kate made a sound that was disturbingly like a growl, and after a minute, Dacia decided it was a laugh. "Wait until the moon goes dark. Three nights from now. Then we'll see some of the sauce taken out of you, miss." Aunt Kate marched out, and Radu followed her.

Dacia shut the door behind them, so that she and Lou stood alone on the balcony. She could feel Lou shaking, and put her arm around her. She was shaking a little, too, and felt like crying. She hated crying.

"I think I hate Aunt Kate. Not as much as Lady Ioana, but I think I hate her," Dacia said, trying to sound flippant and failing utterly.

"I don't hate her," Lou said. "I'm too frightened to hate her. Frightened for all of us. She wouldn't be acting this way unless there was something . . . something really terrible that she was afraid of, too. Dacia, what is going to happen to us in three nights? What's going to happen to us in a month? Will we go to jail for plotting treason?"

"I don't know, LouLou." Dacia hugged her cousin close, taking as much comfort from Lou as trying to give it. "But I'm sure your father won't let us come to harm."

"But my mother? She doesn't care, does she? She's becoming more and more like Lady Ioana." Lou let out a little sob.

"We're going to need more help," Dacia decided. "It looks like Radu's too much under Lady Ioana's thumb." A flash of inspiration hit, and Dacia straightened. "Lord Johnny!"

Lou let go of Dacia's waist and took a step back. "Lord Johnny? But he's in Bucharest with . . . That Awful Man."

"True," Dacia admitted, but refused to be deterred. "But I'm going to write to him all the same. If we need help getting out of the country, I'm sure he could arrange matters. Also, why don't I just ask him outright who that man is? Lord Johnny is a good friend, and besides, I'm sick of all the lies. I need someone to tell us the truth!"

"Radu would if he could," Lou protested halfheartedly.

"But he can't," Dacia said. "Whether or not it's his choice doesn't matter now. He can't, so we need to find someone who can."

"And Lord Johnny can?" Lou looked skeptical, and Dacia felt defensive.

"Well, he's certainly *not* a Florescu, which seems more and more commendable. And he must know the name of the man he was sharing a box with at the opera, so at the very least we'll have that."

"I suppose." But Lou's brow was creased.

"Lou," Dacia said gently, the cause of her cousin's distress finally dawning on her. "Don't you want to know who that man is?"

"I don't know," Lou said, her brow creasing even further. "I'd rather he just disappeared from our lives altogether. But if he knows something . . . about being the Wing . . ."

"Why don't you read the letter, before I send it?" Dacia said. "Then if you think it's too much, I can change it."

Lou looked at the forested view for a long time. "Very well," she said at last. "I suppose it would be good to have another ally."

11 June 1897

Dear Lord Johnny,

I was delighted that you made the acquaintance of my dearest darlingest cousin Lou (Louisa Neulander) on the Orient Express these two weeks past. I am most grateful that you were able to come to her rescue: you are quite the gallant, always scooping up young maidens in distress and delivering them to safety! And now I am afraid that I must beg you for more rescuing, on behalf of myself and Lou. Please say you can refuse me nothing, or I shall be heartbroken!

It is a matter of some delicacy, of course, and I know that I can rely on you to be discreet. It seems that while Lou was traveling to Romania she was accosted on two separate occasions by a man who made very rude remarks to her. This caused her no end of distress, as she is of a most delicate disposition. I had roundly decried the man as a cad, and certainly not of our class; so you must imagine my surprise when I saw you sharing an opera box with him! I shan't hold it against you, we are too good of friends for that, but my dear Lord Johnny, you simply must tell me who that man is, and what business he had saying such awful things to Lou.

And now, just so you will know how much you are forgiven for associating with such as That Awful Man, as Lou has taken to calling him, you can do me one other favor. Lou and I are not enjoying our stay in Romania quite as well as we had hoped. Lou's mother and our aunt Kate (whom you met in London) seem determined to keep us locked in our rooms, and our Florescu grandmother is, to be frank, a terror. We might want to try to stage a quick escape back to Paris. Would you be willing to play a part? Lou's father, my uncle Cyrus Neulander, will aid us, but I know how adept you are at locating carriages and train tickets in the middle of the night!

Please say that you will help us, and I shall forever remain

Yours,
Dacia Vreeholt

# CASA DRAGOSLOVEAN

Lou read the letter over twice before she nodded her approval. It said a great deal about Dacia's real emotions that she was having Lou read it before sending it to Lord Johnny. The tone of the letter was just as brash and confident as ever, but Lou knew now that it was mostly an act. They had to get out of this house, out of Romania. Lou felt suffocated, and found herself rising up on her toes without even thinking about it, as though she could launch herself into the air and fly away.

"I wish I *was* the Wing, whatever that means," she said to Dacia as she watched her cousin fold up the letter and slide it into an envelope. "Then perhaps I could fly away from here."

"As long as you bring back a carriage for me," Dacia said with a quick smile.

"Naturally, I won't leave without you," Lou said.

"Where were you planning on going?" said a man's voice from the doorway.

Both girls jumped, and Dacia let out a little scream. When they saw that it was just Radu, Dacia punched him in the arm.

"Don't you knock before you enter a lady's bedroom? I might have been dressing!"

Red rolled up Radu's face from his collar, clashing horribly with his bright hair. Lou didn't want to see how much redder he could turn, so she quickly put an end to his suffering.

"But she wasn't, so no harm done. Can you do something for us?"

"Yes," Radu said, his high color fading and a wary look entering his eyes. "What is it?"

"I want to send this letter to Lord Johnny Harcastle," said Dacia brusquely. "He's staying in Bucharest, at the Crown and Cross Hotel." Despite their maid in Bucharest taking a dislike to Dacia, she had still reluctantly discovered Lord Johnny's address for them, though by the time she had surrendered this information it had been too late to send him a note. Dacia finished sealing the letter and held it up. "I don't dare give it to a servant to post, I am certain they'll show it to Lady Ioana first."

"What does it say?" Radu licked his lips nervously. "It doesn't tell any . . . family secrets, does it?"

Lou felt a guilty flush rising on her own cheeks. Truthfully, it didn't, but it was looking for answers to some of the family secrets.

Dacia, however, refused to be cowed. At least not by Radu. And Lou found her guilt passing as Dacia read him a lecture on his unbecoming curiosity concerning her *amours tendres*, as she termed them. By the time she was done, Radu was blushing again, and Lou was feeling inexplicably cheered up. They would get their letter to Lord Johnny, he would answer some of their questions, and if they needed to leave suddenly, he would help to arrange it. She remembered his piercing blue eyes, the firm set of his mouth. With her father and Lord Johnny to help them, they would get out of Romania.

"You'd better pay some Gypsies to send it," Radu said when Dacia let him speak.

"How do we find some?"

"Out at the gate of the estate," Radu said. "There are usually a couple of them sitting there. We hire them to run errands or help with house repairs."

"Are you sure they aren't loyal to Lady Ioana?" Lou had seen several Gypsies on their way to the estate, and they frightened her. They had stood and simply stared at the carriage, not with curiosity, but with hard eyes that seemed to be weighing her.

Radu shook his head. "They don't like Lady Ioana. They don't like anyone who isn't Gypsy. But they're loyal to whoever pays them."

"Take us to them," Dacia insisted. "I don't want to deal with them alone."

"No, I'll go," Lou said, surprising everyone, including herself.

Radu and Dacia gawked at her, which made her start blushing again.

"If anyone sees me, they'll think I'm just curious," Lou said. "If they see Radu, they'll know he has a job for the Gypsies, and ask him what it is. If they see you, Dacia, they'll ask you what you're doing as well. I'm sorry, but you're always . . . up to something."

"You have a point," Dacia admitted. She gave Lou a searching look. "Are you sure you want to?"

"Someone has to," Lou said, raising her chin.

"Here." Radu fished in his pockets and brought up a handful of coins, a button, and a crumpled handkerchief. "Sorry." He took back the handkerchief and button, and gave her the coins. "That should be enough for them to post the letter, and consider themselves well paid for the effort."

"I can pay for my own letter," Dacia said stiffly, reaching for her purse.

"But I feel like . . . I know I've let you both down," Radu mumbled. "I'm just not able to . . . I can't do anything else."

Dacia looked like she was going to protest some more, but Lou just took the money and thanked him. She knew what it was like to feel helpless, and it was disturbing that Radu felt that way.

Mustering what confidence she could, and being mindful to keep her back straight, but not straight enough that she looked like she was marching to her doom, Lou went downstairs. The stairs were narrow and shallow, which meant that there were quite a lot of them. They were also made of tile, and the low heels of her shoes clacked loudly as she went down to the main hall. It, too, was tiled, but there was a large rug in the middle, and she practically leaped from the bottom step to the muffling rug. She walked as lightly as she could to the front door, which was so huge that she had to push it open with both hands once she had figured out the latch.

A maid crossed the hall just as she was turning to close the door, and they both froze for a moment. Then Lou summoned her best Aunt Kate Look and said in Romanian, "Close this door; I don't want to let in the draft." And stepped across the porch as carelessly as she ever had in her New York home.

The gravel drive sloped, so she was rather less elegant walking down it than she had been crossing the porch. The gravel rolled out from under her heels, and she had to lift her skirts in the back to keep them from dragging. By the time she reached the front gate, her skirts were crumpled where she'd been clutching them, and the letter was crumpled as well. No matter, it was still readable.

She lifted the latch of the wooden gate, and found it even harder to open than the front door. But when she had moved it an inch or two, she heard a rough voice speaking a language she didn't recognize, and felt someone take hold of the other side of the gate and pull it out of her grip. She let go willingly enough, and stepped through.

A thank-you died on her lips when she saw who had helped her with the gate.

He was a Gypsy, of course. She should have known. He wore a tall hat and a thick, embroidered coat. He glared down at her from a great height, and she felt her confidence sapping away.

"What do you want?" His Romanian was only slightly accented.

Belatedly Lou wondered what she would have done if he'd only known the Gypsy language.

"Oh. I—I want— My cousin and I want—"

"Which cousin?" The man let out a harsh laugh. "There are too many of you to count! You're like rabbits, not wolves!"

"Ah, I suppose . . . but it's Dacia and I, and we—" She held out the letter.

"You want to send a letter?" The man looked at the creased envelope with disgust, and then spit to one side. "The postman comes in the morning." He turned his back on her.

Lou wondered if he would have turned his back on Radu. Or Aunt Kate. Or Lady Ioana. Or even Dacia. She breathed deeply through her nostrils. She was sick and tired of being of no consequence. She was here because no one would suspect her of dissembling if she'd been caught. And now she couldn't even finish the job, because this large, sneering man didn't think her worth his time.

"Now see here!" Her voice rapped out, not in imitation of Aunt Kate, but with its own steel showing through. The man turned, surprised, and Lou glared at him. "I want to send this letter to Bucharest as soon as possible, and no one else can know about it."

He took it from her and studied the address. "Lord John Harcastle," he said, turning over the strange name in his mouth.

"Yes. A young English lord, staying at the Crown and Cross Hotel in Bucharest."

"No."

"No?" Lou wavered a little, then straightened again. "I shall pay you." She reached into her pocket for Radu's coins.

"Yes, you will pay me. But I will take the letter to the young English lord at Poiana."

"No, he's staying in Bucharest," Lou insisted.

"*Poiana*," the man said loudly and slowly. "Yesterday, my brother helped a young English lord find Peles Castle in Poiana. The other man in the carriage, he called this English boy Lord Johnny. They said, they hoped the food is better than Crown and Cross, when they paid my brother."

"Are you certain?"

The man glared at her. He snatched two of the coins from her hand. "Keep the rest. Maybe you will need me again."

"Here." Lou handed him two more silver coins. "If the man in Poiana isn't Lord Harcastle, I want you to send this letter to the Crown and Cross in Bucharest."

The man raised one eyebrow, and then let out a blast of laughter. "Silver in the hand, silver in the blood, but steel in the bones? Very nice." He shoved the coins into one pocket, the letter into another, and then stalked off.

Lou went back through the gate, which she had to leave open because it was too heavy for her to close by herself, and then hurried up the treacherous drive to the house. When she was halfway across the main hall, her mother fluttered out of the sitting room.

"There you are, darling!" She grasped Lou's arms, squeezing with her soft little hands that were surprisingly strong. "Don't you just adore it? I'd forgotten how wonderful the old house was! And the smell of the trees, and the earth! So romantic!" Her mother heaved a little sigh, her eyes far away. Then they sharpened on Lou's face. "Were you just outside?"

"Yes," Lou said, seeing no point in lying. She was a terrible liar.

"Why?"

"Radu said that sometimes Gypsies hang around the gate. I wanted to see one, but there isn't anyone there." Which was not a lie. There wasn't anyone there. Not anymore.

Her mother shuddered. "Stay away from the Gypsies, darling; they aren't our kind of people."

"Yes, ma'am," Lou said with relief.

"They are far better society than Prince Mihai," Lou's father said, coming out of the sitting room behind her mother.

There was a dark cloud in her father's eyes, and Lou felt her knees begin to shake. Perhaps there was no point in waiting to hear from Lord Johnny, and she and Dacia should simply beg her father to take them away right now.

"We're about to have tea, dear," Lou's mother prattled on, ignoring her husband. "And then we're off to tour Castle Bran! You'll simply love it! The most homey little castle you can imagine!"

"I'm sure Prince Mihai's illustrious ancestor Vlad the Impaler found it very homey when he spent a decade there under arrest," Lou's father said coldly.

Lou's mother let go of her arms, a hard look on her plump, pretty face as she rounded on her husband. "And how would you know anything about that? You are not Romanian!"

"No, thank goodness, I am not," Mr. Neulander said, his face just as hard.

Lou took a step backward, away from both her parents. She was on the verge of crying, suddenly, and clenched her fists to stop the tears. She had cried far too much in the past few days.

"Which is why I raised my children to be Americans,"

Mr. Neulander continued. "And which is why, when our tours of Bran and Peles are over, I will be taking our children back to Bucharest. And from Bucharest we will return to New York."

"Our sons will be returning to Bucharest with you," Maria agreed. "But Louisa will remain here."

Lou opened her mouth to protest, and her father shot her a look.

"LouLou should not be here. Dacia should not be here," he said in a low, intense voice. "I would like to insist that you should not be here, and yet more and more, you seem to be turning into one of *them*, and so I will not force you to return with us. But I will take my daughter and niece away from here, if it's the last thing I do."

"It will be."

So silently had Lady Ioana entered the hall that Lou's legs jolted and nearly threw her to the floor when her grandmother spoke. The old woman was standing in the doorway of another room, the light from a window behind her making her white headdress glow.

"Dacia and Maria Louisa belong with us. They belong *to* us. And when you see why, you will not want to take them away. Should you try anyway, out of some misguided sense of honor, you will be removed by force."

"You can't take my daughter——" Lou's father began, a muscle in his jaw jumping.

"She isn't your daughter," Lady Ioana announced.

Lou felt a small cry escape her lips and choked it back.

"She is Maria's daughter," Lady Ioana went on, not looking

at Lou. "This has been explained to you. By all means, take those horrible boys and go. They are yours. Today, tomorrow, it doesn't matter to me. But don't think to try to take the girls.

"You will not long survive my wrath."

Lou looked at her father, willing him to scoff at the old woman's claims. But his face was white with rage or fear or both, and instead he let out an anguished cry of his own and turned his back on his wife, and Lou, and fled.

Lou's legs did collapse, and when Lady Ioana and Maria turned their gaze on her, she was clutching at the tight weave of the Turkish carpet and sobbing.

"Get up, you foolish girl, and wash your face," Lady Ioana ordered. "You are stronger than this, and you must be stronger still.

"In two nights you will find out why you must forget your father."

*12 June 1897*

Something is horribly wrong with Lou, and she will not speak to me. She won't speak to anyone. Lady Ioana said something to her, I know that. And I fear that her parents have quarreled. I certainly hope that they weren't tactless enough to quarrel in front of her. Really, they should know by now that Lou is far too sensitive for that sort of thing! Long before this vile journey, I was convinced that Lou and I should be given a place of our own. No one else in this family has a care for her delicate nature, and I would do far better without my parents and Aunt Kate always shadowing me as well!

Tea was ridiculously awkward. Uncle Cyrus not present, Aunt Maria weepy, Lou silent, and Lady Ioana gloating. Still, everyone else was convinced that a visit to Castelul Bran will be heaven on earth. More later on that, if true. Or if not.

Note: perhaps if this whole thing turns out as horrible as I fear it will, I can use it as leverage in negotiating a private household. There is a darling apartment on Fifth Avenue that would suit the two of us admirably.

# CASTELUL BRAN

Dacia was in love.

"I didn't know there was such a thing as a livable castle," Dacia marveled, gazing out over the green, wooded mountains from one of Castle Bran's balconies. The sun was shining, making the white walls of the castle positively glow, and plotting and treason seemed impossible. "But look at this place, Lou! Couldn't you just live here forever? It's adorable!"

Lou murmured something in agreement, her eyes wide.

Castle Bran sat on a hill overlooking a pass through the Carpathians, where it had been built to serve as the gateway between Wallachia and Transylvania. The walls were plastered and painted white inside and out, and the roof had been newly retiled. The long, low rooms were more cozy than regal, with built-in window seats, and beautifully tiled stoves in the main rooms to keep them warm in the winter. There were ranks of balconies and terraces on every level, looking out over forests and mountains.

"Look at this! There's a miniature sitting room on this terrace!"

Dacia had just spotted the enclosed benches under the eaves. She ducked under the low beams that supported the roof and sank down onto one of the benches before she realized that there was someone already there, sitting across from her.

"Miss Vreeholt," said Lord Johnny politely.

Dacia let out a little scream and rose, hitting her head on the low ceiling. She dropped back down onto the bench and stared at Lord Johnny in shock. What on earth was he doing here?

His blue eyes studied her intensely. "Are you well?"

"Am *I* well?" Her voice rose and cracked. "What are you doing here? I'm not well, I'm all in a muddle . . . but what are you . . . I just sent you a letter!"

Dacia was embarrassed to find herself blushing, and seemingly unable to put together a coherent sentence. She had forgotten how handsome Lord Johnny was up close, with his clear blue eyes and windswept brown hair.

"It's probably on its way to Bucharest right now, yet here you are!" She knew she sounded ridiculous, but she just couldn't stop her mouth in time. Saying that you were going to enlist the aid of a handsome young nobleman was one thing, but sitting face-to-face with him, trying to explain what was happening, was another matter entirely. "The letter, you know. You've missed it. You will miss it."

"This letter?" Lord Johnny reached into his coat and pulled out a folded piece of paper.

Dacia was almost as surprised to recognize her own stationery as she was to see Lord Johnny sitting here in Castle Bran.

"How did you get it so quickly? We sent it to Bucharest only a few hours ago." She reached for it, realized it was addressed to him anyway, and pretended she was just straightening her cuffs. The dragon bracelet rolled around her wrist, and she tucked it into her sleeve, not wanting to tell Lord Johnny who had given it to her.

"A Gypsy brought me your letter just before tea time," Lord Johnny said. "I determined to come here and wait for you as soon as I read it. The Gypsy said that you would be taking the tour this afternoon."

"How did he know that?"

Dacia felt strange, as though she were standing outside of her body. She no longer felt fluttery around Lord Johnny, and the urge to flirt had left her completely. How had the Gypsies known where she would be? Were they spying on her, too? Just like the servants? And probably Radu and Aunt Kate? She put one hand to her head.

"Dacia," Lord Johnny said in a low voice. Just that. Just her name.

She looked at him very seriously and he gave her a tight little nod, encouraging her to say what she needed to say. He wasn't spying for Lady Ioana. He hadn't changed, become a stranger, since last they spoke.

"Our Romanian relations are not . . . what we have expected," Dacia began. "They are not common, or otherwise socially unacceptable, but instead they are . . . frightening." As soon as she said it she realized it was true. She'd never been one to take fright around strangers before, but now . . . "They seem to enjoy frightening me and Lou, especially. There have also been threats of harm to any one of us who puts a toe out of line. It has driven a rift between Lou's parents, and we want to leave before anything worse happens. Can you help us?" She held out one hand to him.

Lord Johnny took her hand, his own palm very warm through her gloves. "We can help you, but it's probably not the way that you think," Lord Johnny said.

Dacia wanted to shout. More riddles! "What do you mean?" she said, doing her best to keep her voice level. "*We?* Who? How can you help us?"

Dacia wanted to run away, just run off into the mountains and never look back. It was all too much. Yet at the same time, she was very aware of the smell of Lord Johnny's cologne, and the warm comfort of the thick-grained wooden bench beneath her hand. She could see Lou and Radu over by the terrace wall. They had seen whom she was speaking with, and drawn back.

"I'm here with a man named Arkady. Theo Arkady. He was at the opera the other night. We're trying to find out some information. Once we have that, we can help you."

"What information? And do you have any idea what that man has said to Lou?" Dacia lowered her voice on this second question, not wanting to call any attention to them. She hoped that Radu would create a diversion if Aunt Kate or Aunt Maria came to see where they had gone.

"Theo told me that he'd spoken to your cousin in Paris, and

he wishes me to convey his most heartfelt apologies. It was most indelicate of him," Johnny said.

"Most indelicate!" Dacia threw up her hands in indignation. "Did he tell you what he said?" She knew that it really didn't matter that much in the grand scheme of things, but she just couldn't let it go. Her Lou had been insulted, and she needed to know that it wouldn't happen again, if they were going to accept this Arkady's help along with Lord Johnny's.

"He didn't actually, but Dacia, I'm sorry, I need to tell you something before we are interrupted." Lord Johnny leaned out of their little nook to look around the terrace.

"That's our cousin Radu," Dacia said. "He can be trusted. For the most part."

"I know who he is," Lord Johnny said, his voice flat. "Listen carefully: you're being presented to the king and queen tomorrow. Prince Mihai will be there. I want you to watch him. Make sure he doesn't slip away alone. I am trying to arrange an invitation myself, but you'll be able to get closer to him. If he says anything to you, anything suspicious, I want you to try to remember it, so that you can tell me later."

"You mean if he seems to be plotting treason?"

Lord Johnny's eyes widened. "He's already approached you about his family's plan?"

"*His* family's plan? Have you met my grandmother?" Dacia's voice cracked.

Lord Johnny's expression was grim. "Ah, yes. So you know of your family's involvement? We really must speak soon, when we have more time. And privacy. I also—"

"Miss Neulander! You are here! And where is she? Where is your fair cousin?"

A young man in a gray suit had leaped from the doorway into the middle of the terrace, startling Lou and Radu, and was turning in a rapid circle. Dacia and Lord Johnny stared out at him from their little hiding place.

"Will Carver? I don't believe it!" Dacia recovered herself and stepped out onto the terrace. "What are you doing here?"

Will stopped turning in circles and snatched at Dacia's hands, holding them to his heart.

"Miss Vreeholt! No, Dacia! My dear Dacia! You have to come with me right now," he cried. "You're in very grave danger!"

"Mr. Carver—Will, I mean," Dacia began, still a bit dazed by his sudden appearance. She noticed suddenly that he had a rather weak mouth and bulging eyes. Her time abroad in the company of Lord Johnny and Prince Mihai seemed to have raised her standard for male beauty. "Whatever do you mean? How did you find me?"

She freed one of her hands, and found herself automatically feeling at her hair to make sure it was in order. Then she realized that she didn't care if Will saw her with her hair mussed. Yes, her taste in men had changed a great deal in the past weeks.

"I called at your family home in Bucharest, and your uncle Horia Florescu was kind enough to tell me where to find you!" Will squeezed her other hand even tighter and she attempted to extract it without success. "There is a terrible evil stalking the streets of Bucharest! I've come to take you back to civilization before it's too late," he told her. "I only just put it all together, and I came as quickly as I could!"

"Put what all together?" Dacia managed to remove her hands from his grip. Lord Johnny was looking at Will Carver with a cynical expression, and she was still turning over what the young American was saying.

"I read a novel," Will began. "A terrible, sickening work of trash! Nevertheless, it seems to have the ring of truth about it. It was set in Romania, and I thought nothing of that beyond hoping that you would never read it and see your mother's country defamed!

"But I began to be plagued by terrible nightmares and suspected that much of this novel was in actuality true. I got on the next train for Bucharest, thinking only to reassure myself that you were well, but as I journeyed my fears began to be realized! The terrible signs of evil from this very book were all around me: wolves running free in daylight, without a hint of fear. Swarms of bats that nearly blotted out the moon at night!"

Radu hissed and Dacia saw that his eyes were wide and he was clenching his fists.

"Oh, for heaven's sake, Radu," she said in disgust, frowning repressively at her cousin. "Go on, Will, I'm afraid I still don't understand."

"I'd like to know more myself," Lord Johnny said. Dacia was about to chide him for mocking poor, silly Will, but a glance at the British lord showed that he was deadly serious.

Will hardly needed any encouragement. He seemed, rather, to relish the audience. Especially when Lou took Radu's arm, as though looking for comfort. Dacia rather thought, though, that she was preventing Radu from punching Will, which seemed unnecessarily dramatic on his part.

"And then," Will went on with great flair, "when I arrived in Bucharest I was horrified to find that it was too late: I saw your name in the paper, linked to the very family this novelist has seen fit to expose as the monsters that they are!"

"I'm sorry, is any of this supposed to make sense?" Lord Johnny raised an eyebrow. "I'd been hoping for something more concrete."

"*My father* sent you here?" Radu looked astonished. "Who are you? Did you tell my father about the wolves and the bats?"

"He's Dacia's beau from New York," Lou said in a low voice.

"Hmm," Radu said. "Was he prone to hysterics in New York?"

"Hysterics?" Will was indignant. "Am I the only one here concerned for the safety of this delicate beauty?"

"Wait. Stop." Dacia held up one hand. Will Carver had a very artistic temperament, and she was used to interpreting his sometimes complex sallies. "You read a novel, set in Romania, about a Romanian family who—"

"Are monsters. *Literal* monsters," Will supplied eagerly as Dacia began to smile. "As well as having the power to summon beasts like wolves and bats. Their name is Dracula."

Dacia froze.

Everyone on the terrace froze. Lou made a small noise, but otherwise didn't move.

"What do you know about the Draculas?" Radu spoke first, stepping forward. He had one arm around Lou now, and he put the other around Dacia to move her away from Will. A good head taller than Will, Radu loomed over him, his expression menacing enough to make Will shrink back. Dacia wanted to prod him to make Radu stop, but she was suddenly afraid of her cousin. There was a look in his eyes that told her not to tease him, not now.

"They're, ah, vampires," Will Carver said in a small voice, and his cheeks colored as though he was finally aware of how ridiculous it all was.

Dacia burst out laughing, a wave of relief rushing over her.

When she was in England she had found a copy of *Carmilla*, the scandalous novel about vampires set in the forests of southern Europe, and read it in her room at night. And as a child she'd heard the old folktales and legends of things that fed on human blood from her Romanian tutor. But Mihai a *vampire*?

She shook her head and laughed again, and for a brief, sweet moment she thought that everything would be all right, that Lady Ioana's treason was only talk, more nonsense taken too seriously. Soon she and Lou would go home without suffering anything more than the humiliation of having a grandmother with a nasty temper.

But Lord Johnny didn't laugh, nor did Radu. And Will looked desperate to prove that he wasn't a fool, so he began to speak again, babbling about dungeons and a Dracula who stole young ladies to feed his horrible appetite.

"He doesn't just *control* the vermin; he can turn himself into a wolf, or a bat, or even a mist," Will added, as though this last impossibility was the most damning piece of evidence.

Dacia closed her eyes. In the golden afternoon sunlight, standing on the tiled terrace of the ancient castle, Will Carver truly did not seem as dashing and romantic as he had in the drawing rooms of New York. He was wispy, and apparently rather lacking in intelligence. Dacia opened her mouth to say that it was impossible for anyone to turn into a bat, but Lou spoke first.

"The Claw, the Wing, and the Smoke," she said softly.

Dacia felt the whole world tilt.

Lou turned to Radu and said in a much louder voice, "You will find out what novel this was, and bring me a copy. I am going back to the estate." And she marched away without looking to see if anyone was following her.

"Agreed," Lord Johnny said in a strangled voice. "Carver, was it?" He put a comradely arm around Will. "You and I need to talk. Radu, you had better make sure that the young ladies get home safely. And if you can locate a copy of . . . ?"

"*Dracula*, by a Mr. Bram Stoker," Will said, still sounding embarrassed but trying visibly to rally. "It was just published this year."

"Yes, *Dracula*. I wouldn't mind having a look at it myself." Lord Johnny nodded stiffly at Dacia. "I will do my best to see you tomorrow, Miss Vreeholt."

Dacia could only nod stiffly herself by way of reply. She let Radu take her arm and lead her away. They passed through more whitewashed rooms with dark wood floors, but she didn't see them. Down in the courtyard, Lou was waiting by their carriage.

No one said a word all the way back to the Florescu estate.

### THE DIARY OF MISS MARIA LOUISA NEULANDER

*12 June 1897*

*I am the Wing.*

# PELES CASTELUL

The king and queen were out driving when Lou and her family arrived at Peles. The housekeeper was only too happy to take them on a tour of the palace, though, starting with the music room and ending with the guest bedrooms, which were rather plain and narrow and linked together in an odd way. Lou admired the glass ceiling of the foyer, and tried to look suitably impressed by the fact that it could be cranked open on sunny days. She peered at the grates that provided heat in the winter or cool air in the summertime, powered by an enormous boiler system down in the cellar, and saw one of the bathrooms with its modern fittings, making small noises of interest over these innovations even though she was feeling sick and anxious.

The royal couple returned, and the palace tour ended abruptly with the Florescus being herded into a room full of antique weapons and left there. Dacia and Radu immediately began exploring the spears and sabers nailed to the walls, but Lou's mother and Aunt Kate looked as though they were going to have fits.

"And they just leave us here, cooling our heels, for who knows how long?" Aunt Kate's face was pinched with displeasure.

"There's not even a chair to sit in," Maria said by way of agreement.

"We have had this appointment for a week now," Aunt Kate went on. "They should have at least had the courtesy to be at home when we came."

"We arrived an hour and a half early," Dacia pointed out in exasperation. "We wanted to tour the palace, and we did. I don't see how this is some kind of snub."

Aunt Kate and Lou's mother gave her quelling looks.

Lou didn't even bother to try to soothe them. Just getting up that morning and getting dressed had taken all her energy. She spoke only when she absolutely had to, and couldn't bring herself to eat. Her mother tried to press her, but Aunt Kate had come to her aid and told Maria to leave her alone. Dacia, too, seemed to respect that Lou needed space, though she was normally one to try to jolly people back into good humor.

Of course, Lou reflected, Dacia was dealing with the same shocks that she herself had received, and probably felt much the same. Lou had felt too drained that morning to notice whether Dacia had eaten anything, either.

They had only been in the weapons room for a few minutes when the butler appeared. He led them to an elegant parlor, with a large harp standing before the windows and several brocade sofas. On one of them sat the queen, Elisabeth, a handsome woman wearing a plum-colored gown and a lace veil over her hair. King Carol the First stood near the windows in a green uniform, a book in one hand.

Even Lou, from the depths of her despair, could see that it was a prop. The king wanted to look like he was in the middle of reading a book, even though the book was closed and he was standing, stiff, several paces away from any chairs.

King Carol was afraid of them, Lou realized with a jolt. Did he know of her family's plan? She wondered why he had agreed to see them at all. Was he sizing them up?

"Your Majesties," Aunt Kate said, curtsying. They all followed suit, except for Radu, who bowed. "Thank you for receiving us."

"It is our pleasure," the king said in a voice that was anything but pleased.

He was in his fifties, and had a beard shaped like a coal shovel. Lou found that she pitied him. He was the first king of Romania since the Ottoman Empire had finally been thrown off and the states of Wallachia and Moldova had been united. Many battles had been fought on Romanian soil, sitting as it did between Europe and the Near East, and many more would probably be fought in the future. But for a brief shining moment Romania had triumphed, and there was peace throughout the land. Then here came her family, plotting treason with the Draculas, trying to bring down this stately king and his kind-eyed wife.

And it seemed that the king knew of it.

Queen Elisabeth welcomed them graciously and held out a soft hand. They all lined up to kiss it while Aunt Kate murmured their names.

"My sister Mrs. Maria Louisa Florescu Neulander. Radu Florescu, the son of my brother Horia. My nieces, Maria Louisa Neulander and Dacia Vreeholt, both of New York."

"Ah, yes, you were born in America," said King Carol.

Dacia nodded. Lou looked at the queen's eyes, seeing the sorrow behind the kindness.

"And you are visiting your mothers' homeland for the first time?" The king had a deep, calm voice. Lou found it soothing.

Another nod from Dacia. "Yes, Your Majesty," she added.

"How delightful to meet you," the queen said. Her voice was light, cultured. "It is so good to see you again, Ana Katarina." She looked at Lou and Dacia with a ghost of a smile. "Did you know that your aunt was once one of my attendants?"

Both girls shook their heads, wide-eyed. Aunt Kate, a lady-in-waiting to the queen? The queen against whom their family was plotting?

"She was indispensable," the queen said, nodding at their surprise. "I was very sorry to see her go to America with her sisters, but I understood that the lure of the new and exotic was much stronger than the need to stay and pour my tea." Queen Elisabeth had a little twinkle in her eyes now, and Lou observed that it made her look younger.

"And are you back for good, Katarina?" The queen looked up at Aunt Kate with a hint of challenge, and Lou found herself reassessing the older woman. She had lost her only child years before, and grief still weighed on her, but there was steel beneath it.

"That rather depends on my nieces," Aunt Kate said coolly. "They are going to be deciding how long they will stay in Romania tomorrow night."

"Oh, is that right?" The queen looked only mildly interested, but the king's face had gone tense and white.

"We're having a family dinner, and hoping that will provide

entertainment enough to entice them to stay," Aunt Kate said smoothly.

Lou couldn't be sure, because of the beard, but she thought that the king swallowed.

She couldn't stand the tension any longer. Her mother was staring over the queen's head as though Her Majesty wasn't even there. Radu hulked behind them like a mute bodyguard. Aunt Kate was being oddly enigmatic . . .

"Your Majesty," Lou said to the king, her voice barely above a whisper from disuse. "I am so honored to be here. Thank you for all you've done for our country." She gave another little curtsy.

King Carol looked as if he'd been struck by lightning.

"Thank you, Miss Neulander," he said hesitantly.

The tension in the room was humming now, and Lou looked at the strings of the harp to see if they were vibrating. They weren't, but Lou still felt that they should be. When the butler knocked they all flinched, and Lou almost shrieked, but she bit her lip just in time.

"Prince Mihai Dracula, Lord John Harcastle, and Mr. Theophilus Arkady," the butler announced.

Prince Mihai, Lord Johnny, and That Awful Man came in and bowed to the royal couple. After greetings had been exchanged, much to Lou's shock, That Awful Man turned and bowed to her.

"Miss Neulander, I wish to beg your forgiveness for my behavior at our first meeting, and the occasion after that. It was very bad of me, and I hope that I have not caused you lasting distress. Please accept my humblest apologies."

Lou felt her cheeks turning red, but for once it was with anger and not embarrassment. Everyone was looking at her, and it was unthinkable that she should refuse his apology, but she truly wished she could. He hoped that he had not caused her lasting distress? Of course he had, and she was sure that he knew he had, and Lord Johnny knew as well! Dacia had put him up to this apology, and now she was forced to accept.

Prince Mihai did not seem to think that it was fair, either.

"What is that you say? You offended this young lady?" He gave That Awful Man—Mr. Arkady, Lou supposed she should call him—a wrathful look.

"We were on the same ship, coming from America," Arkady said, his spine straightening. Lou noticed that he was very tall, taller than Prince Mihai or Lord Johnny, and that he was not much older. "I wished to make the young lady's acquaintance, but am sadly lacking in social graces."

"I can imagine," Prince Mihai sneered.

Lou felt as though she had been rescued from one bad situation and thrown into another. She no longer needed to accept or decline Mr. Arkady's apology; no one was even looking at her now, but Prince Mihai and Mr. Arkady seemed on the verge of coming to blows. She did not find the idea of having men fight over her exciting. And why did Prince Mihai care? She had a sneaking suspicion that Prince Mihai just loved to cause trouble, and she didn't feel like catering to his whims.

"It's all in the past," she said calmly, and turned back to the queen. "I believe you write books, ma'am?"

The queen seemed to understand, and smiled at Lou in a knowing way.

"Indeed I do," she said. "I find that it gives me a deep sense of fulfillment."

"I should very much like to read one of your books," Lou said, ignoring her mother's poking at her side, and That Awful Man's stares.

"You are a good child," Queen Elisabeth said. She looked over Lou's shoulder, at Dacia and Radu, who were standing side by side. "I can see in your eyes that you two are also very good. I shall send you some of my books; I think you will enjoy them."

"Thank you, Your Majesty," Lou said, and heard Dacia and Radu echo her.

But the queen was not finished. "Ana Katarina," she said, turning to Aunt Kate, "the world grows ever more terrible. Youth should be treasured, not forced to leave their innocence behind too soon."

"Elisabeth," King Carol said with a warning in his voice.

But the queen only looked at Aunt Kate, and so did everyone else. Aunt Kate stiffened, and her face was still. It was not one of her famous, quelling Looks, but another expression entirely, one that made her look older, almost as old as the queen.

"The world is hard," Aunt Kate said finally. "And sometimes we have to make the decision to be just as hard."

"Come now," Prince Mihai said jovially. "The world doesn't have to be as hard as all that! Some decisions are very easy to make! I have known your family all my life, and I find that they make decisions very easily. They are loyal, intelligent, and courageous, as well."

Dacia made a strangled sound.

"Dogs are also loyal, intelligent, and courageous," Lou said, rather louder than she had intended.

She heard a soft huff of breath from Dacia, and her cousin took her arm. "Quite, LouLou! Do you recall my father's old beagle? The very characteristics that Mihai has just listed!" She turned her bright eyes on Prince Mihai, and Lou could see that her cousin was no longer as enamored of the prince as she had been. "Now it seems that you no longer have room to take Mr. Arkady to task for his manners, since you yourself have just given our family an even more left-handed compliment!"

"Really, Mihai," King Carol rumbled. "I do not think that this is the time or the audience for your particular . . . grievances."

"It is never the time for my grievances," retorted Prince Mihai. "But it will be, soon. Your Majesty."

The venom in his voice caused Dacia to gasp and Lou to take a step back. It did not appear to surprise anyone else in the room, however. Aunt Kate merely raised her eyebrows, giving the room in general one of her Looks, and then beckoned to her nieces.

"I think that should be our cue to leave," she said. "Please forgive us, Your Majesties. I fear we are not good company."

"It isn't you, dear ladies," the king said in a low voice as they curtsied.

"It seems to be all of a piece," Aunt Kate said enigmatically, but the queen understood, and gave a small, bitter laugh.

"Oh, Ana Katarina, do think about what I said, my dear. For the sake of your nieces, if not for yourself."

Lou was expecting her aunt to make some disparaging remark, or to put the queen off with a cool reply at the very least, but instead Aunt Kate merely bowed her head and said, "I will consider your words."

"And that," Dacia whispered to Lou, "is the most surprising thing of all."

Lou could only nod and take Radu's offered arm, releasing Dacia. Any strength she might have had was gone, and she felt like a marionette with the strings cut.

13 June 1897

Dear Lord Johnny,

   I am sorry that we did not get a chance to speak more privately yesterday at the palace. And you hardly need me to spy on Mihai, since you arrived together, and we left soon after. I find that I was not at all amused by Mihai's heavy-handed attempts at chivalry, if that is what they were. Or by his equally high-handed treatment of Their Majesties, who seemed all kindness and honor.

   What is afoot?

   You surely know, and you must tell me, particularly as it concerns me, my dear Lou, and our family. I would ask you to call, but the household is in an uproar preparing for this evening. There is to be a special dinner and then a ball . . . I think. An entertainment of some kind, at any rate. It is most odd. Lou and I are being petted and groomed as though we were about to be married . . . Horrible thought! If you know anything more that concerns me, I demand that you reply at once!

   Dacia V.

*13 June 1897*

My papa has gone, and he has taken the twins with him.

They are only going as far as Hungary, to a hotel in Buda-Pesth, and there they will wait for me. My papa promised that he would send for me as soon as the family would allow it, and from Buda-Pesth we will go to Paris so that Dacia can get her fill of shopping, and see the cathedrals and romantic little streets.

This is what my papa told me, but I know that it is false comfort. He cannot send for me, any more than I can leave. I am being trussed and dressed like a lamb for the slaughter, and I do not know if I will ever see my dear papa again. Nor do I think he left of his own free will. I believe that he left with my brothers out of concern for their safety as well as his own. I do not blame him for leaving me behind, as Lady Ioana has made it clear that she wants me here, and I do not think I am in the kind of danger that my father and brothers are in.

But I am in danger. We all are.

So, good-bye, darling Papa! I love you so! And David and Adam, my little brothers: be good, and know that I love you also!

*Maria Louisa Neulander*

# IN THE FOREST OF SINAIA

Dacia wished that Romanian food weren't so *heavy* as she stood between Lou and Radu, waiting for Lady Ioana to speak. They had dined well, in the traditional manner, which meant several courses of grilled meats, cabbage, potatoes, and more spicy mamaliga. She wished that she hadn't tied her sash quite so tight, and slipped her fingers under the edge of the thick red cloth to try to loosen it a bit.

She was busy trying to do this when Lady Ioana took her place in the middle of the crowd. The entire Florescu family was there, and had eaten somberly at the feast in the massive dining room with its heavy table and low-beamed ceiling. But now they were all standing in the clearing behind the manor, and this was stranger and more ominous than eating in near silence in a room that had torch-smoke-blackened beams.

There were no formal gardens here, only a little grassy area before the trees of the forest took over. There was a large flat rock in the center of the clearing, and Lady Ioana stepped up onto it without any assistance. For an old woman who carried a cane, she could certainly move well when she needed to, Dacia reflected.

No longer fiddling with her sash, Dacia gave her grandmother her full attention. A stillness had fallen over the family that made Dacia even more nervous than she already was. Radu was making a noise low in his throat that she could just barely hear. Looking at his face, which showed his whole attention focused intently on Lady Ioana, Dacia wondered if he even knew he was making the sound at all.

Lou's cold hand slipped into Dacia's, and Dacia squeezed it by way of reply. Whatever it was that everyone had been hinting about was going to happen now, that much was clear. But what was it? Dacia looked around, but could see little beyond the ring of torches that had been placed in tall holders around the clearing. It was the dark of the moon, and though the sky was bright with stars, the forest loomed black, blocking the starlight.

"It has come, my children," Lady Ioana announced. "The time has come. The Son of the Dragon is ready to take his place on the throne, and we are poised and ready to aid him. But before we can do that, we must teach our two youngest members— the two daughters who the dreamers told would one day lead us to glory—the way of our people!"

"What?" Lou whispered, but Dacia had no answer.

"From darkness into the light," Uncle Horia said in a hoarse whisper, more to himself than anyone else. "Not to glory, from darkness into the light."

Dacia couldn't even think about what that meant. More growls had arisen from more throats, and now she saw movement in the ranks. People stepping forward, swaying back, making tense little motions, tightly controlled. Their faces strained toward Lady Ioana, and Dacia saw Aunt Kate lick her lips in a weird, hungry gesture that was more unnerving than anything else she had seen thus far.

Lou must have seen it, too, because she clutched Dacia's hand even tighter. Dacia didn't mind.

"Daughters belong to their mothers, and sons to their fathers," Lady Ioana said. "But we have not had daughters to initiate into our ways for a very long time. Not since Ana Katarina, Maria Louisa, and Ileana Ioann were themselves young maidens. It is always a pleasure to look upon the daughters of our family, and see them take on their new forms."

Lady Ioana had an expression on her face that was not pleasure, but a vulgar gloating. And what did she mean, to take on their new forms? Lady Ioana stopped addressing the family in general, and looked directly at Dacia and Lou.

"The time has come, daughters of my daughters," she said. "To teach you who you really are." She lifted her carved cane and brought the tip down on the stone with a sharp crack.

The growling was louder now, louder and higher and coming from all around them. Dacia pressed close to Lou as Radu's entire body convulsed, and he folded over until he was crouched on the ground. Everyone was on the ground, on all fours, and the growling had risen in pitch and volume until it was now a howl forcing its way out of dozens of throats.

"What's happening? What are you all doing?" Lou's voice was halfway between a sob and a whisper.

"Miss Dacia will be first," Lady Ioana said in a silky voice.

Lou let out a scream as Uncle Horia grabbed her from behind, locking his thick arms around her shoulders to tear her away from Dacia. Dacia shrieked as well, and reached for Lou, terror making her whole body shake. Cold sweat ran down her back, and the hair on the back of her neck lifted and prickled.

But before she could snatch at Lou's grasping hands, a sound behind Dacia made her whirl around. It was coming from Radu . . . but the thing that crouched behind her now was not Radu . . . could not be Radu.

Where Radu had been, there was a shredded pile of clothes, and a very large wolf with reddish-brown fur.

Its golden eyes looked at Dacia, and she knew. It *was* Radu. This was her family's secret, their strangeness, their arrogance, and all things that they were.

Beyond Radu, Aunt Kate slithered out of her white-and-red gown, panting, and stood tall in the moonlight. Then she transformed into a slender white-and-gold wolf. For a moment before her transformation, she had been standing naked without an ounce of shame, but that didn't shock Dacia, nor had the expression of sheer joy on her aunt's normally cool face. Nothing could shock Dacia anymore.

Or so she thought.

She saw Aunt Maria shed her own gown and stand there, pale and plump in the torchlight before she gave a little screech and leaped into the air to become a bat the size of an eagle. Lou's heart-rending cry brought a sob to Dacia's own lips, but even then she was not shocked; she was calm and cold and rapidly moving to a place beyond fear.

Until Lady Ioana looked at her once more, and said, "Run."

Then Lady Ioana's clothes dropped away and she, too, became a bat, a silver bat that flew straight at Dacia's face. Lady Ioana raked her needlelike claws down Dacia's cheek, scattering droplets of blood on the ground.

Dacia saw that only she, Lou, and Uncle Horia were still human, and that Radu and the other wolves were staring at her and her bloody cheek with hungry eyes, and that there was a cloud of giant bats about her head.

And Dacia saw that no one was looking at Lou, and she knew what must be done. She had to protect Lou, just as she'd always protected Lou.

So she ran.

She ran into the forest as fast as she could, dodging between wolves and around rocks and trees. In her Romanian shift, unhindered by a corset or high-heeled shoes, she ran as she had always dreamed of running, out and away, as swiftly as she could.

But the exhilaration of being able to run freely was marred by the pain slashing her cheek, and the sounds of pursuit behind her. She sobbed and prayed as she ran, but she knew in her heart that no one would come to save her.

—ɯ—

Lou struggled against Uncle Horia's grip. Dacia was gone, and once her white gown had disappeared into the woods, the wolves who had been their cousins, their uncles and aunts, had all followed her. The bats, too, had followed, but Lou could not look at them as they went.

Her mother had become a bat.

One of those creatures had been her mother.

Radu had changed, Aunt Kate had changed, but there was something more human about the wolves. Their eyes, perhaps. Or perhaps it was seeing the creature that had been her mother flapping its velvet wings, just over her head, that had so horrified her. Whatever the case, Lou could not dwell on it another moment or she thought she would lose her mind.

It was better, instead, to think about Dacia. Dacia was being chased, hunted, by wolves and bats, through a dark forest. What would they do when they caught her? She couldn't evade them for long: she didn't know the forest, and she was encumbered by her gown—her white gown that almost glowed in the darkness—and by her human body, which was not meant for running through the forest with its tangled undergrowth and fallen logs.

"They're going to kill her," Lou moaned.

Uncle Horia tightened his grip on her arms. "We do what we must."

Lou felt hot tears running down her cheeks, and she leaned forward, straining against the iron-hard grip that held her back.

—❦—

As she ran, Dacia felt her fear replaced by hate. She hated Aunt Kate, Aunt Maria, Uncle Horia, Radu, Lady Ioana . . . all of them. But most of all, she hated her mother. Her mother, Ileana, had known this terrible secret when she sent her here. Her mother had known what they would do to her, her first-born child, and she had sent her anyway, with only Aunt Kate to watch over her. Her mother was probably a wolf; she had the figure for it, or lack thereof. Dacia snorted, which caused her breath to come short and she tripped over a large tree root.

She let out a scream of pure rage and tore off her shoes and stockings. She tore off her sash and apron, and shook her hair loose, since it was falling out of its braids anyway. What did it matter that she was half-naked and dirty and bloody and barefoot? She was no longer Miss Dacia Vreeholt of New York, who went shopping at the fashionable warehouses with her friends all day and attended all the best parties at night. She had stopped being Miss Dacia Vreeholt of New York the moment she set foot on Romanian soil.

If she had ever been that person at all.

That part of Dacia that had always yearned to run and shout and scream came to the fore. She heard the snarls and howls of wolves hunting for her, smelling her blood on the wind. She saw dark flickers above her, black on black, and knew that the bats were there in the trees, watching her, but she didn't care anymore.

She didn't care about anything but getting away, getting free. The hem of her white gown tangled around her ankles. Dacia tore open the drawstring collar and let it fall down past her shoulders, her hips, to huddle on the ground. She leaped out of the circle of white cloth and ran.

—❧—

Lou had stopped struggling. She knew it wouldn't do any good: Uncle Horia was twice her size and as determined to hold her as she was determined to get free. Instead she stood in his grip and strained with her soul. She tried to see through the thick trees and the darkness to Dacia. She tried to feel with her heart if her beloved cousin was all right, and she prayed as hard as she could for something to happen to end this terrifying ordeal.

Then she heard the howling of the wolves change. A note of triumph, a call to those lagging behind.

Lou wept, straining forward with every particle of her body, reaching for her cousin until she thought her heart would burst. She had to reach Dacia.

Lou shattered into a million tiny motes, carried on the wind.

—∞—

Surrounded, Dacia backed up the side of the mountain. All around her, gleaming with a light of their own, a light that had nothing to do with the brightness of the stars above, were wolves. Wolves who had once been her family, her cousins and aunts and uncles. She had kissed them, embraced them, eaten with them, talked and laughed with them. They had sent her little gifts on her birthdays and at Christmas. She had written thank-you notes in return, had sent letters and gifts on their birthdays.

And now they surrounded her, with fangs bared, eyes shining, hungering for the blood that continued to drip down her cheek. In the forefront of the pack she saw Aunt Kate, pale and deadly but just as beautiful as she was in her human form. Dacia swiped a hand across the blood on her face, and held it out to Aunt Kate.

"Is this what you want?" She shouted it at her aunt. "Come and take it!"

For a moment, she was distracted by the sight of the blood on her fingers. In the starlight it looked very dark, and there were flickers in it, like silver. Then she turned her eyes back to Aunt Kate, who was creeping closer, ready to pounce.

Dacia let out a snarl of her own. She was not going to stand here, naked and vulnerable, in a dark forest, and let her own aunt attack her. She leaped at Aunt Kate, hands outstretched.

And changed.

She landed in front of Aunt Kate with all four paws firmly on the ground, her body transformed into something lithe and powerful and wondrous and strange.

The other wolves fell back, deferring to Aunt Kate, but Dacia continued to stare into her aunt's golden eyes. In this form it was a challenge; Dacia knew it in the core of her being. But all the same she continued to stare.

—m—

Lou was not a bat, flapping through the air on wings of taut velvet, nor a wolf running through the forest on silent paws. She was a swirl of white, of mist, of nothingness. The wind carried her up and she fought it, trying to force it to take her to Dacia until she was exhausted. She stopped fighting, and then she saw how she could slip through the streams of the air, flowing down and over, until she swirled among the trees where the wolves crouched, tense, and watched two slim shapes in the center of a small clearing.

With shock, Lou saw that the two wolves in the middle were Aunt Kate and what must surely be Dacia. She had fur the dusty-gold color of Dacia's hair, with large dark eyes. The two females were circling each other, while the others looked on. Lou floated over to Radu, and slipped a tendril of thought into his ear.

*What are they doing?*

*Aunt Kate leads the wolves; she is our queen*, Radu replied, the thoughts floating out of him and into her mind. *Dacia must bow to her.*

He turned his head and let out a yelp of surprise when he saw Lou, but she was already swirling away, moving toward Dacia.

The other wolves all whined and edged around Lou uneasily. She drew herself into a column. She could sense how easy it would be condense, to change back into her solid, human form, but she was afraid to. Dacia might need her help like this, and she didn't know if she would be able to do it again.

And then there was the pleasure she felt in this form. There was a natural feeling to it, as though she were at last at peace. She could, at last, fly.

While the wolves were staring at Lou, Dacia made her move.

⸻

She would not bow to Aunt Kate. Aunt Kate had done this to her, as much as her mother or Lady Ioana. She saw the other females fall into ranks behind her aunt, and would not take her place among them. This might be her fate, to be this thing, this animal, but it would be a cold day in hell when she exposed her belly to Aunt Kate like a lapdog begging to be petted.

A strange mist slid out of the trees and hovered near Radu.

It was Lou, Dacia could smell her, but she had no time to be astonished, or to mourn with her cousin over their fate. The other wolves were looking toward Lou now, and she saw Aunt Kate's ears swivel.

Sensing that her aunt's attention was being drawn away, Dacia leaped forward once more, only this time she did not land in front of her aunt. She landed on top of her, opening her jaws wide to grasp Kate's throat in her long, strong teeth. Her aunt fought, growling and clawing, trying to twist her neck free. But Dacia let herself go heavy, clamping down with her jaws for an eternity of time. Flesh ripped as they rolled across the ground, a rock bit into Dacia's hip, and one of her aunt's claws gouged her left ear, but still Dacia held on. In her mind, she ranted, cursing her aunt for everything, calling down damnation on them both and the entire family as well.

And then it was over, and Aunt Kate went limp. Dacia waited another heartbeat, then two, before she released her jaws and stood. The other wolves came forward, crawling and whining, but she turned her back on them and fled higher up the mountain, into the trees, running faster and faster on her four legs.

When she stopped at last, exhausted, she found she could not wear her inhuman form another moment, and she rolled on the ground, howling, until the howls turned to screams and she was naked and cold and dirty and scraped and human.

Mist swirled through the trees, then condensed into the smoky shape of a girl. Then the smoky shape became solid, became Lou, and the two cousins held on to each other as tightly as they could and sobbed.

THE DIARY OF MISS MARIA LOUISA NEULANDER

*13 June 1897*

*I am the Smoke.*

# CASA DRAGOSLOVEAN

The next morning, Lou woke with the sun. She threw open her curtains and stared out at the forest, so green and beautiful in the early morning light. When the maid came in, she was so startled to see Lou up and around that she nearly dropped the tray of hot chocolate she was carrying.

"Thank you," Lou said, taking the mug before it could fall. She had moved across the room so gracefully that she couldn't stop smiling.

For the first time in her life, Lou felt beautiful. She felt swift and light, as though she'd lost the heavy weights that had been keeping her tied to the ground. Her terror of the night before had been pushed to the back of her mind, which was now largely filled with memories of what it had been like to slip through the air, flying above them all.

She continued to smile when the maid went to her wardrobe and showed her the Romanian gowns that had been placed inside. They were less elaborate than the one she had discarded the night before, and had colors other than red decorating the white linen, but Lou shook her head all the same.

"I'll wear the pink Parisian morning gown," she said.

"Lady Ioana said that—"

"I prefer the Parisian mode of dress," Lou said. "If you'll just help me with my corset?"

The maid looked nervous, but didn't run to Lady Ioana to tattle. She got out Lou's chemise, corset, bustle, and stockings, and laid out the gown and the lace-edged petticoat that went underneath it while Lou washed at the basin.

To her delight, Lou found that her gown fit so well that her corset did not need to be laced all that tightly. For the first time, she felt that the corset merely enhanced her figure rather than struggled to contain it, and the smoothness of her linen underthings and the airy weight of the silk gown thrilled her. The maid put Lou's hair up in a simple twist, tweaking the natural curls at the front so that they fell just so over Lou's forehead. Pleased with the effect, Lou thanked the girl and went down to breakfast.

To find no one else there.

She looked at the fried tomatoes and sausage on the sideboard and gave a little shudder. It was all so heavy! In the end she ate rolls with jam and drank mint tea, and when the breakfast room was still empty she went to find Dacia. Crossing the front hall, she heard raised voices from the sitting room, but the thick door muffled the exact words. She thought about eavesdropping, but then decided that she honestly didn't care. What could they do to her?

She was the Smoke.

She went back upstairs to Dacia's room. The door was closed, and she couldn't hear any noise within the room. She knocked, but didn't get an answer. The maid, coming down the hall with Lou's nightgown over her arm, shook her head sadly at Lou.

A sudden panic clutched at her, driving away her euphoria. She tried the door, but it was locked. She went to her own room and out along the balcony to Dacia's other door. Sure enough, Dacia had not locked the outside door, and Lou went in without knocking.

Dacia's bed was neatly made, and the room was empty.

A hundred thoughts flashed through Lou's mind as she stood frozen in the doorway. Dacia had fled. She had eloped with Will Carver, or Lord Johnny, or even Prince Mihai.

Goodness, there were a lot of people she could imagine Dacia eloping with!

Or perhaps Dacia had gone to Bucharest. To Buda-Pesth. To Paris, London, or New York. Becoming a wolf had made her ill, and they had taken her to a doctor. Or, most likely, Aunt Kate had decided to take vengeance on her niece for her loss of position.

Radu had carried Lou back to the house last night, after he had turned back into a human, and Uncle Horia had taken Dacia. But had he brought her back to this room at all? Lou cursed herself for not looking in on Dacia.

As Lou hurried across the room to the door that led into the house, she heard a strange choking noise.

Lou felt herself start to dissipate into Smoke and got herself under control just in time. The noise had come from the other side of the bed, near the wall. She grabbed up the heavy pewter candlestick on the bedside table and crept around the bed.

Dacia was huddled on the floor in her chemise, her hair matted and her face red and swollen from crying. She looked up at Lou with bloodshot eyes, made all the more vivid by the long black-and-red scratch down her pale cheek.

"I want to die," Dacia croaked.

"Now what have you done?"

As soon as the question left her mouth, Lou wanted to slap herself, but Dacia didn't seem to care.

"I'm a monster, LouLou," Dacia sobbed. She made a sudden movement as though to grab the hem of Lou's gown, but checked herself and huddled against the wall again. "A monster! I almost killed Aunt Kate last night! I took off my clothes and ran through the woods naked! Our family turned into monsters, and I did, too!" Dacia's sobs were dry and horrible to hear, and Lou could see that her cousin's red eyes no longer had tears to cry.

"If you are, then I am, too," Lou said practically. "But I don't feel like a monster. I feel wonderful."

"That's because you are," Dacia softly. "You're beautiful, like a forest spirit. I'm an animal, a hairy animal that bites and kills and likes the taste of . . . the taste of . . . blood!" She pressed her face into her knees.

Lou was a little sickened by this last revelation, but didn't feel that there was any need to dwell on it. She needed Dacia up and dressed, because even with her newfound sense of beauty and strength, she didn't particularly want to face Lady Ioana alone.

"Dacia, stop wallowing at once!" Lou ordered her cousin. "Have a bath and get dressed. You will feel so much better."

"But then what?" Dacia asked hollowly, looking up. "It doesn't matter if I ever get dressed again." She let her head droop, shoulders heaving. There were leaves caught in her hair. She looked up at Lou again. "You look beautiful," she said suddenly. "That's a good color for you."

This sign of the old Dacia encouraged Lou. She rang for the maid to prepare a bath. The girl tried to look past Lou at Dacia, but Lou shut the door in her face.

She pulled her cousin to her feet. Dacia swayed like a willow wand, and Lou braced herself to catch the taller girl. But then Dacia righted herself, and looked around with reddened eyes.

"I can never leave here," she said. "This will always be my room."

"Stop being dramatic," Lou ordered. "We're leaving today."

"What do you mean? What did Lady Ioana say?" Dacia bit her already ragged lower lip. "Where are they taking us now?" Her voice was hardly more than a whisper.

Before she answered, Lou led Dacia to the bathroom, where the maid was fussing about with bath oils and towels. Lou dismissed her with a jerk of her head. "They aren't taking us anywhere," she told Dacia when they were alone. "You and I are going to Bucharest, and then on to Buda-Pesth to meet my father and brothers."

"We are?"

"Yes," Lou said, pushing Dacia into the bathroom and closing the door behind her. "We are. So hurry and bathe and get dressed," she called through the door.

"Trying to lie in bed and be regal, was she?"

Lou turned to find Aunt Kate standing there, looking arch and sour at the same time. It was not a pleasant combination. She was wearing a traditional gown, and Lou thought she looked like some archaic queen. Which she was, or had been until last night.

"Was it hard?" The question slipped out before Lou could stop it.

"I beg your pardon?"

"Was it hard to live in New York all these years?" Lou clarified. "Away from the other . . . the others?"

Aunt Kate didn't answer for a long time. She didn't seem angry, though, so Lou relaxed very slightly.

"Yes," Aunt Kate said finally. "It was. But Lady Ioana ordered me to go, and I went. That is the way of our family."

"But you were the leader of the Claw, weren't you? Their queen?"

"Lady Ioana is the leader of the family," Aunt Kate said. She sounded as though she were reciting a lesson. "She is the true queen."

As her aunt moved to walk around Lou, Lou stepped to the side to block her.

"And now Dacia is the queen of the wolves . . . the Claw."

Aunt Kate winced, and put one hand to her throat, where a filmy silk scarf did not quite conceal the place where Dacia had bitten their aunt. "I believe that has been established," she said.

"I see," Lou said, her brain whirling. She fixed Aunt Kate with her gaze, and saw her aunt actually squirm a little, avoiding her eyes. "One more question?"

Aunt Kate just looked over Lou's shoulder. She didn't agree, but she didn't walk away, either, so Lou plunged ahead.

"Will my brothers become the Smoke as well?"

"No," Aunt Kate said. "Girls inherit their talent from their mother, boys from their father. Your brothers will take after your father, and be perfectly human. Likewise, if Ileana's child is a boy, he will be of no interest to Lady Ioana. But if it is a girl, she will need to come here and discover her true self." She sighed.

Lou blurted out more questions, since Aunt Kate didn't leave. "Why am I the Smoke, then, if my mother is the Wing? Why are you the Claw? And Aunt Ileana . . . she's the Claw as well, isn't she?"

"Yes, she is." Now Aunt Kate brushed a hand against her cheek, as though Lou's questions had begun to annoy her. "It's only the talent for transformation that is passed down. The form is determined by one's . . . inner self, I suppose." Aunt Kate looked past her again. "Is that all?"

"Yes, thank you," Lou said, pleased to have finally gotten some answers.

Aunt Kate started to walk on, but stopped suddenly and came closer to Lou. Lou almost backed away from her aunt, steeling herself just in time.

"My grandmother Ana was the Smoke," Aunt Kate said softly. "The last one until now. The Smoke are always women, and first among our family, above the Claw and the Wing." Aunt Kate looked over her shoulder, and leaned closer to Lou.

"You have no girl cousins here in Romania, but girls have been born. And died."

Lou felt dizzy. "You don't mean . . . how . . . not Lady Ioana?"

She gasped out the question, not even sure she understood it herself.

"My mother likes being a queen," Aunt Kate whispered. "She would have married Mihai's grandfather, if he would have had her, but he chose another.

"Then the prophecy came, and how much easier to put a puppet queen on the throne beside a young king? All she had to do was make sure no one took control of the family from her." Aunt Kate's smile bore a ghost of the love she had once shown Lou and Dacia. "I did my best to protect you. I told her in every letter that I was sure you were the Wing. Told her I had tasted your blood, looked into your eyes, consulted an American seer . . ."

"But you knew?" Lou could barely form the words.

"Oh, my dear," Aunt Kate said, putting one hand on Lou's cheek. For the moment her face softened, and she was the beautiful Aunt Kate that Lou had always known. "I could tell from the time you learned to walk that you were meant to fly. Higher than all of us."

She went to her own room and locked the door.

Lou stood for a moment longer in the passage, frozen, and then finally summoned the strength to carry on to Dacia's room. Dacia was in the bath, so Lou selected a green morning gown and laid it on the bed. She rang for the maid and asked her to help Dacia dress, and then Lou walked stiffly along the balcony to her own room.

Lou sat down for a moment on a chair. Then she got up and sat on the edge of the bed. Then she got up again, opened the shutters, took a breath of air, and fought down a little sob.

"I need to do something," she said aloud. "I need to do something or I'll have the vapors like some silly miss at her first ball."

She sat at the little writing desk and carefully composed a letter to her father. She could not bring herself to tell him what she had just learned, so instead she informed him that she and Dacia would be leaving within the next few days, and promised to send a telegram with the information on their train once they had tickets in hand. When she was done she took a moment to admire her own handwriting, which was just as neat as ever and bore no sign of how badly she was shaking.

Lou thought about putting the letter on the tray in the main hall for one of the servants to post, which she had planned to do earlier, but didn't feel quite that confident. Instead she went down to the front gate. There was an old Gypsy man there she didn't recognize, and she gave him the letter and some money.

"I heard howling in the forest last night," the old man said, smiling toothlessly at her.

"I didn't notice," she said with a quelling look.

The old man cackled with laughter, but it was easier to ignore than Lou would have thought. She went inside the gate and pulled it shut behind her.

# THE DIARY OF MISS DACIA VREEHOLT

*14 June 1897*

    *I never meant for this to happen! What have I done? All I wanted was to run, to be free, to do what I felt like doing just once in this life! I've never hurt anyone, not even when I was going to go up north with Lord Johnny! It seems too stupid for words now. We were only going to <u>pretend</u> to elope so that he could spy on that man from the Treasury! But Aunt Kate caught us . . . and now I've caught Aunt Kate, so to speak. First with Mihai's uncle, and now . . . this. I always wanted to be a leader, but of society, not of this. I see how childish it all was; everything in my life was just a stupid game until now. If only I could have been a fairy-tale queen, in a beautiful palace, with nothing to do but dance and be beautiful.*

    *Now I am a queen of darkness and terror.*

# CASA DRAGOSLOVEAN

The gown laid out on her bed made Dacia shudder. She didn't want to wear Parisian gowns, or even her old New York gowns. For all Lou's determination, Dacia knew that all that was behind them now. Even if Lady Ioana let them return to New York, why would they want to? Could they honestly sit in front parlors with their old friends, drinking lemonade in summer and tea in winter and talking about parties and engagements, when they knew that they were ... different?

Dacia was a wolf. She could feel it there, beneath her skin, all the time now. She could drop her dressing gown to the floor and transform in a matter of seconds if she wanted to. She no longer cared whether Jenny Darville invited her to be a bridesmaid for her wedding. She never wanted to see Jenny Darville again, or anyone from New York, in case they guessed her secret.

Will Carver's face popped into her head, and she shuddered, causing the maid to look at her fearfully. The girl was trying to help her into her underthings, but Dacia was standing and staring out the window. If this little maid, who probably knew all about Dacia and the rest of her family, could look at her like that, how would Will look at her? Would he recognize that there was something different about her? Or would he be too caught up in his art to notice? This last thought was surprisingly bitter.

Just a few weeks ago she had been waiting for Will to propose. Everyone in New York had been waiting, too. Dacia's friends had been green with envy, her Vreeholt relations beside themselves with delight. But then it had come to Ileana's attention, and she had insisted that Dacia go abroad before she made any rash decisions. Dacia had of course leaped at the chance to travel, ignoring the baffling idea that marrying Mr. William J. Carver, of the Manhattan Carvers, was a rash decision.

But now she knew why her mother wanted her away from Will.

Dacia knew now that she should be grateful to her mother. Will was not half so dashing and handsome as Lord Johnny, but he was from an old and wealthy family, and was currently considered the best catch in New York. And, with his artistic temperament, he was far less boring than most New York bachelors. She'd even fancied herself in love with him, though really she was in love with the *idea* of him: rich, admired, and artistic.

He would have made an eminently suitable husband, but Dacia could no longer be an eminently suitable wife. Because of her mother's legacy, this wolf that hid within her, Will would not—could not—have anything to do with her. She thought of his ravings at Bran about the monstrousness of the Dracula family and felt sick. They weren't the monsters: she was.

She brushed a hand against the scratch on her cheek. Though it had seemed deep the night before, it was healing well and she didn't think it would leave a scar. In the moonlight, the drops that had fallen from it had had a silver glow to them . . . and just now in the bath the dried blood had been as black as soot. The memory made her shake, and the maid looked even paler and more frightened.

"Just go, then," Dacia said, not wanting to feel the girl's hands trembling as she helped Dacia dress.

When the maid had gone, Dacia put the green silk gown at the back of her wardrobe where she wouldn't have to see it and be reminded of her old, good life. She took out a traditional gown, embroidered in red and blue, and put it on, grateful that she didn't need help with the simple garment. She even got the apron and sash in place without too much trouble. Then she braided her hair in a long plait and left her room, trying not to look timid as she checked the corridor first. She didn't want to run into Aunt Kate.

Lou popped out of her room when Dacia passed it, as though she had been waiting for her cousin to emerge. She looked startled when she took in Dacia's choice of clothing, but she didn't say anything. Instead she took Dacia's arm and led her downstairs.

"I have something to tell you," Lou whispered as they went down. "But I can't say it just now."

Dacia summoned the will to look at her cousin but couldn't make her mouth move to ask what it was Lou had to say.

From behind the sitting room door came the sound of voices. Dacia thought she could hear Lou's mother and Uncle Horia despite the thickness of the wooden door. Everything seemed louder today, and the sunlight streaming through the open windows on either side of the front door was far too bright.

"They're talking about us," Dacia said, her voice dull.

What more was there to say? They had done exactly as the family had expected. No, that wasn't true. Lou had not changed into a bat, but an enchanted being of mist, and Dacia had challenged Aunt Kate and won her place in some sort of primitive duel. But what did it all mean?

"Still?" Lou wrinkled her noise. "It's been hours!"

Dacia's heart sank even further, though she hadn't thought that was possible.

"Oh, well, we'd best beard the lion in her den," Lou said, trying to sound cheery and almost succeeding.

Lou rapped on the door and the voices within stopped. Taking this as a sign to enter, Lou lifted the latch and went in, dragging Dacia along behind.

"Good morning, Lady Ioana," she said, nodding to the old woman. "Uncle Horia. Mother."

Uncle Horia stood and bowed to Lou, only to sit again hastily when his mother shot him a terrible look. Aunt Maria fluttered a bit as though she might rise, then subsided, and Lady Ioana turned her attention to the girls.

"Good morning," their grandmother purred. "I hope that you both slept well. I am surprised that you did not stay abed longer. You both had quite an exciting night."

"Yes," Lou said, and there was a tightness in her voice that hadn't been there before. "Quite exciting. I slept all right, but Dacia did not sleep at all. Which is part of the reason why we wanted to speak to you."

"Oh?" Lady Ioana raised her eyebrows.

She was smiling. Dacia hated her grandmother's smile. It was a look of pure evil, in her opinion. Bat or no, Lady Ioana most often looked like a cat that was letting a mouse get within a hand's breadth of its home before she dealt the killing blow.

"Dacia and I need to go back to Bucharest now," Lou said. Her voice was very even, but Dacia could feel in the additional pressure from Lou's hand on her arm that her cousin was not as calm as she seemed. "We would like to order the travel carriage."

"You *need* to go back to Bucharest?" Again the smile.

Dacia felt like her stomach was filled with ice. She wanted to run from the room, and only Lou's arm in hers kept her from fleeing.

"Maria Louisa, don't be silly," Aunt Maria said, waving a handkerchief at her daughter as though wiping her request away. "There is so much to discuss! And so much to teach you!"

"Dacia is very shaken by the events of last night," Lou pressed on. "And, although I love it here"—a trace of wistfulness showed in her voice—"I don't think it's the right place for us to be right now. I would like to go back to Bucharest today and then on to Buda-Pesth. We'll say good-bye to the Szekelys, and other acquaintances we've made in Bucharest first, of course." She nodded at her mother, as though convincing Aunt Maria that she would observe all the formalities of polite society.

"The Szekelys?"

Lady Ioana's eyebrows could not possibly go any higher, and her smile could not get any wider, either, Dacia thought. The ice was creeping its way up her throat from her stomach.

"A charming family that we met just before we left Bucharest," Lou supplied.

"I know the family," Lady Ioana said. "I know all the important families in Bucharest. In all of Romania!" She banged her cane on the floor, and Dacia jumped. "And do you know why?" She didn't wait for them to answer. "Because they are of so little concern to us! We are so different from them, so far above them, that they are as insects crawling on the ground beneath our feet!"

"After last night, we thought you would understand," Uncle Horia said. There was a line between his brows and he looked baffled by Lou's request. "We are not like them. We have our own concerns, which other people cannot understand."

"Like treason?" Dacia's voice broke shrilly through the ice that was consuming her from within.

"It is not treason to restore the rightful ruler to the throne," Uncle Horia said, not very convincingly, to Dacia's ears.

"Taking over Europe is not restoring a rightful ruler to the throne," Lou pointed out. "Besides which, Dacia and I are Americans. We really should not be part of this."

Lady Ioana made a rude noise. "Americans! You are your mothers' daughters, and Romanian! We should have brought you here years ago!"

"I'm afraid I feel far more American than Romanian," Lou said, rather primly.

Even as she resolved not to say another word, Dacia found herself speaking. "I just don't understand. If Mihai's family has the greater claim, why does no one but our family talk about it?"

"Young ladies do not need to concern themselves with politics," Aunt Maria said. "You are here to add your support to the family, and to do as you are told!"

Dacia pulled at the drawstring collar of her gown. Her aunt's words angered her, and in the rush of heat from her anger, she felt her soft gown chafing. A bitter taste filled her mouth, and she fought the transformation, smothering a wail of despair. Would it always be like this? Would fear or anger or surprise always make her change? She was distracted, fortunately, by Lou's answer.

"I don't think so, Mother," Lou said with shocking coldness. "I don't think that it is a good idea at all for us to sit quietly and wait for you to tell us what to do. Not if it's treason. I don't like Prince Mihai, and if we are to take part in Romanian politics, it seems to me that King Carol has much more to recommend him."

Aunt Maria drew in a shocked breath. "Maria Louisa! How *dare* you! Our family has guarded the Dracula family for four hundred years! If Prince Mihai told you to bring him the moon—"

"I'd laugh in his face," Lou retorted. "As you yourself have told me all my life: I am from two very great families, and I take orders from no one."

"You will take orders from me, little girl," Lady Ioana said. She was not smiling now, and it seemed much worse.

"Why should I?" Lou asked. "I am the Smoke."

Lady Ioana's wrinkled face flushed dark and her teeth seemed to sharpen. "You will listen to me now, you spoiled thing—"

But Lou was clearly not in the mood to let her finish. "*I am the Smoke*," she snapped. "Like your mother, Lady Ioana."

Dacia could not understand why Aunt Maria and Uncle Horia both flinched at Lou's words, or why Lady Ioana seemed unable to reply, but at least Lou's argument seemed to be working, which was better than Dacia could say for her own feeble attempts to fight.

"And Dacia is the queen of the Claw," Lou said. "In case you've forgotten." Her hard, very un-Lou-like gaze found Uncle Horia's, and he looked away. "We won't be taking orders from anyone. You can try to lock us in our rooms, but I doubt very much any lock could hold me." She gave Dacia's arm a tug. "We'd better order the maids to pack," she said. "Please order the carriage for us, Uncle."

Stricken mute, Dacia allowed Lou to lead her out of the parlor and up the stairs to Lou's bedroom. Dacia slowly collapsed on a chair in the corner, staring at the new Lou. Lou, for her part, threw herself on the bed, kicking her legs in what looked like a tantrum. Dacia started to rise again, alarmed, but then she realized that Lou was laughing.

"Why didn't you tell me that talking back felt so good?" Lou demanded.

*14 June 1897*

*Dearest Papa,*

*Dacia and I are on our way to Bucharest, so you must forgive my handwriting; this carriage is not very well sprung. Lady Ioana did not try to stop us from leaving, but is showing her disapproval in other, smaller ways, like lending us the oldest carriage in the stables. It is very childish of her. Nevertheless, we will be there tomorrow, and spend a day saying good-bye to some new acquaintances. We shall take the Friday train to Buda-Pesth, and hope to see you and the twins at the station on Sunday afternoon.*

*We now both know what it is that made you so anxious for our safety. It was a shock, but I can assure you that I am quite recovered. Dacia, on the other hand, has taken it very badly, hence our hasty departure. I am hoping that time and distance from Lady Ioana will restore her.*

*I hope that the twins are behaving themselves. Tell them that if they are, I shall bring them both a present. Radu brought me some sugared plums that are simply divine, and I want to find more. I will buy a box for each of the boys IF they can be good.*

*All my love,*
*LouLou*

*P.S. Since I know you are wondering: I do not know when, or even if, Mama will be joining us. You will have to inquire of her directly. She is not speaking to me at present.*

# STRADA SILVESTRU

In Bucharest Lou felt herself breathe a little easier, which she hadn't thought possible. She was so light already that she thought she might float away at times in sheer excitement, and seeing the elegant boulevards of Bucharest made her positively giddy. Not even the revelation about Lady Ioana and what she'd done to the other girls of the Smoke could keep Lou down, for during her journey she had made a silent promise that she would bring Lady Ioana to justice for what she had done.

When they pulled up in front of the mansion on Rua Silvestre, Lou sprang from the carriage before the footman could even offer a hand to help her. She smiled brightly at Dacia, who emerged from the carriage blinking and wincing, as though the sunlight were far too bright. It was a lovely day, but there were enough clouds in the sky to keep it from being too glaring.

"Coming?"

Dacia didn't answer.

Lou studied her dear cousin and friend. Dacia had hardly spoken the entire journey from Bran, preferring instead to stare out the window and answer any of Lou's comments with monosyllables. Stripped of her usual fashionable clothes, her hair down, and her face so remote, Dacia looked fragile and yet wild at the same time . . . entirely unlike herself. It was the only mar on Lou's good cheer. She hoped that once they were safely away from Romania, her cousin would recover, but she didn't know what to do if she didn't. Dacia had often talked of getting a small apartment for the two of them in New York. It had always seemed too scandalous for Lou to contemplate, but at present it seemed like just the thing to help Dacia, and Lou knew that her father would not refuse her if she asked.

Yes, that was the answer. A place of their own, far from here, and perhaps college in the fall, for Lou. She let out a little laugh and squeezed Dacia's arm. Yes.

Lou's giddiness was dampened considerably when Prince Mihai arrived moments later. The cousins were still standing in the entrance hall, so they could hardly pretend they were not at home when the prince pushed past the butler who had answered the door as though he weren't even there.

"You are back at last!" He made an expansive gesture, as though he wanted to embrace them both.

Lou stepped back a bit, and so did Dacia. Lou saw that her cousin was looking at Mihai with terrified eyes.

Unable to cast manners aside completely, Lou invited the prince into the parlor, though she was determined to get rid of him as soon as possible. She had to fight down years of training to avoid ringing for tea. She removed her hat, a delicate confection of lace and feathers, and set it on a small table, jabbing the long hatpin into it with unnecessary force. Dacia sank onto a sofa as though she were near fainting, of which Lou approved, as her semi-prone posture prevented the prince from sitting next to her.

"How fortunate for you that we have just returned," Lou said politely after a short silence. "I must warn you, it's been a tiring day." She stopped herself just before she mentioned changing out of her travel clothes. Mihai always made such statements sound so *intimate*. "And when did you get back from Peles?" She tried to keep her manners in place, all the same.

"Yesterday," he said. "The longest day of my life!" He gave Dacia a smoldering look.

"I'm very sorry to hear that," Lou replied.

Dacia stood up.

"You *know*, don't you?" she asked in a flat tone. "You know all about us. About our family. So just say whatever it is you want to say and then go."

Prince Mihai stood as well. His flirtatious manner dropped away like a cast-off cloak, and he looked at Dacia with an expression that was so hard it was frightening. Lou rose to her feet, feeling herself tensing and lifting out of her shoes a little bit. If Mihai threatened her, she could simply dissolve and fly away.

But Dacia didn't have that luxury, so Lou forced her heels back on the ground.

"Good," Prince Mihai said. "Since you are both still alive, I am guessing that you have successfully made the transformation into your true shapes."

Lou felt thoroughly grounded now. She didn't answer him, and neither did Dacia; and in any case he seemed to not need an answer. As he had said, they were both still alive. Lou had not allowed herself to question what would have happened if she or Dacia had failed to transform.

In light of Aunt Kate's revelation about the fate of the other Smoke girls, Lou had no doubt that Lady Ioana would have had them killed if they'd failed. Even now she might be planning on having Lou murdered, to get rid of the only living Smoke and ensure that she, Lady Ioana, remained head of the family.

"And you know of my plans to take the throne?" Mihai asked appraisingly. "The throne that rightfully belongs to me?"

Now he waited for an answer, so Lou nodded. Dacia didn't move.

"Excellent," Mihai said. "I have other plans as well, you know. Deeper plans beyond just getting back my illustrious ancestor's throne and bringing Europe to its knees."

He looked at Dacia, and his blatant gaze made Lou blush. Her blush turned to anger, though, when she saw how Dacia's hands began to shake, and the feverish color that stained her cousin's pale cheeks.

"A queen who is also a shape-shifter?" He smiled. "Who could rip the throats out of anyone who displeases me? Ah! Such a thing will make me powerful beyond measure! And what could be more natural?" He pointed to the bracelet on Dacia's wrist, and Lou noticed that her cousin was wearing the heavy gold bangle that Mihai had sent her. "The sign of our people is a wolf-headed dragon! We are meant to rule the world together!"

Before either of the cousins could move, Mihai seized hold

of Dacia and kissed her hard on the mouth, his hands grasping at her back, her buttocks. Dacia made a strangled noise, and her fists beat weakly at his shoulders.

Lou exploded into mist, her clothes falling to the floor in a heap.

Mihai pushed Dacia away, temporarily sated, and she fell backward onto the sofa. He noticed Lou's clothing, and looked up with a grin, his lips red and wet. "Where did you fly off to, little bat?"

Lou forced herself to take on her own form, but only half-way, so that he could see her there. She did it between him and Dacia, with her arms outstretched to warn him off.

"The Smoke!" Mihai's eyes widened and then narrowed. "Very interesting. Perhaps you would be even more useful to—"

Lou tried to move away from Mihai, but without leaving Dacia unprotected. She went too thin, like a narrow wall of mist, then pulled herself together too hard. She almost became fully human—and therefore nude—just inches from Mihai's awful leering face. She dissipated again, whirling between Mihai and Dacia in an attempt to protect the one and fend off the other.

"Get out of our house!" Lou screamed it with all her might, but she had no voice. Instead she made a high, rushing noise, like the wind through the trees, and she moved toward him. When her misty hands came into contact with his chest, he shuddered and turned pale. "Get out!" she screamed again, another whoosh of sound.

Mihai took two quick steps, as though he would break into a run, but then he stopped himself. He grinned at Dacia and

Lou, and put his hat on with care. "I'll get what is mine," he told them. "I always do!" He slammed the front door shut on his way out.

Lou turned back to Dacia, who was huddled on the sofa, sobbing. Lou returned to her human form and grabbed a silk-fringed shawl from one of the chairs to cover herself. She sat down by Dacia, holding her cousin tightly.

"I hate him so much," Dacia choked out. "But what am I going to do? Who else will marry me now?"

Startled, Lou drew back. "What? You surely aren't considering marrying *Mihai* just for the sake of being married, are you? Dacia, don't be ridiculous! Someone much better will fall head over heels in love with you, and he won't care if you can turn into a . . . a frog! You cannot marry Mihai and let him order you to kill people!"

"*Can* I refuse? I don't know anymore," Dacia said, tears streaming down her face.

"I'm sorry, is this a good time?"

Lou looked up, mouth agape, to see Lord Johnny and That— Mr. Arkady standing in the doorway. When they saw Lou's gown on the floor and the way she was holding the shawl over herself, both men blushed.

She drew herself up, pulling the shawl closed at her neck.

"We have had a most trying day," she informed them with as much dignity as she could muster. "Prince Mihai has just left us and is no longer welcome anywhere near Dacia or me, and I am naked beneath this shawl.

"So to answer your question, my lord: this is a terrible time."

The gentlemen looked politely shocked, and Lord Johnny started to say something, but Lou cut him off. She didn't want them to leave, despite her condition. And Dacia's. In fact, it was because of Dacia's condition that she wanted them very much to stay.

"But I can hardly think that a better one will present itself," Lou said before Lord Johnny could get a word out. "We have many questions, which I believe you can answer. And you *will* answer them!"

"I see," Lord Johnny said, coming into the room. He appeared to be recovering from the shock of her state of undress, as well as her asperity.

Mr. Arkady, on the other hand, couldn't seem to take his eyes off her legs. He caught her staring back at him, and blushed an even duskier color.

"Mr. Arkady," Lou rapped out. "Kindly remove your jacket and put it over my legs. Without looking."

Mr. Arkady did so, while Lou ignored him and helped Dacia pull a handkerchief out of her sash. Then she gave her attention to Lord Johnny.

"Now, my lord," Lou said. "I want to know everything about the Dracula family, our family, and why you happen to know so much about the both of them to begin with."

FROM THE DESK OF MISS DACIA VREEHOLT

15 June 1897

Dear Mother,

I hate you, I hate you., I hate you.

Lou insists that we return to New York, but I am not going to get on any ship that is headed toward you. I don't care where I go, but it must be as far from you and your evil family as I can get. I would rather end my life than transform into a beast again, and I loathe you for giving me this life. For giving me this life, and then refusing to tell me that it was cursed.

# STRADA SILVESTRU

The inner change that had come over Lou was almost as shocking as seeing her turn into Smoke. Dacia couldn't believe that it was Lou, her shy, easily embarrassed *Lou* who was sitting beside her—naked, no less—demanding that Lord Johnny answer their questions.

Which, to Dacia's further surprise, he did. He seemed only slightly discomfited by Lou's lack of clothing or Dacia's clear distress. In fact, he seemed to have expected to find them . . . well, not undressed, but in distress.

"You know the story of Vlad Tepes?" Lord Johnny looked at them both with his bright blue eyes.

"The Wallachian prince who impaled his enemies?" Lou wrinkled her nose. "Of course."

Dacia and Lou's governess had taught them the history as well as the language of their mothers' country. Stories of Vlad, the hero of the Wallachian people, had been de rigueur.

"Despite his mad rages, and his penchant for impaling his enemies... and anyone he perceived as an enemy... Vlad Tepes was loved by the common people," Lord Johnny said. "He was a just ruler, a strong protector, a builder of churches. The peasants felt safe at night, knowing that their prince and his soldiers were on guard."

Lou nodded impatiently. "I told you we know all that," she said. "Although I still don't understand revering a man who impales his enemies." She grimaced. "But I didn't think he had any descendants," Lou added. "I was startled when I heard that Mihai was a Dracula." The name Dracul, or Dragon, had been awarded to Vlad Tepes's father for his battle prowess. It was not exactly a common Romanian surname.

"Vlad's son, Vlad III, survived," Arkady said. "He did his best to regain his father's glory, but his line died out two generations later, thank heavens. It was rumored that Tepes was mad, and the family has been plagued by violence and signs of insanity. But Tepes had other wives."

"Other *wives*?" Dacia spoke without thinking, startled by this piece of scandal on top of all the others.

Lord Johnny blushed. "It was common at the time."

"Mihai's several-times-great-grandfather was born *after* Tepes's assassination," Mr. Arkady continued. "His mother was Hungarian—the daughter of the emperor himself! She knew that her father would kill her if he found out, so she hid, had the child, and then returned to court to marry a man of her father's choosing. For many years, this branch of the Dracula family lived in obscurity in Transylvania, waiting for their chance."

"Their chance?" Lou's eyebrows raised, and for a moment, Dacia could see a resemblance between her cousin and their grandmother, Lady Ioana.

Lord Johnny drew a deep breath. He was sitting on the sofa opposite Dacia and Lou, leaning forward with his forearms resting on his knees. He looked exhausted.

"Yes," Lord Johnny said.

His face was grim, and he looked careworn. Dacia made a small move to reach out to him, and then caught herself and hid her hand beneath Lou's shawl.

"There was a prophecy that Vlad Tepes would return to rule again," Lord Johnny said, as though telling them the direst news they would ever hear. Perhaps it was, but Dacia felt beyond fear at this moment. She had seen and heard too much in the past week, and was numb from her heart to her toes. "He is rather like King Arthur in my own country, in that respect. Mihai believes that he is his ancestor reborn. And this time, he wants more than just Wallachia; he wants all of Romania."

A line appeared between Lou's brows. This was normally a sign that she was upset, and the old Dacia would have leaped to protect the old Lou from whatever it was that had bothered her. But the new Lou appeared more thoughtful than upset, and the new Dacia did not have the strength to defend anyone. She could still feel Mihai's wet lips on her own, and she suddenly rubbed her mouth on the sleeve of her dress, chafing her lips on the embroidery.

"I'm sick to death of prophecies," Dacia muttered. Lou squeezed her hand.

"Then why didn't the Dracula family make their claim years

ago?" Lou shook her head. "King Carol isn't Romanian, but he was put on the throne because people went looking for a king!"

"First the Draculas were in hiding," Mr. Arkady said, taking up the thread again. "Afraid that those who had killed Tepes would seek to destroy them as well. Then for several years, there were no likely heirs." He grimaced. "There have been incidents . . . many of Mihai's ancestors have died from violent confrontations or ended their own lives. Mihai's father was dead before Mihai was born, and his uncle has no interest in being a king."

"Do you mean Mattias?" Lou asked.

"Even so," Mr. Arkady said, nodding. He looked a tad confused at the significant look Lou gave Dacia at the name. Or perhaps he was only confused because Dacia did not return the look, but merely stared at the fringe of the shawl draping Lou.

Dacia did not want to think about Aunt Kate.

"But now they have Mihai," Mr. Arkady said, after clearing his throat.

"Yes. Now they have Mihai," Lord Johnny echoed, his voice dark. "Handsome, intelligent, *charming* Mihai. The family is pinning all their hopes on him. They've groomed him from the time he was a small child to come to power."

"By taking the throne from King Carol?" The line between Lou's brows deepened, then smoothed out. Dacia noticed that Arkady was watching this, too, with great fascination. "Because now King Carol has brought Romania together."

"Exactly," Lord Johnny told her, nodding. "The states are united, and there is talk of annexing Transylvania. It's a powerful nation now, prosperous."

"How does our family come into this?" Lou pulled her shawl

tighter about herself, and then reached under it for Dacia's hand, squeezing tightly again. Dacia found she did not have the strength to squeeze back.

"When Princess Anna, Vlad Tepes's Hungarian wife, went into hiding in Sighisoara, it was the Florescu family that hid her. You come from an old, respected family, and they also have a certain . . . reputation."

Now Dacia felt her own eyebrows rising. "Reputation?" Her voice rasped a little.

Lord Johnny looked at the floor, pulling at his cuffs as though discomfited.

"The Florescus are rumored to possess magical abilities," Mr. Arkady said finally.

Dacia thought that she might be sick. They knew. Lord Johnny knew. Their lives were ruined, and all because they were born into this horrible family. No wonder he couldn't look at her. No wonder they weren't all that startled to see Lou naked, herself in traditional dress like a peasant. Their family was beyond the pale, and Lord Johnny knew it very well.

But Lou was shaking her head. "Oh, surely you don't believe such things!" She laughed, and Dacia thought that she was probably the only person in the room who knew Lou well enough to recognize that it wasn't her real laugh. "Magic? Honestly, Mr. Arkady!" If Lou had had a fan, she would have slapped Mr. Arkady's wrist with it. "It's like that awful novel that Will Carver was raving about!"

The look that Mr. Arkady gave Lou made Dacia wonder how closely this man had been watching Lou, and for how long. He certainly looked like he knew her laugh was fake.

"Miss Neulander, I am being perfectly honest," the young man said in a stiff tone. "Lord Johnny and I have seen things that I think neither of you ladies would credit." He did not look as if those things had been pleasant.

Now Lou's laugh was genuine, but it had a slight edge to it, and the hand that held Dacia's was damp. "You might be surprised about that," she said.

"I have now read that novel," Mr. Arkady continued, "and I—"

"I told you," Lord Johnny interrupted him. "I told you that it was too late. We should have done something, protected them somehow." He rose to his feet and crossed to the sofa where Dacia and Lou huddled. He knelt down and put one hand on the arm of the sofa near Dacia, but without touching her. "What did they do to you?"

Dacia looked at Lord Johnny's earnest face. His eyes were so blue, and he needed a haircut. Her heart shrank at the thought of seeing his expression turn to disgust when he found out what she was.

"You still haven't answered *our* questions," Lou said. "Why are we still tied to the Dracula family? It was four hundred years ago that Princess Anna went to them." She tossed her loosened hair out of her eyes. "And you say we have magic? What of it?"

Lord Johnny straightened, a little taken aback at Lou's businesslike words, but Arkady looked appreciative. It was Johnny who answered, however.

"Well," he said, "Anna gave them her child to raise, and a great deal of gold to sweeten the prospect. The Florescus were respected, but Anna made them wealthy as well. In return they raised her son, also named Vlad. He was trained in arms, educated, and unfortunately hotheaded. He died in a tavern brawl when he was only twenty-two, leaving behind his young widow and infant son.

"By then, the Florescus had established themselves as the guardians of the Dracula family, and after all these years, they continue to protect the family: hide them when needed, support them, act as bodyguards, even. In return there is wealth, status, and the promise that when a Dracula sits on the throne of Romania, a Florescu will stand beside that throne."

"Or sit on the one next to it," Dacia said without thinking.

Lord Johnny looked surprised, but he nodded. "Yes, there have been some marriages back and forth, but not many. The Draculas, I'm afraid, seem to think of your family as more in the vein of trusted servants." He had the grace to look embarrassed.

Dacia wanted to scream. She didn't know what held her back, really. Her life was ruined, Lou was naked and unashamed; why couldn't she do something unladylike and just start screaming and tearing out her hair? But she was already anticipating the disgust on Lord Johnny's face when he learned the truth about her; she couldn't bear to have him think she was mad as well.

"Mihai wants to marry Dacia," Lou said in a matter-of-fact tone. "So you can see why we were so upset when you arrived. He had just left, after making his attentions vulgarly clear."

"Did he hurt you?"

Lord Johnny's whole body was rigid with tension, and he stretched out a hand to Dacia, but she was afraid if she took it, he would feel how clammy her palm was. Also, if she moved she was fairly certain that Lou's shawl would be disarrayed, and Mr. Arkady would see more than her fine legs.

"No," she managed to answer. "But it was most unpleasant."

Her voice sounded missish, and she hated herself even more. *Most unpleasant*. It was the kind of thing she had been taught to say if a gentleman pressed her hand too warmly. Not if he groped her and tried to . . . her mind rejected the memory.

"You must help us," Lou said decisively. "We want no part of Prince Mihai, or his ambitions. But tell us first: Why do you know so much about it, and why do you care? Can you help us?"

Lord Johnny looked to Arkady for confirmation, and the other young man nodded. They both took deep breaths, and then Lord Johnny sighed. He sank down on a small ottoman, near enough that Dacia could have reached out to touch him, if she had wanted to. If she hadn't been too frightened.

"We are part of an organization with members all over the world," Lord Johnny said. "It's called the Society of Saint Gabriel the Archangel."

"That's a mouthful," Lou said. "Are you monks?"

Mr. Arkady muttered something in Turkish that made Lord Johnny look at him sharply.

"No, it's not a religious order," Lord Johnny said with a little cough. "It was once, but it's not now." He stopped himself from saying something and then plunged on. "Centuries ago, our ancestors encountered monsters, things you cannot even imagine, and pledged that we would keep the world safe from them. Our men—and women—are fighting this fight all over the world as we speak. And for now, Theo and I have been sent to Romania to protect King Carol."

"Why?" Lou asked simply. "King Carol and his wife seem kind, but why all this fuss?"

"As you know, Romania straddles the divide between the Eastern and Western cultures of Europe," Mr. Arkady said. "So it is both important and sadly rare for the land to be united under a good, strong king. If Carol stays in power, we believe that Romania will remain a peaceful bridge between east and west. If Mihai takes control, he will use this country's position to spread his diseased rule across Europe."

Dacia felt as if a weight had lifted from her heart. It would be all right. It would all be all right. She smiled at Lord Johnny, and he smiled back, blinking at her rapid change in expression.

"So you're here to get rid of Mihai?" She slipped her hand out from under the shawl as smoothly as she could, reaching for Lord Johnny.

His smile faded, and he didn't take her hand. He tugged at his cuffs again, and looked at Mr. Arkady, who got to his feet.

"In a roundabout way," Arkady said, his expression grim. "Our orders mostly concern your family, Miss Vreeholt. We are here to stop the Florescus.

"As John said: our society keeps the world safe from the monsters."

## THE DIARY OF MISS MARIA LOUISA NEULANDER

*15 June 1897*

Am I a monster? I don't feel like one. I don't feel like anything, not when I am the Smoke, anyway.

Therein lies the attraction.

I am so very tired of feeling gauche, or embarrassed, or silly, or plump. I am so tired of people looking at me, judging me: What am I wearing, how much did it cost, how is my hair arranged, who is my family, have I been invited to this party, that ball? It is so very wearying to be a part of New York society! There is so much to remember, so many rules and traditions, like the steps in a dance that goes on and on. I feel like Marley's Ghost in Mr. Dickens's Christmas story, all wrapped about with chains of my own making.

But when I am the Smoke, those chains are gone, and I am free. I become giddy just thinking about it. Imagine if I was at a party and someone was horrible to me, like Justine Coombs. I know that Dacia likes her, but she is so sly I simply cannot. Imagine if she were to make some comment to me at a party, and everyone was watching to see if I would blush or cry, and instead I just disappeared? Just floated away to a place where no one was looking at me? It would be heaven!

And now it seems that Lord Johnny and Mr. Arkady have

been watching our family, because they believe we are monsters. I am not sure what to think! It certainly explains Mr. Arkady's rude behavior, but not Lord Johnny's obvious attraction to Dacia (which I think she is oblivious to, despite their earlier time together). I do not feel like a monster. I think that perhaps Dacia does, though. And dare I say that Lady Ioana falls into the "monstrous" category even when not transformed into a bat!

I will have to take Lord Johnny aside and ask him to speak more circumspectly about it. Dacia needs to be handled much more delicately. It is apparent that the gentlemen's secret society is much more accustomed to dealing with monsters than with young ladies.

# STRADA SILVESTRU

You are mistaken," Lou said politely to Mr. Arkady. "We are not monsters."

"Of course not!" But he didn't sound at all convinced. "You may not know this, having been raised in America, but some in your family have strange powers that they use in the service of the Draculas. They are the ones we have come to stop, my dear young ladies. Horia Florescu, your uncle, is very well known to our Society, I'm afraid."

Lou felt that there was something they were not saying. Both men were tense, as though they were communicating silently, trying to decide how much to tell the cousins. She had thought for a moment that they knew what had happened at the family estate the night before, but now Mr. Arkady acted as though he was sparing her a shock.

Dacia had withdrawn the hand she'd extended to Lord Johnny and was pale and shaking. Lou was very worried about her, but first they needed more answers. Although it was a relief to have gotten as many as they had already.

"Then why were you spying on Prince Mihai at Peles?" Lou asked.

"Hmm," Mr. Arkady said, and he looked at Lord Johnny.

"No," came the other's reply.

"They have asked, and they deserve to know," said Mr. Arkady.

Lord Johnny slumped back on his ottoman.

"Your uncle terrifies us," said Lord Johnny. "Your grandmother terrifies us. Even Radu, your cousin—"

"Terrifies you?" Lou couldn't keep the tartness out of her voice. No fire had been lit in the parlor fireplace, and she wanted to put her clothes back on before she caught a chill. "Please tell us why, and stop dawdling."

Lord Johnny gave her an astonished look, but Mr. Arkady smiled at her.

"I fear I must be blunt," Lord Johnny warned.

"Please," she replied.

"Many of your uncles, aunts, and cousins are shape-shifters," Lord Johnny said tentatively, as if his words themselves were explosive. Lou supposed that, had the night before never happened, they would have been. When he got no reaction from either Lou or Dacia, he continued in the same almost timid vein. "In fact, to the best of our knowledge, they all are. They can turn themselves into bats or wolves. Until a few decades ago, some of them could also turn into an amorphous form called the Smoke, but that form has been lost. It was always rare."

Lord Johnny made a dismissive gesture. Lou bristled at the

implication that the Smoke was of little consequence to him. It was of very great consequence to her. She didn't say anything, though, and the young men began looking from her to Dacia and back, waiting for a reaction that was not coming from either cousin.

"You knew," Lord Johnny stated, horror dawning on his face. "It is as I feared!"

"What do you fear?" Dacia said dully.

"You have been exposed to these terrible secrets," Lord Johnny said. Somehow he managed to not sound half so hysterical and, well, silly as William Carver had on the terrace at Castle Bran. But only by half.

Lou arched her eyebrows. "Why do you think we came back to Bucharest alone?"

She realized that she was daring them to accuse her of being a monstrosity. Perhaps it was unladylike of her to have taken all this in stride. She supposed that she should be having hysterics herself, or be in bed with smelling salts and cold compresses. But what good would that do? And with Dacia's reaction to all this, Lou needed to be the strong one now.

"What do you fear?" Dacia's voice was barely a whisper.

"You have seen them . . . take on their animal forms?" Mr. Arkady said before Lord Johnny could answer. The Turkish man looked eager, like he wanted her to describe it. Well, she wasn't without some sense of decorum, and she was not going to indulge his curiosity.

"Yes, we have," she said. "But how is it any business of yours?"

"In their animal forms the bats spy on the enemies of the

Draculas, and the wolves . . . hunt them," Mr. Arkady said. Lord Johnny made a noise but didn't interrupt.

"I beg your pardon?" Lou felt a sudden trickle of sweat start down her back beneath the shawl. Hunt?

"They hunt down their enemies, the enemies of the Draculas, and they . . . dispose of them," Mr. Arkady clarified. "Prince Mihai's father was the first Dracula in generations to acknowledge his ancestry and there were many who set themselves against him. King Carol had just taken the throne, and his supporters tried to strip Mihai's father of his title to avoid conflict. Many of them were found dead, savaged by animals, the others disappeared. If Mihai's father had not died soon after, he could have deposed Carol.

"And it was the Florescus who did the dirty work. Without them, Mihai can only sneer and make empty threats."

Dacia made a small noise, and Lou tried to put her arm around her cousin, but it dislodged the shawl, showing all of her arm and most of one shoulder. She froze, although it hardly mattered at this point.

"You're accusing our family of murder?" Lou could hardly speak the words.

There was a long silence. Then Mr. Arkady nodded at her.

"I am sorry, ladies. But I'm afraid there is proof," Lord Johnny said gently. "That is how Theo and I got this assignment: the last person charged with observing the Florescus died a few months ago. In his final message, he said that he had been discovered. He named your uncle Horia specifically as having threatened him. His body was found in the woods near Rasnov a week later."

"Is that why you approached me, in London?" Dacia's voice cut across the thick silence in the room. Her eyes were fixed accusingly on Lord Johnny. "Not because you'd always wanted to meet an American heiress? Not because I seemed bold enough to undertake 'a little adventure,' as you called it. But because you had been told to watch my family?"

Lord Johnny ducked his head, unable to meet Dacia's eyes.

"So that's the real reason why you asked me to accompany you to Gretna? Not because you were supposed to watch that man, but because you were watching me?"

"Oh, no!" Lord Johnny looked up, eager to redeem himself. "That was true! I do work for the Home Office, and they did need me to follow that man. He's been selling secrets to a faction of Scottish separatists! He's the one who told the press I had gambling debts, to try to ruin my credibility. I asked you to help because I thought that you seemed game for it." He winced at the way the words sounded. "At the time I wasn't assigned to . . . I mean, I knew of your family, but wasn't supposed to . . . I just thought you would think it was fun . . ."

"Oh," Dacia said, mustering a small amount of her usual dignity. "That's all right then. *If* it's true."

"It is true," Arkady said. "He was taken to task by our superiors for it. We are not supposed to get quite that close to any of our subjects. Even if we are not specifically assigned to watch that particular, ah, *person*."

Dacia leaped to her feet, nearly dumping Lou off the sofa. Lou's shawl slipped off and she scrambled to recover it. To her relief no one was watching her: all eyes were on Dacia, whose face blazed with anger and pain.

"Very well," she snapped. "Now you've answered our questions, and we thank you. Please leave. We have done nothing wrong, and I will not be the subject of another crass investigation. If you want to help us, keep Mihai away. If you don't want to help, just go. Lou and I are leaving for Buda-Pesth as soon as may be, and this will be nothing but a horrible memory."

"Dacia, please," Lord Johnny begged. "I never meant to hurt you! Of course *you* aren't under investigation! As soon as I met you I assured my superiors that you were innocent. I don't know what horrible things you've witnessed, but I know that you have no part in any of the horrors that your relations perpetuate! You are young ladies of breeding, not monsters!"

"Good day, Lord John," Dacia said. She continued to stand, very straight, while the young lord and his companion, baffled by her harsh expression, made their good-byes.

Lou did her best to smile graciously from her precarious position on the sofa. She was sure that the shawl was not covering much of anything at this point, but the gentlemen were too polite to ogle. Mr. Arkady averted his eyes as he retrieved his coat, and by the time they left, Lou was blushing in places she hadn't known a person could blush.

"What do you make of it all?" She waited until they were quite alone to say anything.

Dacia was still staring at the wall across the parlor. At Lou's question, she slowly collapsed to the floor.

"We're monsters, LouLou," she said. And then she didn't speak again.

Lou rang for the maid.

"Have a footman carry Miss Dacia to her room," she ordered when Nadia entered. "She's had a shock. And help me into my clothes. Yes, right here! I need to make arrangements to leave Bucharest as soon as possible, so don't bother unpacking our trunks. And no, I don't have any message to send to Lady Ioana." Lou stopped, and took a ragged breath as the girl turned to find a footman. "Wait! I do! Get me a footman, help me dress, and then send a telegram to the estate in Sinaia."

"What would you like it to say, miss?"

Lou felt a smile spreading across her face. The maid's normally smug expression faded as she saw that smile. "The Queen of the Claw and the Last Smoke bid you farewell. Stop. They shan't return. Stop."

## THE DIARY OF MISS DACIA VREEHOLT

15 June 1897

My name is Dacia Katarina Vreeholt. And I am not a monster.

My name is Dacia Katarina Vreeholt. And I am not a monster.

My name is Dacia Katarina Vreeholt. And I am not a monster.

My name is Dacia Katarina Vreeholt. And I am not a monster.

My name is Dacia. My name is Dacia. My name is Dacia.

I am not a monster.

# STRADA SMARDAN

The maid helped her into bed, and Dacia decided to stay there. She was comfortable, she was warm, and she was safe. There was no need for her to ever leave her bed again. This would be for the best. If she never left her bed, then there would be no one to call her a monster, no one to point fingers at her. She cuddled the blankets around her neck, savoring the smell of lavender and the smoothness of the linen. Yes. She would stay here.

Somewhere, outside her room, Lou was making plans for them. She loved Lou, both the old Lou and the new one, and she trusted that Lou would do the right thing. If Lou told her it was time to get out of bed, she would, but until that moment, she would just lie here and pretend that the last month of her life had never happened. No Mihai. No Lady Ioana. No Lord Johnny.

If they made it back to New York, Dacia would ask the new Lou to get them that apartment on Fifth Avenue. The new Lou would do it, she felt sure. They could live there very quietly, and never have to see their mothers again.

After a while Dacia dozed.

When she woke up she was disoriented. Her mouth felt awful and sticky, and she was very hungry. She wiped at her gritty eyes and sat up, trying to look around, but the curtains blocked any light.

Dacia had always hated napping. She always woke up feeling more tired, and grubby besides. Today was no exception, and she had the added problems of not wanting to leave her bed and not knowing where anyone was. The house felt far too still.

Surely Lou had not gone out without her? But perhaps she had, to purchase train tickets, or to visit the Szekelys. Dacia would miss them, but she would rather appear rude by not telling them good-bye than risk them learning about her true nature. Her stomach growled, though, at the thought of the tea cakes the Szekelys were probably offering Lou, and she decided that staying in bed didn't mean starving. She stretched one hand out of the blankets to ring the bell.

Two minutes later, she heard the door open.

"I'd like a glass of cool water, please, Nadia," she said. "And something sweet. Is there any cake?"

Nadia didn't answer, but Dacia heard the girl approach the bed. She smelled something beyond the odor of the lavender and starch on the sheets. To her acute nose it didn't smell like Nadia, it smelled like sweat . . . male sweat. She struggled to sit up, tangled in the sheets.

"Hello, Dacia," said Radu.

"Oh, Radu! Must you keep startling me this way?" She threw a pillow at him. He dodged it.

"I'm sorry," he said.

"You should be," she grumped, lying down again.

"No," Radu said. "I'm sorry for *this*."

And he scooped her up, blankets and all, and carried her from the room.

She writhed and kicked, calling out to Nadia as they passed the maid in the corridor. But the girl just scurried away and the footman stared blankly at the opposite wall. Radu carried Dacia right out of the house and into the late afternoon sunlight, where a carriage waited. He threw her inside and followed, slamming the door shut behind them. As soon as the door was closed, the carriage lurched into motion, driving at breakneck speed through the streets of Bucharest.

"What are you doing? Take me back right now!"

She punched Radu in the chest, bruising her knuckles and making his breath come out in an *oof*. He just huddled against the back of the seat, though, and didn't look at her. There wasn't much to look at, since it was a closed carriage and all the shades were tied down. She snatched at the door handle, and Radu reached out and grabbed her arm.

"Don't," he said. "You'll fall and get hurt. And you're not dressed."

She realized that part of the reason why he wasn't looking at her was embarrassment. She was in her drawers and a simple shift, but that was all.

"I'm wearing more than Lou was when Lord Johnny and

Mr. Arkady came," she snapped. "You remember them, they're the gentlemen who came to find out how many people your father has killed . . . ?"

"What? Who came?" Radu's face went paper white, in sharp contrast to his hair.

"Lord Johnny. And Theophilus Arkady. The gentlemen we met at Bran, and then at Peles. They work for an organization that has been watching our family. They know what we are, and they are trying to find out if Uncle Horia murdered one of their number." She paused to let that sink in, then added, "Well, they know he did, and now they're trying to stop him, and Lady Ioana, and the rest of our family from killing anyone else in the service of the Draculas!"

She hadn't thought it possible, but Radu went even paler, looking directly at her for the first time.

"Damn Archangels," Radu said. "What did you tell them?"

"Nothing," Dacia said. "Nothing they didn't already know. They've been watching the family for years . . . and you knew about them, didn't you? You call them . . . Archangels?"

"Of course we know the Society of Saint Gabriel," he sneered. Then his face changed. "Did they hurt you?"

She was startled by the very idea. Despite his secret agenda, Lord Johnny was still a gentleman! "No, they didn't hurt me," she snapped. "Unlike you, who tried to kill me last night! And now you've kidnapped me! What is going on, Radu?"

"I'm under orders," he said, and now he looked away again.

"Whose orders? Lady Ioana's?" She froze. "Where's Lou?"

"This doesn't concern Lou," he said softly. "She'll be all right."

"Who gave you orders, Radu? Was it Mihai?" Her voice cracked on the name. "Radu, where are you taking me?"

"I can't tell you."

"You'd better tell me, or I'll turn into a wolf and bite you right now," she said from between gritted teeth.

Radu looked straight into her eyes.

"Are you commanding me as the queen of my pack?"

Now it was Dacia's turn to pale. She hadn't really thought about what she was saying, but she'd regretted the threat as soon as she'd spoken it. She looked at Radu, at his hazel-gold eyes. He was watching her intently, leaning forward a little in his seat.

Here was power, she realized. She'd once enjoyed ordering around the young men of her acquaintance, having them bring her little gifts, flirt with her, dance with her. She'd ordered Radu around in quite the same way: he was her devoted slave, she the princess. And now it was true. She had beaten Aunt Kate.

Dacia was a queen.

"As the queen of your pack, I order you to explain this to me!"

He bowed his head. "My queen, I had no choice. I came to Bucharest to make certain that you and Lou were all right. My father, who is now at odds with Lady Ioana, sent me to escort you to Buda-Pesth and Uncle Cyrus.

"As soon as I arrived in the city I was stopped by one of Mihai's servants and ordered to his house. He told me to abduct you and bring you to a hotel. You'll be kept there until you agree to marry him."

"And you're going to do this?" She punched him again.

"I don't have a choice," he said miserably. "They're going to . . . Mihai's already sent word to Lady Ioana . . . they're going to kill my father."

"She wouldn't!"

"Of course she would," Radu said impatiently. "Don't you understand? We exist to bring glory to the Draculas! If we fail, we have no reason to live."

"Ridiculous," Dacia told him. "We exist because we are from an old and noble family, one with great power. There is no decree from God that says we have to obey Mihai! He wouldn't even be alive if it weren't for us; he should be groveling at our feet, not the other way around." She drew in a deep breath. "The Dracula family can go hang for all I care!"

Radu smiled at her sadly.

"Don't look at me like that," she snapped, wanting to slap the smile from his face. "Stop this carriage at once. I'm commanding you, Radu, to take me back. Tell the coachman to turn around at once!"

"I can't," he said.

"Yes, you can."

"No, I really can't," he told her. "The coachman isn't— The coachman is Mihai's uncle."

"Aunt Kate's lover, Mattias?"

"That's right." Radu made a ghastly attempt at a smile. "He usually doesn't get involved, not since Lady Ioana sent Aunt Kate away. But now he's perfectly ready to help."

"Why . . . oh!" Dacia understood at once. "If Mihai can marry me . . ."

"Then there's no reason to keep Kate and Mattias apart anymore."

"Why did they have to be apart?" Dacia asked, wondering if she could distract him long enough to leap out at the next crossing. "I should think Lady Ioana would have been pleased."

"The prophecy says two Florescu daughters would lead our family to glory," Radu said.

"Out of the darkness and into the light," Dacia corrected him. He nodded, like it was the same thing, but to Dacia's mind it wasn't the same at all.

"Their fathers were supposed to be from the New World," he continued. "Lady Ioana sent her daughters to New York and ordered them not to come home until they'd . . . produced . . . two girls who seemed like likely candidates."

"That's awful," Dacia said. The carriage had slowed but she didn't even try to escape; she was too appalled by what he'd said. "Good heavens! It's like she was breeding dogs!" Her cheeks burned with the absolute vulgarity of it all.

"You've met Lady Ioana," Radu said, uneasy. He looked out the window, and didn't relax until they had speeded up again. "Aunt Kate fought, in her own way, by refusing to marry at all, and Mattias has waited for her to return."

"I'm very happy for them," Dacia said.

She was trying to be facetious, but she realized that it was true. At least some good was coming of this all. She just hoped that Aunt Kate and her true love got to remain together, after she and Lou were gone. Because there was absolutely no way she would marry Mihai.

Dacia would die first; on that matter she was perfectly resolved.

The coach halted at last, and it dipped and creaked as the coachman got down. He opened the door a crack and peered inside. Dacia drew her blankets around herself with as much dignity as she could, remembering Lou's example from earlier that day. It was late afternoon, and golden sunlight highlighted a handsome man with dark hair barely threaded with gray, a neat mustache, and a carefully blank expression.

"Let me out at once," Dacia said.

"Very well, *doamna*," the man said without a trace of irony. He helped her down with a courtly gesture, and then ushered her toward a tall building.

Dacia stiffened and put one hand to the neck of her shift. It was now or never.

"I think not, *doamna*," Mattias Dracula said.

He raised his hand, and she saw the loaded pistol concealed in the folds of his overcoat. Dacia started to think herself into the body of the wolf anyway, but he jerked his chin and she realized: he wasn't pointing the pistol at her. He was pointing it at Radu, who stood slump-shouldered beside her.

Dacia looked around for help. There were dozens of people on the street—they were in the middle of the shopping district. She felt her cheeks start to burn with helplessness as much as embarrassment, and looked up as Mattias ushered them inside the oddly narrow building. The man at the desk smiled blandly as though he saw young ladies wearing only blankets enter his lobby every day, and Dacia wondered how much money Mihai had given him. Dacia used one of Aunt Kate's Looks, and the man wilted as he showed them the elevator. It was so tiny that only Radu and Dacia could fit inside, but the stairs wrapped around it, and they watched Prince Mattias make his way up, trying to keep pace without appearing to hurry.

"Radu, you have to help me escape," she whispered. "I order you to do so as your queen . . . and I beg you to, as your cousin."

"I will," Radu said. He was staring upward as the elevator rose, his face sickly in the barred light. "I don't care anymore if they—if they kill me."

"Go to Lord Johnny," Dacia instructed. "He's staying at the Hotel Bucharest. Tell him everything. About this, the plot against the king, whatever you know. We can't let Mihai win."

"I know," Radu said.

With a loud clank, they reached the seventh floor. Radu opened the doors, but Prince Mattias hadn't gotten to their floor yet. Radu closed them again, and tried to press the button for the first floor.

"I don't think so," Prince Mattias said. He reached the top just in time to grab the door and wrench it open. "One more flight, Your Majesty."

He gestured with the pistol and they marched up one last narrow stair. At the top was a plain wooden door. Prince Mattias produced the key and opened the door with a flourish. The hall was so narrow that Dacia had to pass uncomfortably close to him to enter the room.

"Not you," Mattias said when Radu tried to follow.

Before she could protest, Prince Mattias slammed the door and locked it from the outside.

Dacia looked around the small room with its slanted

ceiling. It was what she imagined an artist's loft would be like, with a simple bed shoved under one slope, a table and chair under another. There was a tiny but quite modern bathroom, and a broad balcony. She dropped her blankets and ran out onto the balcony. She could see the rooftops of Bucharest all around her; this weirdly narrow building was one of the tallest in the district. She looked down, thinking to call out to the passersby, but she was so high that she felt dizzy and had to step away from the balcony wall. She looked to either side of the balcony, wondering if she could climb down, but the roof slanted too sharply. She wouldn't be able to escape as a wolf or as a young lady.

Gathering up her blankets, she went back into the little room and lay down on the bed. Really, what else did she have to do? She was a prisoner now.

15 June 1897

Dear Papa,

I am writing again because Lord Johnny Harcastle and his associate Mr. Theo Arkady have just told us everything they know about the Dracula family and our own Florescu relations. This is a great deal to think about, as you can imagine. Did you know Mihai's history, and what his family has been planning? Is that why you objected to him courting Dacia? If so, why did you not speak up?

Dacia's shock has become a terrible depression over the entire matter, and I grow more concerned for her by the minute. Prince Mihai wants to marry her and use her to gain even more power. I must get her out of Romania at once.

I will purchase train tickets for us after I post this letter.

Love always,
LouLou

# HOTEL BUCHAREST

It was, thank heavens, very simple to buy tickets to Buda-Pesth. In fact, Lou wondered if she should use the helpful travel agent to book tickets through to Paris, and then New York, for all five of them. But in the end, she only bought tickets for herself and Dacia to get to Hungary. She would rely on her father to do the rest, and for the first time in her life she worried that he might let her down.

She was having rather mixed feelings about her father, now that she had more time to think. He had left her with Lady Ioana despite knowing that something terrible was to happen. And how many of the particulars did he know? Did he expect her to turn into a bat, as all the others had? Did that disgust him? But that meant he had to know what her mother was, and her father had always loved her mother deeply.

Had his life been threatened? And the twins? Since they had not inherited the Florescu power, as Aunt Kate claimed, Lou knew that Lady Ioana would hardly scruple to get rid of them. She would as soon kill Radu as look at him, and he was of the Claw, after all.

And she'd killed the others. Those who were the Smoke. Infants.

She put it out of her mind so that she wouldn't start to cry right there on the street.

No wonder it had been so momentous when Lou's mother and Aunt Ileana had married outside the family, even if they had done it at the urging of Lady Ioana. How to explain your family to your spouse? She wondered, then, if her mother really had. Her parents had seemed very much in love until they had arrived in Romania . . . had her mother kept the secret all these years, only to spring it on her husband now that she was not entirely human?

Lou determined to give her father the benefit of the doubt until she heard his side of the story. It could not have been a comfortable thing, to find out that your wife and daughter were monsters. Every so often Lou saw the image of her mother transforming in her mind, and her breath would catch and her steps would falter. She wondered if it would have been easier if her mother had been the Claw. Lou was terrified of bats, and to see her mother's body shrink and twist, sprouting wings . . . She shuddered.

All the same, Lou didn't shy away from the word *monster* the way Dacia did. It was the simplest way to describe what they were. They could change their shape and become something *other*. Was that not an excellent definition of a monster? It wasn't something that she'd always dreamed of being called, of course, but really, what was the point in fighting it now? Why not embrace it? It made her feel powerful, and beautiful, and special.

If only she could convince Dacia to feel the same way...

The carriage pulled up to the house on Rua Silvestre and Lou got out, busily thinking of ways to cheer up Dacia. Seeing Lord Johnny again wouldn't do the trick, it would only make her worse. But Will Carver was another story. Yes, Lou decided. She would invite Will Carver to dinner. He would see that they were well, they would tell him that Mihai was not a vampire and that they had cut off contact with the Draculas, and he would return to his usual sketching and flirting with Dacia. Flirting with him was sure to be a good tonic for her cousin. And they really ought to call on the Szekelys tomorrow, before they left. That might be even better.

She was halfway across the parquet floor of the front hall when she knew something was wrong. Lou froze, head cocked to one side, and listened.

Dacia had been asleep when she left, but the house was still too quiet. There were no footmen, other than the one who had escorted her to the travel agent's office. There were no maids bustling about, drawing the curtains against the setting sun, or offering to take her gloves and hat.

"Nadia!" Lou did her own best impression of Aunt Kate. It was not as good as Dacia's, but it worked well enough. "Nadia, where are you?" She called up the stairs, but with control so that her voice didn't shriek.

There was a rustle, and then the girl came from the direction of the kitchen.

"Yes, miss?"

Lou looked her over. Nadia had her hands clasped demurely in front of her starched white apron, and a smug smile on her face. She was hiding something.

"Out with it," Lou said, once again evoking Aunt Kate at her frostiest.

Tossing her hair, Nadia stuck her lower lip out. "I don't know why you're taking that tone with me, miss. *I* haven't done anything."

The older sister of two terrible little brothers, Lou knew better than to get into this game. "Well, if you haven't done anything, who has?"

Shrugging, Nadia said, "It's nothing to worry about. Mr. Radu arrived."

"Anyone else?"

"No."

"And where is Mr. Radu now?"

"I don't know," Nadia said.

"Fine. Where is Dacia?"

"With Mr. Radu."

"She wasn't dressed, and I haven't been gone that long!"

Nadia just shrugged again.

Lou left the infuriating girl behind and ran up the stairs, but she stopped halfway up when she heard Nadia's answer.

"I told you I don't know where they went, but Prince Mattias was driving."

Lou froze.

"Prince Mattias . . . ?" Nadia taunted. "Prince Mattias *Dracula*? Prince Mihai's uncle."

Lou flew back down the stairs and snatched her hat and gloves back from the maid. Calling out for the footmen, she ordered the carriage brought back around. While she was pulling her gloves back on, she turned on Nadia.

"You don't have any idea where they went?"

"No, miss."

"You helped Dacia to dress, and didn't say or hear anything?" Lou had never wanted to shake someone so badly in her life.

"She didn't get dressed, miss." This was the real thrill, at least to Nadia. Her glee over the scandal was plain on her face. "Went out in her underthings."

"If anything has happened to Dacia, I'm going to leave you tied up in the forest for the wolves to find," Lou said to her, and watched the other girl's face pale. "Are you certain that you don't know anything more useful?"

"No, miss," came the chastened reply. "They only left half an hour ago, though."

"They could be anywhere," Lou moaned.

When the carriage pulled into the front of the house, she hurried toward it and pulled herself inside without any assistance. Then she sat there, numb. Where could Dacia be? How would she find her? She didn't even know what the carriage they had taken looked like. Did it belong to the Dracula family, or the Florescus?

When the coachman asked for the third time where she

wanted to go, she gave him the hotel address that Lord Johnny had given her. They would surely know how to find Mihai, she thought, blushing a little. She had done her best not to be embarrassed before, but for some reason, fully dressed in a crisp French walking gown, she could not stop thinking about how she had ordered Mr. Arkady to put his coat on her legs.

Concern for Dacia overruled Lou's feelings, and when she alighted at the hotel she was back on the warpath. She marched into the lobby, a footman trailing behind her, and told the clerk at the main desk that she needed to speak with Lord John Harcastle and Mr. Theodore Arkady right away.

"Theophilus," the man said, staring at her.

"I beg your pardon?"

"Mr. Arkady. Theophilus Arkady. Not Theodore." He quailed a little at her expression. "I will just send them both a message. Whom shall I say is here to see them?

"The Smoke," Lou said. "I will be in the restaurant."

She sailed into the very fine restaurant, was immediately seated by the maître d', and ordered tea and cakes for three. Inwardly, she felt a clock ticking away, reminding her of how much time was passing. But she could hardly march into Lord Johnny's hotel room, and this wasn't something she wished to discuss in the middle of a hotel lobby.

To her gratification, the tea, the cakes, and the two gentlemen arrived in only a pair of minutes. The gentlemen appeared surprised by her presence; she supposed that because of her message they hadn't known whom to expect, but they hid it well until the waiter had left the table. Lou shook her napkin out, placed it in her lap, poured them all tea, took a cake, and then looked seriously at Lord Johnny.

"Radu and Prince Mattias Dracula have abducted Dacia," she said in a low voice.

Lord Johnny, who had just raised his teacup to his lips, nearly spit tea across the table at her. At the last moment, he turned his head, and merely choked. Mr. Arkady slapped him on the back, his brows drawn together.

"You are certain of this?" he asked, while his companion recovered and wiped his mouth and streaming eyes with his own napkin.

"Where did they take her?" Lord Johnny asked before Lou could answer. "When did this happen?"

"I don't know where," Lou said, smiling brightly at a passing waiter as she stirred sugar into her tea.

Lou had no idea how far the influence of the Dracula family extended. Anyone here could be a cousin, a friend, or even a spy for Mihai. How well known were Lord Johnny and Mr. Arkady? Were the Draculas watching them?

"It was about an hour ago," she told them. "Radu went into the house on Rua Silvestre and took Dacia. She was upstairs sleeping. Prince Mattias was driving the carriage. I was out, and didn't know until half an hour after they had left."

"Why would Radu take her? Why is he helping them?" Lord Johnny demanded.

It galled Lou to say it, because she loved Radu . . . or the person she had known as Radu, the cousin who had written them playful letters. But that cousin was gone, she told herself.

"Radu is a loyal member of the Florescu family," Lou said, and couldn't keep the bitterness out of her voice. "As you told us yourself: the Florescus exist to aid the Dracula family. If Prince Mihai ordered Radu to bring him Dacia, Radu would do it. And he did. Now we have to find out where they've gone."

"Your message said . . . Are you really the Smoke?" Mr. Arkady was looking at her with great admiration.

Lord Johnny was not, however. "She was only trying to get our attention, Theo," he said. "Miss Neulander cannot possibly be—"

"Yes, I am." Lou interrupted him. "That is why I was . . . undressed when you called on us earlier. I had just transformed in order to scare away Prince Mihai."

"You are the first Smoke in generations, then," Mr. Arkady said eagerly. "I should very much like to see it. It is a rare gift and—"

"*It is not a gift!*" Lord Johnny's voice rose. Lou shushed him, and he looked around, abashed. "I'm sorry. But this is a terrible thing! You have my deepest sympathies! It is no wonder that poor Miss Vreeholt was so traumatized this morning seeing you . . ." His voice trailed away as the reality struck him. "Dacia didn't . . . did Dacia . . . is she . . . ?"

"The Claw," said Lou tartly. "And the queen of the pack, moreover. She challenged our aunt Kate, and won."

"How amazing!" Mr. Arkady looked as though he might applaud. Then his brow clouded. "Of course, that gives Mihai all the more incentive to marry her. Any of your relations whose loyalty is more for the Florescu family than the Dracula will still follow Dacia."

"How will we find her?" The feeling of a clock ticking in her head became even stronger. She had to get Dacia out of there—wherever *there* was—before Prince Mihai forced her into marriage or worse.

"We'll send a message to the Dracula town house," Lord Johnny said. Whatever disgust he might be feeling at finding out about Dacia and Lou was quickly swept aside, to Lou's relief. "Find out if Mihai is at home to callers."

"Would they leave Bucharest, do you think?" Mr. Arkady was crumbling a cake between his long fingers. "Take her to his family estate? The castle here is in pieces, but Targoviste, perhaps."

"There's a castle in Bucharest?" Lou was startled. She'd spent very little time here, but surely she would have noticed a castle rising up among the buildings!

"As I said, it's in pieces," Mr. Arkady repeated, not unkindly. "It was Tepes's residence, but all that's left is a few pillars and the cellars. Another day I would love to show it to you."

Lord Johnny frowned at him. "Yes. A day when Dacia hasn't been abducted!"

Lou and Mr. Arkady shared a chastened look.

"If they are going to Targoviste, they will still be on the road," Lord Johnny said. "Unless they went to Snagov . . . surely not." But his eyes flashed at the thought and he and Mr. Arkady looked even more tense.

"What's Snagov?" Lou had to ask twice before they remembered that she was there.

"A church, on an island," Mr. Arkady said tersely. "Built by the Dracula family. It's very isolated."

"A church?" Lou felt like a plucked harp string. If Mihai had had Dacia taken directly to a church . . . her head reeled.

Then something happened.

"So high up," she murmured. A sudden vision of a copper drainpipe came to her, and the feeling of a rain-laden breeze touching her bare shoulders. "I don't think that will hold my weight . . ."

She looked up and realized that both gentlemen were staring at her.

"Are you quite well?" Mr. Arkady half rose, concerned.

"I'm sorry," she said. "I don't know what came over me! I suddenly felt faint . . . well, I felt as though I were on the roof of a building, and I—" She stopped babbling.

Lord Johnny reached across the table and gripped her hand. "Did you suddenly feel faint, or did you suddenly feel . . . Dacia?"

"Pardon?"

"You're very close to your cousin. Did you feel like you were seeing something else? Like you were in another room, or another person? Have you ever felt like this before?"

"What do you mean? I—I haven't—" Lou stopped.

Hadn't she? Hadn't she always known when Dacia was happy or sad? And those flashes, like being dizzy, only what she was seeing was some other room. Or a roof, in this case.

"Miss Neulander," Lord Johnny said. "We cannot begin to understand what powers you might have in addition to your . . . transformative gift. You and your cousin are very close, as close as sisters, and both very powerful." He looked at her, urging her to understand.

"So you think that I just saw what Dacia was seeing?"

"It's very possible," Lord Johnny said.

"Well, she wasn't in a carriage," Lou said. "And she wasn't in a church."

"Come upstairs with us, Miss Neulander," Lord Johnny said, rising. "And we'll find out where she was . . . is."

## Rembrandt Hotel
### Smardan Street, Nr. 11, Bucuresti

To Whom It May Concern:

My name is Dacia Vreeholt, and I am being held against my will on the top floor of the Rembrandt Hotel. I have been imprisoned here by the will of Prince Mihai Dracula, with his uncle, Prince Mattias Dracula, and my own cousin Radu Florescu acting as his accomplices. I beg of you to help in my rescue by giving this note to the police. Lord Johnathan Harcastle, at the Hotel Bucharest, may also be of assistance, as will my cousin Maria Louisa Neulander of Nr. 32 Rua Silvestre.

I can offer a generous reward in return for my safety and freedom.

Signed,
Miss Dacia Vreeholt

# THE REMBRANDT HOTEL

Dacia found that it was not as easy to sleep her captivity away as she had thought. The strain of being abducted had made every nerve in her body stand on edge, and she could not lie still. She got up to prowl around the room, searching in the empty wardrobe and in the drawers of the small writing desk, which held nothing but stationery and an old fountain pen.

She closed the desk, annoyed. She was wearing her comforter like an ancient Roman toga, and she gathered it up and went to sit on the end of the bed in a huff, springing back to her feet as soon as she touched the mattress.

A pen and paper! She felt like a fool for not thinking of writing to the police. Or Lord Johnny. She dropped the comforter and went back to the desk, taking out paper and pen with shaking fingers. Then she stopped to think about what to write. She needed to sound urgent but not hysterical, and the promise of a reward would be helpful. Once she'd gotten it just right she folded the note and printed "Please help!" on the outside.

Dacia carried it out to the balcony and was about to throw it over the edge when she realized that it would probably waft on the breeze and end up in a rain gutter or something equally useless. She carried it back inside and looked around, but couldn't see anything that would weight it down. At least not anything light enough she dared to drop off a balcony. She supposed that she could tie it to a lamp, but that might hit someone on the head and make them less inclined to help her.

At last, for want of anything better, she stuck the pen inside the note and crimped the edges so that it wouldn't fall out. She wouldn't be able to write any more letters, but what was there to say? Either Radu would muster up his courage and help her, or someone would find the note and help her, or she would be stuck there until she starved to death, because she had come to the conclusion that death was preferable to marrying Mihai.

She tossed the paper over the edge of the balcony, throwing it toward the middle of the narrow street so that it would catch more attention. Then she waited and watched. It was getting toward evening, and there was very little traffic on the street. It was narrow enough that few carriages passed by, and there were no pedestrians. She had a sinking feeling that the only person passing would prove to be Mattias, or worse, Mihai.

Then a woman came along the street. She was expensively dressed, with a large hat that made her look like a walking flower basket from Dacia's point of view. She had a parasol, and an attendant footman laden with bundles. Dacia felt her breast swell with hope. Here was someone who wouldn't be afraid to speak to the police, to help a young lady in need! Dacia leaned forward over the edge, even though it made her dizzy to do it, willing the woman to see her letter lying there, just a few paces away.

The woman passed right by the letter without once looking down. Of course. A well-bred lady would hardly pick up some trash off the street, Dacia realized with despair. She gave it another try.

"Hello! Hello there!" Dacia cupped her hands to her mouth and shouted down at the woman. "Help! Please help!"

The woman did not even look up, though her footman looked around, as though confused as to who was yelling. He didn't raise his head, though, and Dacia gave up when her voice cracked. Even if they did look up, what would they see? A deranged, bare-armed girl waving at them?

She turned and looked at the roof again. There was a copper rain gutter running along the edge of it. She'd heard that burglars used rain pipes and gutters as ladders, but didn't think that it was a skill she could master quickly enough to avoid falling to her death. However, the Rembrandt Hotel was one of the narrowest buildings in Bucharest, and though the building next to it did not have a balcony on the same level, it did have an attic window with a small ledge. Dacia wondered if she could creep along the rain gutter to that window, and climb inside the building next door.

She took a few steps toward the side of the building, gathering up her own courage. It was no use waiting to see if someone would pick up the letter, or if Radu would actually try to save her. She needed to save herself.

Dropping her comforter, Dacia started for the wall, thinking to climb on the low wall surrounding the balcony, and then onto the roof. She reached for the top of the wall, palms wet with sweat. She began slowly raising her knee, trying to find a toehold.

"Dacia! What are you doing?"

Dacia froze, one foot still on the balcony, the other braced against the side of the hotel. Radu was standing in the doorway, a valise in one hand and a shocked expression on his face.

"Were you going to try and climb up the roof?" He dropped the valise with a thud. "You could fall to your death!" He hurried over and grabbed her around the waist, peeling her off the wall.

"I would rather die than marry Mihai," she snapped, but didn't fight him as he carried her into the room.

"I brought you some clothes," he told her.

"Oh, thank heavens. I didn't want to die in my underthings," she said, briefly postponing her climb down the hotel facade.

As she took the valise from Radu, she noticed that he was blushing and averting his eyes. She smacked him on the arm, hoping it left a mark.

"Are you truly embarrassed to see me like this? It's your fault I'm here!" She flared her nostrils. "And you've seen me turn into a monster anyway!"

She lugged the valise over to the bed and found that it was full of Romanian-style gowns. She was a bit disappointed: it would have given her a sense of superiority to face Mihai in her French wardrobe. On the other hand, without a maid it would be far simpler to dress herself in the loose Romanian style.

She wrinkled her nose at the unfamiliar smell rising from the clothing and studied the blue-and-yellow embroidery. Of course, Radu could hardly go back and make small talk with Lou while a maid packed her things. But whom did these clothes belong to, and how had Radu gotten them?

As though sensing her thoughts, Radu said stiffly, "They were my mother's. They are quite clean." He fingered a bit of the embroidery. "She didn't like wearing the Florescu red all the time."

"Oh. I'm sorry," Dacia said, chastened. "Thank you."

"It's all right," he said. "I wanted to tell you: you didn't turn into a monster, Dacia," Radu said earnestly. "You turned into a wolf. A very beautiful, powerful wolf."

"That's what you think," Dacia said briskly, taking out a gown, sash, and apron. "I see it somewhat differently. But then, I'm not under the thumb of Lady Ioana and the Draculas."

"Dacia, I—"

"If you want to help me, you'll get me out of here," Dacia said. She was pushing down thoughts of Radu's mother, her late aunt Mina, who had died when Radu was twelve. She had been a Florescu by blood and marriage, Uncle Horia's second or third cousin. Had she been the Claw? What had she been like? Would she have approved of her son abducting Dacia? "If you're not going to help," Dacia went on, "then you can go. It's bad enough that I have to live with this curse; I don't need to have my own family betray me as well."

"We're not monsters, Dacia. We have a great gift," Radu said with such dignity that she turned to look at him. "You can turn into a wolf anytime you choose! No! It is not just a gift: it is *power!*"

They were silent for a long time.

"Be that as it may," Dacia said at last, putting aside the little thrill that had run through her at the thought of having this power, as Radu termed it. "Is serving the Draculas how it was meant to be used? Is that all there is for us?"

"Lady Ioana says that we live to serve the Draculas," Radu said bitterly. "That is why God made us this way."

"I don't believe that for one minute," Dacia retorted.

Radu smiled faintly. "Neither does my father. Nor does Aunt Katarina."

"Then what do they think?" The gown trailed from Dacia's hands, all but forgotten.

"I don't know if anyone knows why we are what we are," Radu said, gazing out the window. "But I know what I feel. I feel like the Lady of Shalott."

"What?" Dacia dropped the gown in astonishment, and would have burst out laughing, if Radu's face had not been so serious.

"In Lord Tennyson's poem," Radu clarified, red staining his cheeks but his eyes still on some distant vision. "*'I am half sick of shadows,' cried the Lady of Shalott.* I am not half sick, I am full sick of being a shadow."

"From darkness into light," Dacia said.

Radu's gaze sharpened, and he turned to look at her. "My father says the prophecy has nothing to do with the Draculas. There is no mention of them in it."

"Actually," Dacia said. "I think it has *everything* to do with the Draculas."

She stooped and picked up the crumpled gown. "I'm going to get dressed now," she announced. "And then I'm getting out of here. Lou must be frantic! Are you going to help me or not?"

"Of course I'll help, but they'll kill us both if we're caught," Radu warned, one hand on the latch.

"My dear Radu," Dacia said. "You do remember that anytime you choose, *you* can change into a wolf as well?"

15 June 1897

Dear Aunt Kate,

   Your former lover, Prince Mattias, has abducted Dacia.
Prince Mihai ordered the abduction and plans on forcing her
to marry him, or so I assume from his previous behavior toward
her. Mr. Theophilus Arkady and Lord John Harcastle are
helping me rescue her.

   If you have any sort of fondness left at all for your nieces, or
if you have any respect for your queen, you will assist us.


                    Lou

# THE HOTEL REMBRANDT

Being in a gentleman's hotel room was of course a very damaging blow to a young lady's reputation, but Lou was not concerned. Dacia's kidnapping trumped matters of social status in Lou's mind, and both men had seen Lou mostly naked just that morning, anyway, she remembered as she entered the very masculine hotel suite.

Lord Johnny invited her to sit on the sofa and then went to pull the curtains.

"Well, Miss Neulander," Mr. Arkady said, sitting across from her. "If you are truly seeing flashes of what your cousin sees, this may help us more than you know.

"Though it is frowned upon by the Society, I have some little skill with magic." He spread his hands in a self-deprecating gesture. "I think I can help you to locate her."

"What are you going to do?" Lou drew back.

He gave her a reassuring smile, but that didn't help. The last time she had seen magic, her mother had turned into a bat.

Although she felt her own, personal transformation that night had been a thing of wonder, she didn't particularly want to see Mr. Arkady turn into a creature in the middle of Lord Johnny's suite.

"I want to help you see clearer," he said.

"Are you sure it will work?" Lord Johnny paced the room, checked and rechecked that the door was locked, and peered out the windows several times. He stared into the mirror over the sideboard and adjusted his tie, making it even more crooked.

Mr. Arkady just gave him a look, and he subsided. Lord Johnny muttered something and took a chair across from Lou, slouching like one of Lou's brothers being tiresome. Lou wondered if he was in love with Dacia. She was sure that Dacia was in love with him, though he wasn't her usual sort of beau, like the immaculate Will Carver.

Clearing his throat, Mr. Arkady brought her attention back to himself. She caught herself staring at his long lashes and dark, dark eyes and blushed, and he cleared his throat again.

"Yes, well, Miss Neulander," he said hurriedly. "I am going to burn some incense, and have you breathe in the smoke while I play the flute."

Lou felt her eyebrows climb to her hairline. This was unlike any magic she'd ever seen. But then, her entire knowledge of magic consisted of her family turning into wild creatures in a dark forest.

"It is perfectly safe," Mr. Arkady went on. "And it will help you to think better. Concentrate on your cousin. See if you can pick up any clues about where she might be."

"All right," Lou said.

She tried to sound nonchalant, as though this were something she did every day. When Mr. Arkady gave her a sympathetic smile and reached over to squeeze her hand, she knew she had failed in her nonchalance. They both blushed, and he busied himself lighting some sticks of incense that were planted in a brass bowl of white sand on the table near Lou's elbow.

Once the incense was smoking, Mr. Arkady reached into the inside pocket of his jacket and pulled out a small flute. About the length of his hand, it was wood, painted red, and carved with angular patterns. He placed it to his lips the way one would play a clarinet or an oboe, straight on, rather than sideways.

"It's the shepherd's flute of my people," Mr. Arkady explained. "A bit different from the Western flutes that you are used to."

"All right," Lou said again, because she didn't know what else to say.

He began to play, very softly. The flute had a beautiful sound, like wind chimes. He wasn't playing any tune that she could detect, only a series of long, soft notes that flowed into one another. After a minute, Lou found her eyes closing as the soft flute played on.

Lou thought about Dacia as she leaned against the high arm of the sofa, unable to open her eyes. She just breathed in the exotic scent of the incense and murmured her cousin's name. Where was Dacia now? Was she well?

And then Lou *saw*.

Dacia was standing in a narrow room with a sloping ceiling. She had just finished dressing in a traditional Romanian gown and was still tightening the sash. The room was small and the furniture plain but good quality. Lou had the distinct feeling that it was a hotel room.

Dacia stiffened and raised her head, sniffing at the air.

Lou opened her eyes. For a nauseating moment, she could see both Dacia's hotel room and Lord Johnny's. She coughed, choking a little from the incense, and the vision cleared.

"Did you see her?" Lord Johnny leaped from his chair to kneel in front of Lou.

"She's not far from here," Lou said, her voice faint. She coughed again. "It felt high, and narrow . . . a hotel room. A rather strange hotel room. The ceiling sloped, and the room wasn't very big, but the furniture was nice enough."

"Are you sure it was a hotel?" Lord Johnny asked, perplexed. "And nearby? There's nothing like that around here."

Lou coughed again. "I'm sure."

"It had a bed?" he pressed. "It wasn't an office? Or the back room of a shop?"

"It had a bed," Lou said. "There was copper, something copper out the window . . . A shutter? A . . . balcony!" She sat up straight. "I've seen it! I think I've seen it! Isn't there a hotel near here that is very, very narrow? With a peaked roof with copper facings on the balcony? We passed it when we were having lunch with the Szekelys!"

"That Dutch hotel, on Smardan Street," Mr. Arkady said with a small cry of recognition.

The sick feeling came back, and Lou's head pounded. No . . . someone was pounding on a door . . . not Lou's door, the one where Dacia was. The pounding . . . it wasn't pounding, it was knocking . . . but it scared her all the same.

"It can't be Radu," Lou said as Dacia's fear stabbed through her heart. "It can't be Radu, it must be *him.*"

Prince Mihai.

"I have to go to her," Lou said.

Then she was the Smoke.

Her clothes fell away and she swirled out the window that Lord Johnny had opened in his fidgeting earlier.

Lou slithered through the air. She was reminded of the way dragons were depicted in ancient Chinese art, as though they swam through the clouds. She hoped that no one looked up and saw her . . . and then wondered why it mattered. What would they see? Would they understand what they were looking at? Would they care?

It was a relief to ask questions whose answers didn't matter for once.

She followed her senses to Dacia. She would not be able to describe it to anyone, but it was as if she could smell and hear and feel her cousin with the same sense organ. As she got closer, she could almost taste Dacia as well.

The tall, narrow hotel that contained Dacia was not far from the hotel where Lord Johnny and Mr. Arkady were staying. Lou curled herself around the chimneys and then swooped down to the balcony, following the rain gutter that Dacia had tried to climb.

The door was closed, but that didn't stop Lou for very long. She merely poured herself through the keyhole and into the room, ignoring the cramped and oily feel of the lock in her frantic journey to Dacia. She took her human form between her cousin and Prince Mihai, who didn't notice her until she had finished her transformation.

"Lou!" Dacia threw her arms around Lou's neck from behind, and Lou turned around, hugging her cousin fiercely.

"Are you all right?" Lou glared over her shoulder at Mihai.

The prince smiled at Lou, holding out his hands to show that he was unarmed.

"I have not harmed a hair on her head," he said with a smooth laugh. "I only wanted to ask her a very great favor . . . but first, let us find you some proper garb, Miss Neulander!"

Lou looked at her bare arms and almost shrugged. It was becoming sadly normal for her to find herself undressed in company. Dacia let go of Lou to snatch up a Romanian gown from the bed. Lou stepped away, her back still pointedly turned on Mihai, who just laughed again. She was sure he was staring at her backside.

Dacia slipped the gown over Lou's head, and Lou wriggled her arms into the sleeves and got her head through the collar as quickly as she could. Dacia tied the drawstring at the neck with quick fingers, and just like that, Lou was decent. She decided that there was a definite difference between having Mr. Arkady peek at her legs and Prince Mihai leer at her.

"Now," Lou said brusquely, facing Mihai. "Just because you haven't assaulted my cousin does not mean that you haven't harmed her!" She planted her fists on her hips so that she wouldn't slap the prince. "You will release her at once!"

"My dear Louisa—I may call you Louisa, may I not? Or per-haps LouLou, though that is such a silly name!" Another unc-tuous smile that made Lou want to slap Mihai even more, and he just went on talking without pausing for an answer. "Your dear cousin is free to leave at any time! I am sorry if the manner of my bringing her here caused either of you distress!" He looked from one to the other as though the idea that being kidnapped might be traumatic had never before occurred to him.

"Is she?" Lou folded her arms, frankly disbelieving.

"But of course she is! I am not a monster!"

Dacia flinched at the word, and Lou's eyes narrowed. Mihai continued to smile as though he hadn't noticed, but Lou was certain he'd used that word on purpose.

"Excellent," Lou said. She took Dacia's arm, hoping that her cousin could not feel how tense she was. "Let's go."

"Ah-ah!" Mihai waggled a finger at them. "There is one small condition."

Dacia made a noise in her throat and Lou sighed. Of course there was a condition. How like Mihai to toy with them like this.

"You may leave," Mihai said, "as soon as Dacia agrees to become my wife. We will go straight to a church . . . and then you may go wherever you like!"

Lou snorted. "Do you honestly think that she would marry *you*? And do you really think that you can keep her here forever if she won't?"

"Forever? Oh, no," Prince Mihai said with a light laugh. "In fact, I don't have more than an hour to wait for her to make up her mind. *I have other things to do today. The priest is waiting at a church on Calea Victoriei.*

"So let me make this all much clearer: Dacia can decide to marry me now, of her own free will, or she can refuse. But please understand: if she refuses, I will simply force myself on her, and ruin her more effectively than simply being abducted in her underthings has already done. And if she still refuses I will tie her to this chair and force her to watch while I have my way with *you.*" He said all this in a reasonable tone, as though saying he was going to order a tea tray from the hotel restaurant.

"You're mad," Lou choked out, bile rising in her throat.

Mihai frowned at her. "You will keep a civil tongue around me, girl," he said. "I am your king!"

"You're mad," Lou said again, her voice shaking. Mihai's face filled her vision. She recognized him, suddenly, as the dark man from her nightmares. The man whose words turned to blood when he spoke.

"I will possess Dacia, then I will possess all of Europe," he announced.

Dacia made the little noise again, and crumpled to the floor.

"You—you—you *monster!*"

It was all Lou could think to say as she followed Dacia down. She was relieved to see that her cousin had not fainted, but merely folded in on herself, to crouch on the floor of the hotel room while Mihai loomed over them.

"Dacia?" Lou tried to pull her up, but Dacia was too limp. Her expression, oddly, was thoughtful.

"Overcome by your love for me, Dacia?" Mihai sneered.

"Get out!" Straightening, Lou pointed an imperious finger at the door.

"You really don't understand, do you?" Mihai said. "Dacia must choose. Now. She can be married before or after our . . . wedding night." He smiled, and Lou thought she might be sick. "The choice should be fairly simple, now that I have you in my power as well—"

"Hardly," Lou interrupted. "I should like very much to see you stop me from going anywhere I please . . . and bringing help to free Dacia!"

And then Lou knew that she would have to leave Dacia. Mr. Arkady and Lord Johnny had reached the hotel; she could sense them both. But they wouldn't know how to find Dacia's room, and Mihai had no doubt posted guards. She would have to leave Dacia behind so that she could guide them to this room before Mihai could—before he—

Lou put Mihai's threats from her mind and slipped into Smoke, leaving Dacia, Mihai, and her gown behind. She flowed across the floor and through another keyhole, this one leading into a narrow stairwell. She slithered down the stairs, then the elevator shaft, all the while feeling for Mr. Arkady and Lord Johnny.

They were in the lobby, and Lord Johnny had Prince Mattias by the collar.

"Where is she?" The young lord's face was only inches from the prince's. The older man had a sneer on his face that must have been a Dracula family trait.

Lou blew herself between them. Prince Mattias cursed and drew back, and Lord Johnny let out a startled oath of his own.

"Lou! Miss Neulander," Mr. Arkady corrected himself. "Lead the way!"

Twisting around in the air, Lou raced back to the stairs, the men just behind her. Prince Mattias followed, but Lord Johnny turned and punched the prince square in the jaw. Prince Mattias went down with a thud, and Mr. Arkady leaped over him and started up the stairs after Lord Johnny, who hadn't even waited to see his opponent fall.

By the time they reached the top, the men were panting and pulling themselves up by the railing. Far below, they could hear sounds of excitement as someone found Prince Mattias, but the elevator did not clank into life . . . in fact, they passed it on the fifth floor, waiting for some hotel guests who stared as they raced by.

At the top of the hotel, Lou flew through the keyhole once again, frightened by what she might find. It was not as bad as it could have been. Mihai had Dacia on her feet, holding her up by one shoulder in a grip that was painful to behold. With his other hand he was tearing at the sash around her waist. Dacia's face was blank, and she was staring at the wall behind Mihai as though unaware of what was happening.

Lou decided to try something new: she slipped into her discarded gown, and then returned to her human form. Her arms were at her sides, and the gown was twisted around her torso, but Mihai barely registered her entrance. She slipped her arms through the sleeves just as Mr. Arkady burst into the room, having smashed the door open with his shoulder.

Lord Johnny leaped into the room after him, a pistol in his hand.

"Dacia," the young lord cried out. "Are you all right?"

"She's fine," Prince Mihai said. He pushed her down on the bed. "And soon she will be more than fine: she will be my bride, and a princess!" He shrugged off his own coat in a swift motion, oblivious to Lou, who was trying to lunge around him and grab Dacia.

"You whoreson! Release her!"

Lord Johnny leveled his pistol at Prince Mihai, but the prince only smiled wider. Lou actually felt her hand raise of its own accord, ready to slap the smile right off Mihai's face. She froze, however, just as Lord Johnny and Mr. Arkady did, when Mihai coolly pulled Dacia upright and held her in front of himself.

"Go on and shoot, if you have the stomach for it," the prince said.

"Release her, you coward," Lord Johnny said, his voice just as cold, despite the sweat running down his temples.

"Oh, I don't think so," Prince Mihai said. "This is what I've wanted all my life, you know, all my family has wanted for generations, and I will rule. With my queen using her power to keep my enemies in their place, it will be much easier. This is my birthright, and no one will keep me from it!"

Lou let out a small cry as Dacia's head lolled and she sagged in Prince Mihai's grip. Lou thought her cousin had fainted, but then Mihai swore. Dacia had only been throwing him off balance so that she could move her head around . . . and bite him, hard, on the arm.

"She bit me!" He slapped her with his injured hand. "How dare you bite me, you vicious little dog—"

"Don't say another word," Lord Johnny said, cocking his pistol as Dacia, freed from the prince's grip, rushed to wrap herself around Lou like a frightened child.

"I have just one more word to say," the prince said, and Lord Johnny moved forward another step.

"Stop him!" Lord Johnny shouted.

Mr. Arkady lunged forward as Prince Mihai shouted a strange word and threw a handful of choking dust in his face. He leaped over Mr. Arkady, shoved Lord Johnny hard to the ground, and ran out the door.

When they had stopped coughing, and checked to make sure that the prince was indeed gone, Dacia wiped her face on her sleeve and looked at Lou. Her expression was like a person waking from a long sleep, then she drew a deep breath and pulled herself taller.

"Well!" Dacia put one arm around Lou's waist and rested her other hand on her hip. "Can you believe the nerve of him, calling me a monster and a *dog*?"

"Appalling," Lou agreed. She faced the two young men. "So, what next? I am determined to slap that smile off his face, and I suppose it's up to us to stop him from taking the throne while we're about it."

"Us?" Lord Johnny said, setting his jaw. "Now, ladies—"

"Think very carefully about what you say next," Dacia warned. "I'll bite you, too, if I have to."

Lou was so pleased to see Dacia returning to her normal spirits that she clutched at the nearest set of hands and laughed. Then the laughter turned to blushes and *hmm*-ing when the nearest set of hands proved to be Mr. Arkady's.

## THE DIARY OF MISS DACIA VREEHOLT

15 June 1897

Perhaps I am a monster. But does it really matter?
I still can choose whether or not I make the change, and I
still can choose what I do with my life. I hope that aiding
Lord Johnny and his cohorts will redeem my soul
somewhat.

If I even have a soul.

# THE HOTEL BUCHAREST

"Where do you think they'll strike?" Lord Johnny was leaning over a map that had been spread on the table in his hotel suite.

"If they want to attack the king and queen, they'll go to Sinaia, won't they?"

Lou had changed back into her Parisian gown when they had reached the gentlemen's hotel. Her hair had come loose, and she kept fidgeting with it. Finally Dacia took her cousin's dark curls and fastened them with a ribbon so that they hung down over one of Lou's shoulders. Her own straight hair she had braided, but decided against pinning across her head like a coronet. With the traditional garb she wore, it would make her look like some peasant milkmaid. She'd also taken the time in the hotel suite's bathroom to adjust her gown so that the neckline had a nice swoop, and the sash was smooth and tight. It almost made her look like she had a bust.

"But do they want to attack? How strong are their forces?"

Mr. Arkady took a pencil and drew a circle around Sinaia on the map.

"Mihai is done biding his time," Dacia told them. "He said that everything was in place, and the last step was to marry me." She couldn't repress a little shiver.

Lord Johnny reached over and squeezed her hand where it rested on the map. Dacia felt her heart and stomach trade places, and concentrated very furiously on the map until Mr. Arkady cleared his throat and Lord Johnny moved his hand.

"Why you?" Mr. Arkady asked. "Forgive me, and you are both lovely and strong young women, but why have you caused such a stir?"

"There's a prophecy," Dacia said. She did her best to make light of it. "A prophecy, mind you, as if we weren't on the eve of the twentieth century!" She forced a laugh, and Lou stared at her.

Dacia wanted to explain, but felt suddenly shy in front of Lord Johnny. Also, she hadn't quite worked out her own feelings on the topic yet. Yes, a prophecy was a silly thing to plan one's life around in this day and age, but what if it was true? Turning into a wolf had seemed impossible three days ago, too. And what if the prophecy could be turned to her advantage, used to manipulate her family into overthrowing Mihai?

"The prophecy Lady Ioana spoke of?" Lou frowned. "It was rather vague, wasn't it?"

"Radu told me more," Dacia said. "Apparently it's about two girls who will have fathers from the New World, and will return to Romania to lead our family from darkness into light. Which Lady Ioana thinks means to glory at Mihai's side." She snorted.

"So they sent..." Lou trailed off. The lines between her brows went deeper than ever.

Dacia put an arm around her. "They sent Aunt Kate, my mother, and your mother to New York specifically to find American husbands, so that we would be born," she said gently.

"How very...calculated of your grandmother," Lord Johnny said.

"She's not the most doting grandmother, it's true," Dacia said. "In fact, she—"

"She killed them," Lou blurted out. She gave a long shudder.

"What? Who?" Dacia asked, drawing away from Lou to look at her face.

Lord Johnny and Mr. Arkady stared as well. After a minute, when Lou just stared over their heads, clenching and unclenching her fists, Lord Johnny softly asked her who it was Lady Ioana had killed.

"The babies," Lou said, her face a mask of horror. "That's why we have no girl cousins our age. Why there hasn't been a Smoke in generations. Lady Ioana killed them. Her own daughters. Her own granddaughters. The Smoke leads the family, not the Wing." She let out a strange little laugh. "I guess there would have been a lot of us. And now there's only me."

"No," Dacia said, pulling Lou close again. "I don't believe it. Who told you this?"

"Aunt Kate," Lou said. "She lied for me. She told Lady Ioana I was the Wing, but she knew I was the Smoke."

"I still don't believe you," Dacia said, feeling like her head was packed in wool. It was just all so much! Too much! "I believe she said that to you," she said, not wanting to call Lou a liar, "but I can't imagine it to be true! Not even of Lady Ioana."

Mr. Arkady looked apologetic. "Sadly, Miss Neulander, that is in keeping with what we know of your grandmother. We also have records of eight Florescu girls being born to your aunts and uncles, but none survived their first year. We did not know why until now."

"No," Dacia said weakly. "No, no, no!" She sank down on the sofa with Lou. "How could someone be so . . . evil?"

"There is great evil in the world," Lord Johnny said. "That is why we are fighting against it." He sighed. "I'm sorry that you are caught up in this, Dacia. And you, Miss Neulander. But will you help us all the same? You are both in terrible danger, but you are also in a position to be of great help to us. Will you help?"

"Can we?" Dacia said, half to herself.

"Of course we will help," Lou said, blinking as though waking up. "Of course. I'm sorry that I laid the burden of this on you all so suddenly, but I couldn't keep it to myself any longer." She straightened. "I'm fine now, and we will help you, of course. Won't we, Dacia?"

"How can we?" Dacia asked. "We don't even know our own family!" All the plans she'd started to make were crumbling. How do you manipulate a murderer like Lady Ioana?

"But you do know Mihai's plans," Johnny pointed out. "And for all the atrocities she may have committed on her own, Lady Ioana still defers to Mihai in this case."

"Did he confide anything else to you, Miss Vreeholt?" Mr. Arkady asked.

Dacia thought for a moment about throwing hysterics, and then she checked herself. She needed to be strong, so that she could see Mihai brought low. And Lady Ioana, too. She wanted to help Lord Johnny, and his society or brotherhood or whatever it was.

She sat up straighter beside Lou and wrinkled her nose, thinking back. "He said that he had waited all his life for his time to begin, and that time was now. He would marry me to gain a powerful asset against his enemies as he rose to power at last."

"I don't know if slapping will be enough," Lou murmured, and Dacia smiled.

"No, it won't," Dacia said. "But we'll start with that."

"Anyway, then he said that he would sweep away his enemies the way his ancestor Vlad the Third had done, in his own Night Attack."

Lord Johnny blew out his breath in a whoosh. "He said that?" He reached out and took Dacia's hand again. But this time his grip was tight, as though he was urging her to change her words. "He said that exactly? His own Night Attack?"

Startled, Dacia pulled her hand free. "Yes," she said. "I'm certain of it. He said it as though I should know what it meant, but I haven't the faintest idea." She looked from Lord Johnny to Mr. Arkady to Lou, who shook her head in equal bafflement.

Lord Johnny pushed himself away from the table with an oath, and began pacing around the room. He ran his hands through his already unkempt hair and then scrubbed at his face.

"It means that he's attacking tomorrow night," Mr. Arkady said.

"Tomorrow night?" Lou's voice was barely a squeak. "Are you certain?"

"The Night Attack was one of Vlad Tepes's most famous battles," Mr. Arkady explained. "My people—the Turks—had attacked Romania and were holding Bucharest and Snagov. Vlad and his men, dressed as Turks, came to their camp in the night and slaughtered thousands of soldiers. Their aim was to kill Sultan Mehmed, but Vlad entered the guards' tent by accident. While he was fighting them, Mehmed escaped."

Mr. Arkady said this all very drily, with no hint of how he felt that thousands of his people had been slaughtered.

To Dacia's surprise, Lou reached out and gently touched Mr. Arkady's wrist. "How very awful," she said softly.

Now Dacia saw surprise and a hint of sadness on the young man's face. "It was a long time ago," he murmured.

"Or, tomorrow night," Lord Johnny said grimly.

"Why do you say that?" Dacia looked from one to the other. "This Night Attack would have been over four hundred years ago . . . why tomorrow night?"

"Because the Night Attack took place on June 17, 1462," Mr. Arkady said. "If Mihai is hoping to evoke that, to remind people of his illustrious ancestor, then I have no doubt that he will strike on the anniversary of that night."

For a long while, they all stood and stared at the map as though it would have the answers they were seeking. Except for Lord Johnny, who continued to pace.

"Very well," Dacia said when she realized that neither of the gentlemen was going to do anything sensible. "First things first: we need to send a telegram to the palace, to let Their Majesties know that Mihai is planning to attack."

"They have a telephone there," Lou pointed out. "We could telephone. It would seem more urgent and convincing."

"A good idea," Dacia agreed. "Should you make the call, Lord Johnny? I am perfectly willing to, but if they know about your Society, it would be better for you to do it."

"Yes, they know about the Society. I'll call," Lord Johnny said, looking annoyed. Dacia guessed that he was mostly irritated that he hadn't thought of that himself. Men could be that way sometimes. "I'll use the hotel telephone before we leave."

"Are we going straight to Sinaia?" Dacia thought she might like to stop and pack a bag on their way, and opened her mouth to say so, when Lord Johnny answered her question.

"*We* are. By which I mean Theo and myself," he said. "We will take you and Miss Neulander home on our way."

Once again, Dacia opened her mouth to speak, and once again, someone interrupted her. This time it was Lou, but it was still most vexing.

"First of all, you may call me Lou," Lou said. Then she looked at Mr. Arkady. "You may also call me Lou," she said in a softer voice, and Dacia started to make a remark, when Lou continued on. "And second, Dacia and I will be going with you."

"Now, Miss Neu—Lou," Mr. Arkady said in a reasonable voice. "And please, call me Theo, but you really must understand that this is going to be very dangerous, and—"

Dacia decided that it was her turn to interrupt. "Dangerous? Because *our family* will be there? Isn't that who Mihai will be using as his soldiers? Our cousins, our uncles, our grandmother, *Lou's mother?*"

"Hmm." Mr. Arkady—Theo, now—seemed rather at a loss. "That is true, but . . ."

"Didn't you just say you needed our help?" Lou put in.

"Er, yes," Lord Johnny said. "But Dacia, you and Miss . . . Lou have been raised as young ladies, while every other member of your family, including Miss Lou's mother, has been raised to be a fighter."

"I believe that I have clearly proven some usefulness in this endeavor," Lou said with a certain amount of asperity.

"Indeed you have," Theo said warmly. "But I agree with John now: Sinaia will be too dangerous for you. We will find something else for you to do. Here."

Dacia leaned across the map to stare into the Turkish man's eyes.

"I'd like to see you try to stop us from coming," she said in a low voice.

He looked startled, but not, Dacia was relieved to see, disgusted or afraid. Instead he seemed to rather appreciate her ferocity and resolve. He looked at Lord Johnny, who gave a faint sigh of resignation.

"I will telephone Their Majesties," Lord Johnny said. "And some of our colleagues. Then we'll drive to Sinaia."

"Very well," Dacia said, inclining her head in a gracious nod. "Shall we order tea in the meantime? I have no idea when we will have another chance to eat."

She was ravenous, suddenly. And why not? It had been more than a day since she had eaten more than a bite of toast, a mouthful of tea. She felt her stomach start to grumble, and repressed it with stern force of will.

"An excellent idea," Theo said, smiling at her. "It is the way of the soldier on campaign, to eat when you can eat, rest when you can rest. You will make a fine addition to our group."

Lord Johnny made a garbled noise as though he were repressing a protest with his own force of will, and then stomped to the door of the hotel suite. "I'll have something sent up," he muttered, and then stomped out.

The line was back between Lou's brows, but Theo just laughed.

"He will come around," he assured them. "He likes to get his way, but he won't stomp about for very long if he doesn't."

"Well, I should hope not," Dacia said. "Pouting is such unbecoming behavior in a man."

16 June 1897 <stop> Dear Papa <stop> Hope you
and the boys are well <stop> Had to cancel train
to Buda-Pesth <stop> Much happening <stop> New
arrangements soonest possible <stop> Love LouLou
<stop>

# CASTELUL PELES

I believe you," King Carol said, but he looked uncomfortable saying it. "I believe you, yet we've seen no sign of anything unusual." He leaned back in his chair, looking tired. "If Mihai is planning an attack, he'll need more than just a handful of Florescu men to support him. He'll need an army, which he hasn't got."

Lou's eyebrows shot up in surprise, and she almost smoothed them down with her hand. She had a raging headache, and it was painful just to blink her eyes.

She had never been prone to headaches before, and there was something ominous in getting one now. When she'd mentioned it to Dacia on their way into the palace, however, Dacia had assured her it was just the lingering effect of two days' excitement.

"Do you . . . spy on them?" Lou asked when she had her face under control.

"We have had Mihai watched," the king admitted. "In the past, the Dracula family has been more of a curiosity than anything else. They pay taxes and give money to the church . . . the very model of modern Romanian nobility!

"But then Mihai turned eighteen, and suddenly he was everywhere: a private box at the opera, hosting balls, attending the parties of every notable family in Bucharest. The Draculas are usually more reclusive.

"Mihai became well known not only for his social attendance, but for his opinions. Nothing treasonous," the king said as Dacia started to ask. "At least not on the surface. Just a sort of . . . knowing tone, as if he were supervising my rule. At one point he reportedly said that he was withholding judgment on a law, as if it were his duty to rate my legislation."

"Cheeky," Dacia commented, and everyone looked at her. She waved a slender hand in front of her face. "Come now, I can admire his sheer bravado! Even if I do want his head on a platter by tomorrow morning."

She set down her tea and took a small sandwich. Lou had convinced Dacia that she would feel gauche wearing a traditional gown to the palace, and was glad that Dacia had listened to her. Properly corseted and swathed in a finely striped blue poplin and delicate ivory lace, Dacia looked much more her old self, giving Lou one less thing to worry about, so at least she knew Dacia wasn't the cause of her headache.

"The first time I met Mihai," the king continued, "he brought up Vlad Tepes twice during our fifteen-minute interview." King Carol looked at them, to see if they understood, and they all nodded, except for Lou, who feared her head might fall right off if she moved it.

"Take this," said a voice in her ear, and Lou jumped and nearly tumbled off the stiff little sofa where she was sitting with Dacia.

"Goodness!" Dacia clutched at the lacy collar of her gown, dropping her sandwich.

"I am so sorry," Theo said, embarrassed.

"I suppose that's what I get for sitting with my back to the door," Dacia grumbled.

"Thank you for joining us, Mr. Arkady," the queen said. "What were you saying?"

Now Mr. Arkady looked very uncomfortable, and Lou had a moment of schadenfreude at seeing him blush. He held out something to her, a small paper packet of the sort that doctors used to dispense medicines.

"I heard that Miss Neulander had the headache, and brought her a cure," he muttered.

"That is very kind of you," Queen Elisabeth said warmly.

"Yes, very kind," Lou echoed, blushing.

She reached for the small paper packet, and her hand shook. She looked around, saw that everyone was watching, and her hand shook a little more. She told herself sternly that it was only because her head was pounding so.

"Pour it into your tea," Theo said. "And stir until it dissolves."

Lou obediently opened the screw of paper and dumped the white powder into her tea. She put aside the paper and stirred the liquid with a hand that still shook, making her spoon rattle against the sides of the queen's beautiful bone china. When she put the spoon down, the last of the powder having swirled away to nothingness, she looked up and saw that everyone was still watching her.

"I am sorry that you are not well," the king said.

"It's nothing, just a headache," she said, putting the cup to her lips.

The china was so fine that the edge of the cup nearly cut her lip. Her aunt Ileana had a set of bone china, imported from England, and she and Dacia had once been spanked red-bottomed for breaking a cup and two saucers. The shards had been so fine and sharp that they had sliced Lou's fingers, and Aunt Ileana had told her that it was only what she deserved.

Lou drank, grateful that the powder didn't seem to have a flavor. The pain in her head was making her stomach roil, and she didn't want to start gagging in front of Theo ... or Their Majesties. She drank the whole cup while everyone looked on in concern, and Theo breathed a sigh of relief when she was done.

"I can't recall you ever having a headache before, LouLou," Dacia said with a frown.

"I can't either," Lou said. "But we've endured so much these past weeks, it's hardly surprising." She gestured with her teacup, and nearly lost her grip on it. "Whoops!"

"Allow me," Theo said. He was still hovering at her shoulder, and now he gently took the cup and saucer from her. "Are you all right?"

"I'm fine ... aren't I?"

Lou suddenly wasn't sure how she was.

"Why is the room tilting?"

"You're leaning," Lord Johnny said.

"I'm sorry," Lou said, not sure what else to say. She felt decidedly strange, but it was nothing that she could describe, other than that she couldn't seem to straighten herself.

"I've got you," Dacia said, putting her arm around Lou's shoulders and pulling her upright. "What was in that envelope?" Her voice was enraged, and Lou cringed and almost protested that the powder hadn't been her idea, but then she realized that Dacia's anger was directed at Theo.

"I sent one of the Gypsies to get a headache remedy from the apothecary," Theo said, his face ashen. "I told him specifically which apothecary, and which medicine. I've used it myself, I swear!"

Lord Johnny knelt down in front of Lou, staring intently into her face. "Are you sure the man brought the exact medicine you asked for?"

"I paid him well enough," Theo protested. "And I checked the medicine; it looked the same as it always does."

"Was he a tall man, with a double row of silver buttons on his sleeves?" the queen asked.

"Yes," Theo said.

"Oh, no!" The queen put a hand to her bosom, and the king let out an oath. "We have suspected for some time that he is one of Mihai's spies!"

Theo said something in Turkish and sank to his knees at Lou's side. He took her hand, and she felt a bubble of panic in her breast. She couldn't feel her fingers. She tried to wiggle her toes, and couldn't feel her feet, either. When she tried to say something, her lips wouldn't move.

The queen had risen to her feet and was clutching at the king's arm. "We shall ring for a doctor," she said. "Our private physician is not in Mihai's employ, I can assure you."

"I don't think a physician is what she needs," Lord Johnny said.

"But if she's been poisoned, she must have a purge," the king said. He tugged the bellpull before anyone could protest.

"It's not poison, Your Majesty," Lord Johnny said, not taking his eyes off Lou. "At least, it's not any poison I've ever seen." He held up Lou's right hand. Her fingers were transparent.

If Lou could have moved her lips, she would have gasped. But she couldn't. She couldn't move anything, because she had nothing left to move.

She was becoming the Smoke, and there was no way for her to stop it.

"Lou," Dacia said in a quavering voice. "Oh, Lou!"

Theo leaned close to Lou's ear again, as he had when he offered her the screw of paper.

"Lou," he said in his smooth, deep voice. "Oh, my dear Lou! You must change. You must make the change yourself. Perhaps if you take control of this, you will be able to keep yourself in control . . . and change back . . ." But his voice did not sound as though he was certain at all.

Still, it was the best advice that anyone had to offer, and Lou was rapidly losing the feeling in the rest of her body. She could only vaguely sense Dacia's arm around her shoulders now, and she couldn't even feel the panic bursting in her chest with any immediacy.

With an effort, Lou shut out Dacia's increasingly hysterical demands that someone do something, and the voice of the maid who came in to ask why Their Majesties had rung, and the queen's request for a doctor. She shut it all out, except for the sound of Theo urging her to transform herself. She thought for a moment how strange it was to find his voice so comforting now, when only weeks before he had sent her fleeing in embarrassment.

"You called me a houri," she said, though her voice was only the faintest of breaths.

And then she was the Smoke, and Dacia was holding the bodice of her crumpled gown while Theo knelt on the floor, holding a fold of her empty skirts.

## THE DIARY OF MISS DACIA VREEHOLT

*17 June 1897*

Lou is quite correct: dressing well is very uplifting to the spirits. I shall have to tell her; she always assumes that she is wrong. She simply has no confidence, poor dear. You'd think she was Mother's daughter, instead of Aunt Maria's. Or perhaps I am so strong-willed, because of Mother? Something there, I think, but never mind that now.

We traveled through the night to Sinaia, and Lou and I are freshening up in a guest room before we meet with the king and queen. Lou insisted that I put on a Parisian gown, and I find that it is very hard to feel monstrous, or sorry for one's self, when wearing the finest Parisian mode. Also, my corset seems to help my morale, which I find surprising. I feel more protected, but also rather finished, as though now I am my best, truest self: upright and polished. It is a strange feeling.

Lou says that I must stop writing for now, Their Majesties await!

Note: I should replace the white ribbons trimming this gown with the blue ones I bought in Bucharest for Aunt Kate. She doesn't deserve them, anyway.

# PELES CASTELUL

Dacia sat and clutched at Lou's gown in horror. Her LouLou had become the Smoke, but this time not by choice. The way Lou's clothing draped across the sofa seemed so final, like burial clothes waiting for the body to be slipped into them for the last time. Dacia started to sob, but was cut off by a soft touch on her cheek.

Looking around, she saw Lou hovering beside her. Or what had become of Lou. It was only a column of smoke, with no features to speak of, but she knew that it was Lou.

"Are you all right, LouLou? Can you change back?" Dacia dropped the gown and held out her hands to her cousin, sniffling to keep her nose from dripping onto her bodice.

The Smoke swirled about, withdrawing from them all, and became denser. For a moment, Dacia thought she could see Lou's figure forming in the vapor but then it dissolved again, and Lou was nothing but a vague collection of Smoke again.

"We need to find out what that powder was," Lord Johnny said. He sounded so calm that Dacia hated him for a moment, despite the endearing way his hair fell over his eyes.

"Is there any left in the envelope?" King Carol held out an imperious hand for the little bit of paper, that small white square, folded into an envelope, which had caused so much trouble.

Theo handed it to him, his stunned expression quite raising him in Dacia's estimation. He had to reach across Dacia to give the king the envelope, and when he had passed it over, his hand rested briefly on Dacia's shoulder, giving her a small fluttering squeeze. She smiled at him in gratitude.

"When the doctor arrives, I will have him inspect this," King Carol said. "I'm sure he can identify the contents."

"I'm going back to the gates to question the Gypsy who fetched it for me," Theo said. "For the right price, he might be willing to betray Mihai. And it's very possible that it's a Gypsy concoction."

"What shall I do?" Dacia rose to her feet, looking from Lord Johnny to Theo.

The two gentlemen looked at each other, clearly nonplussed.

"You need to be on guard," Lord Johnny said finally.

"Mihai may attempt to drug you as well," Theo pointed out.

Dacia waved her hand, casting aside their concerns. "Meanwhile?"

"I will require your aid," the queen said quietly.

Everyone looked at her, startled, and she smiled back.

"My husband will need to see to the guards around the palace," she said. "And summon more soldiers, if we really are to be under attack tonight. I will meet with the physician, and so must you." She plucked the envelope from her husband's hand and set it on a saucer. She set Lou's cup, saucer, and spoon on the tea table beside the envelope. "Miss Vreeholt, you can describe your cousin's special ability better than anyone else. The physician will need to know."

Dacia knew that the queen was simply trying to pacify her before she made a scene. But it did calm Dacia to know that she was useful. She could help the physician find the antidote. She gave the queen a genuine smile.

"Excellent," Lord Johnny said with relief. "That will be a great help, Dacia." He saw the queen looking at him and amended, "Miss Vreeholt."

"Of course it will," Dacia said tartly, her smile fading. "Now, you'd better go and contact your colleagues, or instruct the soldiers, or whatever it is you were planning on doing. We only have half a day to prepare for the new Night Attack."

Lord Johnny took her hand, clicked his heels together, and kissed her fingers. "As you say, milady, so shall I proceed."

"Oh, just go," Dacia said, fighting down a slightly hysterical giggle at his courtly manner.

"So we shall," King Carol rumbled, and Dacia quickly rose and curtsied to His Majesty. Theo tensely bid the Smoke that floated before the hearth a good-bye, and promised that he would find a cure for her, before bowing to the queen and then pressing Dacia's hand in a comforting manner.

When the king and the two young men had gone at last, the queen sighed. "Sometimes men can be so taxing," she said.

Dacia agreed.

The physician came in a moment later, a satchel in one hand,

and his brow furrowed with concern. "What seems to be troubling Your Majesty?"

Then he noticed the strange column of smoke floating between the two sofas, and the fact that the queen appeared to be perfectly robust. He looked around the room, and licked his lips, his whole face asking the question.

"Dr. Ionescu, do you believe in the supernatural?" the queen asked as if she were making polite conversation.

"I beg your pardon, Your Majesty?"

Dacia noticed that the physician could not take his eyes off Lou, who was keeping very still.

"I asked if you believed in the supernatural," the queen repeated.

He dragged his eyes away from Lou, looked with brief curiosity at Dacia, and then focused on his queen. "I have seen some things in my day, yes, Your Majesty. But why—I mean to say—Oh, damn it all! What is that?" He pointed a blunt finger at Lou.

"*That* is Miss Louisa Neulander," the queen said. "Which is why I sent for you."

"Miss . . . Louisa . . . Neulander?" Although the physician looked to be at least fifty, his voice cracked like a young boy's.

"Her mother is Maria Louisa Florescu," the queen said, as though it were of great import.

Judging from the physician's reaction, it was. The man sagged onto one of the sofas without waiting for the queen's permission to sit. His face was gray, and his eyes, once more, were drawn to Lou.

"Then it is true," he whispered. "It is true!"

"What is true?"

Dacia could not keep the sharpness out of her voice. She sat very straight in her own seat, closest to Lou, her hands folded in her lap. She willed the physician to look at her, to see the elegance of her dress, her hair swept into a smooth, complicated knot, the way she gazed back at him so fearlessly. She willed him to see *her* and gape at her beauty, and not look as though her family were some oddity gossiped about behind closed doors.

Because she knew, she just knew that was what he was thinking. He had heard about the Florescu family, that there was something wrong with them, and now he had seen Lou as the Smoke. Dacia simply could not bear it if this eminent physician went away to carry tales of his own about her family.

Dr. Ionescu did look at her, long and hard. He took in the fine gown, and the way she was sitting; she could see him registering surprise and admiration . . . but then he paled once more.

"You are one of them?"

"I am Dacia Vreeholt. My mother is Ileana Florescu Vreeholt," she said loftily.

It didn't seem possible, but the physician's face went even whiter. He reached up and fingered his right ear, and Dacia saw that he had a scar across the earlobe, and one on his cheek just in front of it, half hidden by his graying side whiskers.

"Ileana," he whispered. "You're Ileana's daughter?"

Dacia nodded, too surprised to keep up her arrogant demeanor.

Nostrils flared in disgust, he leaned forward and raked her

with eyes that were decidedly less than admiring now. "And what are *you?*"

Dacia was about to tell him that she was the person who was going to scar his other ear if he didn't watch his tone, when the queen swooped in to rescue her.

"Dr. Ionescu! I am quite shocked! Miss Vreeholt is my guest, and she and her cousin are in dire need of aid!"

The doctor actually shook himself like a dog, bringing his eyes to the queen. The frown on her face made him turn dark red with embarrassment, and he stammered an apology to Her Majesty, and then to Dacia, who only nodded tautly in reply.

"Forgive me, Your Majesty," he said, and made a little bow. "It is only that . . . I once knew Ileana Florescu . . ."

"You knew my mother?" Dacia leaned forward a little, and the physician flinched back.

"Another time, Dr. Ionescu," the queen said. "But for right now, we have more pressing problems!

"As you can see, Miss Neulander has been transformed into a column of vapor, which among their family is known as the Smoke, I believe?" The queen looked to Dacia, who nodded. "This is a talent that the young lady normally can control. However, she was suffering from a headache, an affliction unusual to her, and took some headache remedy. Almost immediately she became faint and then transformed into the Smoke against her will. The remedy was bought by another of our guests, who had sent a Gypsy to the apothecary for it. We suspect that it was not medicine, but a drug of some kind, and that the Gypsy was a spy for Lady Ioana Florescu."

All this information caused the doctor to sway a little in his seat as he took it all in.

"I see," he said faintly. He cleared his throat. "I don't think that . . . that I can do anything to . . . change the—her—back."

"We are well aware of that," Dacia snapped.

"Now, Miss Vreeholt," the queen said, quietly but with a warning in her voice. She addressed the doctor. "It's not that; it's just that we wanted you to look at the powder that she took, and see if you could recognize the ingredients. It might help us to cure her."

"Cure her? You mean, make her—"

"Make her able to transform at will," Dacia interrupted. She did not want to hear what the physician was about to say. Normal. *Human.* No matter what word his lips had been about to form, she was certain that she would not like it.

"Oh. Yes. I will look at it," Dr. Ionescu said.

He stood up, and the queen rose as well, offering him the two saucers, one with its twist of paper, the other with a teacup and spoon. He looked at them, and sniffed the dregs of the tea.

"She drank from this?"

"Yes," the queen said. "She stirred it into the tea herself. And we all drank from the same pot, so it was not in the tea."

"Very good." He paused, and looked around. "May I use your stillroom? I need a spirit burner, and perhaps some small dishes . . . ?"

"Of course, Doctor," the queen said.

She rang for a maid to assist Dr. Ionescu. When she came,

the maid bobbed a curtsy and held out a tray for the saucers, oblivious to Lou.

As they were leaving, Dr. Ionescu turned to Dacia one last time. Dacia and, she noticed with surprise, Lou.

"I did not mean to offend," he said stiffly, and gave a little bow.

"I understand," Dacia said as graciously as she could manage.

And she did. It must have come as a nasty shock to imagine that he was going to soothe some ailment of the queen's—a fever, perhaps, or a bout of indigestion—only to find that there were creatures of local legend in the palace, and that they needed his help.

"I don't think you do," Dr. Ionescu said. "I—I loved your mother very much, once." His hand rose to his ear again. "But she was a Florescu."

And then he followed the maid out, leaving both Dacia and the queen at a loss.

To my beloved and noble parents,

Think of me with fondness, if I do not survive the coming night, and forgive me if I have offended you. I aligned myself with the Society, despite Father's wishes, because Grandfather and Uncle Joseph turned my foolish head with talk of fighting for the side of righteousness, and of adventure and glory to be had. Instead I have found horror, and sorrow, and now (if you are, indeed, reading this letter) death, though I do not blame Grandfather, nor my uncle. I chose this for myself, and must see it through to the end.

It grieves me that I shall not see you again. It grieves me that the side of the right may not win this battle. And it grieves me to say that I cannot see the world as starkly as Grandfather does anymore. Is everyone born to power a villain? Have these so-called monsters against which we battle chosen the path of darkness? Were they free to choose their path at all? These questions plague me.

Mother, if I die, I beg of you to send Grandmother's amber necklace, which she left to me, to Miss Maria Louisa Neulander of New York City. I know that it was to be given to my future bride, but as there may not be a future bride, I wish this young lady to have it as an apology for the many ways in which I wronged her.

Farewell, my father. Farewell, my mother.

God be with you.

Your devoted son,
Theophilus Xavier Arkady

(Written this 17th day of June, the year of Our Lord,
Eighteen hundred and ninety-seven)

# SINAIA

Night was falling, and Lou was losing herself.

She had to concentrate to hold herself into a column of Smoke. Her body—her Smoke body—wanted to simply dissemble, to waft away on a million currents of air. If it did that, she knew, she would be nothingness.

*It must not happen*, she told herself firmly. *You are Maria Louisa Neulander. Be strong. You are approximately five feet, two inches tall. Hold yourself together. You are curvaceous of figure, a houri!* Just thinking that word sent a scandalous thrill through her. She concentrated on that, on the memories of meeting Mr. Arkady . . . Theo! So dark and dangerous—strange to think that he was only a year or two older than she, and yet his life held so much more. He didn't spend days shopping or going to parties; he was trying to help people by fighting against—

No. She was dissolving. Thinking about what Theo was fighting against, namely her family, was dangerous territory. She had to try something else.

Distressed, she moved around the sofa, wanting to shift from foot to foot in anxiety the way she had when she was younger. The movement forced all her particles together, and she froze in shock. Was that the key? If she kept in motion, would she hold together? She soared around the room, and found that it was true.

Dacia rose in alarm, following her progress around the room. "Lou, are you all right?"

How could she answer? She tried to speak to Dacia as she had spoken to Radu the night before, but Dacia didn't hear her. Was it because Radu had been in his Claw form then? Or was it because she had been forced into the Smoke now? Either way, she could not communicate with her cousin. Nor had she any desire to spend the night swirling around the room like a deranged ghost. There had to be a way she could be of use. After all, they were expecting an attack, and who could say how large Prince Mihai's force would be?

Of course.

She could spy on Mihai. She could find Lady Ioana and the rest of the family, and uncover their preparations. She might even find the cure for what had happened to her. And if she didn't . . . well, she would figure out some way to tell Dacia what she discovered.

Lou went to Dacia and caressed her cousin's cheek with a tendril of Smoke by way of reassurance. Then she went to the window and flowed out a crack between the pane and the frame, and she was in the open air.

Letting her body go as much as she dared, she filtered herself through the air, searching for a sound, a scent, a flavor, that she recognized. Lady Ioana, Prince Mihai, even Radu would do to lead her to their enemies. She let the wind carry her down and around, skirling through the trees that filled the park around Peles Castle.

It was afternoon now. Mihai's force had to be nearby, if they were going to attack at night. An army marching through the streets would attract attention, even if they waited until night-fall. Mihai was too clever for that, she thought. He would have brought his men in slowly, and hidden them somewhere. Vlad the Impaler had come a day in advance, and scouted out the sultan's army himself. It was unlikely that Mihai could disguise himself well enough to get into the palace, but perhaps one of his—

There!

It was Radu, down by the cathedral. It was a very old cathedral, with a monastery surrounding it, and the king had promised to build a larger church for the monks as soon as construction on the palace was finished.

Lou drifted down slowly, pulling herself together into a denser column, but hovering close to the roof in case someone looked up. She crept close so that she could hear Radu and waited for him to say something useful.

But Radu didn't say anything. He was standing across from a monk. The monk's black robes were so faded they were almost purple, and the curly hair hanging below his cylindrical hat was snarled. He held out a hand, and Radu handed him a purse. The monk tucked it into his robes, signed a cross over Radu, and left the monastery.

Lou waited, but nothing else happened. Radu kicked at the

pavement, shoved his hands in his pockets, and then went over to the church and peered through one of the windows. That was all. Lou could not figure out what he was doing, and then something else struck her: Where were the other monks? The devout coming to worship? Where were the sightseers, stopping to admire the centuries-old frescos within the church before they toured the palace? The monastery was empty, except for herself and Radu.

*Oh, Radu! What have you done now?*

Unable to wait any longer, with her Smoky body threatening to dissolve again, Lou wafted down and hovered in front of Radu. He looked at her glumly.

"Hello, Princess LouLou," he said. "Are you spying for the king and queen?"

Lou did her best to pull herself into a human shape, and nodded. She might as well tell the truth; it was hardly a secret.

He took off his coat and held it out to her. "Do you want to change back and talk? The others won't be here for a few more minutes."

*Others?* Lou silently cursed with frustration. She wondered if she could talk to him in wolf form, but how could she get him to transform? She decided to try something else, and touched him on the cheek.

*What others? Just Mihai, the Draculas, and the Florescus, or were there more?*

He shook his head. "You have to change back, or I'll have to change, in order to have a conversation. You and Dacia left the estate before we could tell you more about our talents."

There was no accusation in his voice, just simple statement of fact. And he obviously didn't know that she couldn't change back.

Now she shook her head, trying to make the motion look frantic, willing him to guess that something was wrong. She gestured around the bare courtyard, trying to ask what he was doing here, who was coming, wondering how much information he would give her.

"All right," he said, shrugging back into the coat. "I suppose you saw me pay the priest?"

She nodded.

"All the monks have gone on a holy retreat, thanks to Mihai's generous donation," Radu said, rolling his eyes. "Their cells are all empty." He pointed to the wooden doors spaced evenly around the courtyard. "Do you understand?"

She nodded again. She understood very well. This was where they would conceal their force: in the church.

Radu half turned, listening. "I think they're coming," he said, his voice hoarse. "Go, and tell Dacia and the others . . . quickly!"

But Lou didn't want to go, not just yet. Radu's face was deathly white, the dark circles under his eyes standing out against his pallor. Why didn't he leave? Even if he couldn't bring himself to help King Carol, why did he help Mihai? She held out a hand to him, trying to convey her concern and confusion. He looked at her with dull eyes, and she made a beckoning gesture, willing him to come with her, to change into a wolf and flee into the forest, anything but help Mihai in his evil scheme.

"I can't . . . don't you see?" His voice quavered and broke like a boy's. "This is all I have. I can't go to New York and pretend it never happened. This is my home, my life. Perhaps that makes me a coward; but if so, then that is what I am, and I admit it freely." He looked at the gate once more. "Go, please," he said, buttoning his coat as though he were putting on armor.

Now Lou went, wondering if it was possible for her heart to break when her heart was nothing but Smoke. She understood more than Radu could know. There was comfort in familiarity, but there would be no peace for her in New York society, familiar as it was, not anymore. She was just as trapped, only her cage was prettier.

She began to glide up and over the monastery wall, when Radu ran a few steps forward and called out, "Mihai is at the Hotel Sinaia!"

"What are you shouting about?" Uncle Horia marched into the courtyard.

Lou hid herself by spreading thin and clinging to the roof tiles, straining with her whole body to listen to them.

"I couldn't remember the name of the hotel," Radu said, his face turning red. He was a terrible liar. "The one where Prince Mihai is staying. Then it came to me, all of a sudden."

"Why do you need to know?" His father cuffed him on the shoulder. "Your business is here, just keep your mind on that."

"I've paid the priests," Radu protested. "There's nothing left to do."

"Then pick a cell and wait," Uncle Horia said. "We've lost those girls—I can't lose you, too!" There was unexpected emotion in his voice, but Lou couldn't decide what it was. Anger? Regret?

Radu started to turn away, then turned back. "But, Father, don't you think that means something? There's a Smoke after all these years, and she refuses to help Prince Mihai? Perhaps it is a sign—"

"I don't believe in signs," Uncle Horia said roughly. "I don't believe in prophecies, either! I do believe that we're in a mess of trouble, and we'll be lucky to get out of it alive. Now wait for the others!"

Radu fled, and so did Lou.

She realized that Uncle Horia and Radu didn't know that Lady Ioana had killed the girls who were the Smoke. Perhaps Lady Ioana had only told Aunt Kate so that she could test Dacia and Lou? That cheered Lou: she hated to think Uncle Horia's soul was as black as Lady Ioana's.

Busy with these thoughts, she swooped right over the Hotel Sinaia before she noticed it, and had to flow backward to one of its chimneys. She poured down the chimney and hovered in a fireplace, feeling for voices.

In one room, a stout Hungarian man and his wife were arguing.

Two sisters from Targoviste were plotting to sneak away from their governess and see two young men they had met that morning on a walk.

Lady Ioana was ordering Aunt Kate to find Dacia and bring her back to the hotel.

Lou followed her grandmother's voice until she was coiled just inside the flu of the fireplace in Lady Ioana's room. Or perhaps it was Prince Mihai's room; she could taste his presence as well.

"She is our queen," Aunt Kate said stiffly.

Lady Ioana made a surprisingly rude noise. "Come now, Katarina! You are not mindless animals, foraging in the woods! You fought with the girl, she won. Stop weeping in the corners and do what you were born to do."

"Which is what?"

Lou was startled by the bitterness in Aunt Kate's voice.

"To help the Dracula family return to greatness," Lady Ioana snapped. "If Dacia wants to be a true queen, she'll come with you. If she doesn't—make her come. This is her destiny!"

"Is it?" Aunt Kate said, half to herself. "I wonder. And, I do beg Your Highness's pardon, but do you need a wife to ascend the throne?"

"If you are reluctant to assist me, Miss Florescu," Prince Mihai said, "I would rather you left. I cannot afford to have anyone involved that I cannot rely on."

"You may rely on me," Aunt Kate said, after a long pause.

"Then bring me your niece," Prince Mihai said, as if it were the most reasonable request in the world. "I would rather Dacia, but the other one, the Smoke, would also serve."

"The Smoke?" Lady Ioana's voice was sharp. "She is not the queen for you."

Lou would have shaken her fist at the old woman if she'd had a fist. Of course Lady Ioana didn't want the Smoke, the natural leader of the Florescus, as queen!

"Very well, if it must be Dacia, get her for me!" Mihai smoothed his hair, and Lou saw that his hands were shaking and his eyes looked strange. Had he been drinking?

"No," Aunt Kate said, and now there was no hesitation. "As you say, Lady Ioana: we are not animals. We do not need Dacia to take command of the Claw. I have been trained to lead them, but Dacia has no experience. She bested me by sheer dumb luck."

"I don't care if she is the Virgin Mother of your little pack," Prince Mihai snarled. "Bring her to me!"

"I am not the madam of a brothel; I will not procure girls for you—particularly when that girl is my niece!" Aunt Kate snapped back.

Impressed, Lou did a happy swirl inside the flue. Prince Mihai should really know better than to snarl at someone who could turn into a wolf at will. Her happiness also stemmed from the grand news that Aunt Kate, like Radu, was having second thoughts about following Prince Mihai. And unlike Radu, Aunt Kate was strong-willed enough to do something about it.

"Let me make this much easier for you," Prince Mihai said. "Bring me Dacia or I will kill my uncle and make you watch."

Stunned, Lou lost control and slipped down into the fireplace. She saw Lady Ioana's head twist around, and the old woman pointed a gnarled finger at her.

"The Smoke," she hissed.

Roused from her shock, Lou shot back up the chimney and away.

## THE DIARY OF MISS DACIA VREEHOLT

*17 June 1897*

What a nightmare this has become! Lou is trapped in her Smoke form, perhaps permanently, and we are waiting for Mihai and my own grandmother to begin a war! Should I doubt my own sanity? Surely such things cannot be true! Have I run mad, and these are my hallucinations?

No. It is all too real, and most horribly so!

I have retired to one of the guest chambers, but none of us will sleep this night. Poor Johnny tried to get the king and queen to leave—Bran is nearby, and that castle, for all its coziness, is easier to defend—but they refused. They will stand and face Mihai. It is noble (and romantic) of them, but also very foolish.

I insisted that I be given a pistol, and Johnny showed me how to fire it. He implied that I had other defenses at my command, but I gave him one of Aunt Kate's Looks. I will fight with pistol and with bare fists, if necessary, but never THAT.

Humph. Not at all in the mood to rest, but quite hungry. Is it selfish of me to ring for something while danger looms? It's not as though they'll arm the kitchen staff! I will ring for something filling. Must keep up my strength for tonight's exertions.

# PELES CASTELUL

Dacia ate a ham sandwich and drank a glass of milk, then had a cup of tea. She took her diary out of her reticule again, but could think of nothing else to say except to add that she had eaten, but didn't think it mattered.

She lay down on the bed, got up again, and smoothed her hair in the mirror over the washstand. The guest rooms at Peles were rather odd: plain and narrow, and all decorated the same except for the color. Dacia thought they looked like dormitory rooms at a boarding school, though she had no practical knowledge to support this.

She was in the Lilac Room, which was at the end of the row after the identical Blue and Green guest rooms. The rug, blankets, sheets, and towels were all lilac colored. She picked up one of the towels and held it to her cheek, drawing in a deep breath. She thought about her first shopping excursion in Bucharest, weeks ago, when Radu had followed her to the ribbon shop. She remembered him startling her and then buying her lemonade while they talked.

And Mihai had appeared.

Dacia hung the towel on the bar, feeling sick. Had it been an accident that he had encountered her that very first day, or had he been watching her? In a more vindictive mood, she might have accused Radu of leading Mihai to her at the prince's request, but Radu's uneasiness around the prince was too real.

It didn't matter anyway. It was done now. Mihai wanted her, he wanted power, and he was going to destroy everything and everyone that stood in his way. She decided to burn those lilac ribbons when she got back to Bucharest. They reminded her too much of Mihai.

She opened her reticule and stuck her hand all the way to the bottom, under her diary and pen, her comb and packet of hairpins. Her fingers fumbled out the bracelet that lay at the very bottom. Heavy gold, in the shape of a dragon. A gift from Mihai. Dacia thought about throwing it out the window, or down the commode. Then she changed her mind and put it back. Much better to return it—in person, she thought.

Glancing around the room at the lilac blankets and the framed watercolor of lilac bushes, Dacia found that she could not stay in the room another second. She crossed to the door and went out, closing it firmly behind her. But then she didn't know what to do. Dr. Ionescu was still trying to figure out what was in the powder that Lou had drunk, the queen was resting, and Johnny and the king were closeted with the captain of the palace guard.

Which left her entirely at loose ends.

She smoothed her skirts, her bodice, her hair. There was a mirror across the corridor from where she stood, and she walked over to it. It was far larger than the one in the Lilac Room, and much more brightly lit. She frowned at her hair, with its strange mixture of ash and gold strands. Was there more ash in it now? Was she going gray so young? Not that it mattered, her hair was such an odd color, in this light it almost reminded her of—

A wolf.

Dacia put her fingers to the reflection of her hair in the mirror. Her hair was a mixture of colors, subtle colors that would blend into rocks and trees and earth in a forest. Like a wolf's pelt. Aunt Kate's was much the same, only there was more gold in her hair. Dacia thought of her aunt as a wolf . . . yes, Kate had been more of a gold color than most of the others, while Radu had definitely been reddish.

And then she thought of her mother's hair. Her mother's light brown hair, threaded with gold, but with hairs here and there of a darker hue. Dacia could picture her mother as a wolf. Lean, but not as lean as her sister Kate, with a warm brown pelt, lightly dusted with gold.

But of course, the very idea of the elegant Ileana Florescu Vreeholt shedding her clothes and bending her body into a wolf's shape was ludicrous. The thought of her mother doing anything so . . . so fraught with emotion . . . as turning into a wolf was even more ludicrous, Dacia thought with a flash of anger. You had to feel to transform. You had to *care*.

Dacia turned away from the mirror, and smashed into a

tinkling mass of something. She leaped back and stepped on the hem of her gown. She managed to stay on her feet by grabbing a small marble-topped table. She'd had been standing so close to the mirror to study her reflection that when she turned, she had crashed into one of the elaborate Venetian glass lamps.

Embarrassed, she checked the lamp for damage. It was quite beautiful, with clusters of different-colored flowers surrounding the electric candles. With relief she saw that she hadn't broken any of the tiny glass petals, and started to move away. Which was when she saw the writing that had appeared on the mirror.

She let out a choice oath—a favorite of their head groom at home—and stepped on the hem of her gown again. This time she heard something tear, but she was beyond caring; shaky writing was streaking the mirror, adding another line even as she watched.

Dacia grabbed the carved wooden bowl decorating the little table. She raised it high to smash the mirror, and then saw the name Mihai. She stopped, and let the bowl fall back on the table with a clunk.

"Lou!"

It had to be Lou who was doing the writing! In point of fact, it looked like her handwriting, but much wobblier, like she was writing with her finger . . . or a curl of Smoke. Dacia hurried to read the message, which was already fading.

*Mihai Lady Ioana Hotel Sinaia.*
*Family Sinaia monastery.*
*Kate bring you to Mihai or Mattias killed.*

"Oh, my goodness!" Dacia caught herself wringing her hands like some useless girl in a novel, and forced herself to stop.

*Tell.*

"Oh, yes, yes! Of course, yes," Dacia said, and hurried down the hall to the king's study.

She knocked but didn't wait for the king to invite her in, opening the latch and slipping inside before the sound of her knock had even faded. King Carol was bent over some building plans with Lord Johnny. Mr. Arkady was frozen in the act of writing in a small leather-bound notebook.

"Is Miss Neulander all right?" Mr. Arkady's pen slipped from his fingers and he rose to his feet. "She hasn't . . . I mean . . . is she well?"

He had returned to the palace a little while before, deeply depressed. There were no Gypsies to be found anywhere in town, and none of the apothecaries had sold the man the powder. Lord Johnny speculated that someone in Bucharest had drugged Lou to cause her headache, so that the cure could be offered.

Dacia was putting her money on Nadia.

"She has found a way to send messages by writing on the mirror," Dacia said.

"Astonishing!" Mr. Arkady looked frankly admiring of Lou's new skill.

"What was the message?" The king looked weary, and his question was far more to the point than Mr. Arkady's shining eyes and hushed utterances, at least in Dacia's opinion.

"Prince Mihai and Lady Ioana are at the Hotel Sinaia, the rest of our family are at the monastery," Dacia reported. She lifted her chin. "And Aunt Kate is to bring me to Mihai, or he will kill his uncle Mattias."

Having made her grand announcement, Dacia went to the sofa and sat without being invited. That last message had made her knees a bit shaky, but she would never have admitted it.

"He wants you very badly, Miss Vreeholt," the king said gravely.

"Well, he can't have me," Dacia said in as light a tone as she could manage.

She realized that she was extremely thirsty, and asked the king if they could ring for tea. Dacia had been taught to never eat more than a few dainty bites in front of mixed company, but since becoming the Claw she found herself possessed of an enormous, unladylike appetite. It was time to stop pretending any of the gentlemen present would think of her as a marriage prospect and start taking care of herself. She would need her strength for the night to come: it was hardly the time to worry about fitting into some ridiculous ball gown and start worrying about what to do if they were besieged by her own family.

"I'm not sure that I can take tea at a time like this," King Carol grumbled.

"Nor I," said Mr. Arkady, though he gave Dacia a faint, apologetic smile.

"Well, I can," Dacia said frankly. "I think it's best to keep one's strength up."

"I agree with Dacia . . . Miss Vreeholt . . . Dacia," Lord Johnny said, not meeting her eyes. He cleared his throat. "May I, Your Majesty?" He gestured at the bellpull, which was actually an electric switch affixed to the wall.

"Very well," the king said, and waved a hand for Lord Johnny to ring.

The maid brought more than just tea, and Dacia, Lord Johnny, and even Mr. Arkady feasted on roast beef sandwiches and a salad made of carrots and tomatoes. Dacia tucked in as though she hadn't eaten half an hour ago in her room. The king sat at his desk and frowned. Not at them, specifically, but at the wall, as he thought over what was to come.

At least, Dacia supposed that was what he was thinking about. She couldn't really say, and the king did not speak again for hours. She curled up on one of the sofas and dozed for a while, comforted by Lou, who had slipped into the room and now hovered near the fireplace. Lord Johnny slept as well, though Mr. Arkady paced the room, occasionally shooting them both exasperated looks.

Dacia just frowned at him, even half-asleep. There was nothing else they could do, nothing but wait for the attack to come.

Good-bye.

# PELES CASTELUL

Lou found it harder and harder to concentrate. She tried to go back to the hotel, to spy on Lady Ioana and Prince Mihai again, but felt as though she were swimming through molasses.

Exhausted, she let herself thin out. Mixing with the whole air of the castle, she hovered in every room, a faint haze near the ceiling if you looked up. But no one was looking up. They were looking down, and out of the corners of their eyes as well: jumping at every sound, inspecting each other for signs of betrayal. Several of the maids were huddled in the butler's pantry, weeping, while the butler had drunk most of the sherry and crawled into a closet.

Lou knew all this.

She knew that the queen had written three letters and hidden them inside her Bible. Now the venerable lady was kneeling beside her bed, praying.

She knew that the king was sitting in his study, fists clenched on a plan of the palace and grounds, staring into space with his jaw jutting forward.

She knew that Dacia was dozing with her head on Lord Johnny's shoulder.

And she knew that Theo was sitting on the opposite sofa, staring up and talking softly in a language she thought was Turkish.

She strained to hear him, trying to understand, but instead she heard Mihai.

He was coming in through one of the long windows in the music room. She didn't know how he had gotten past the guards and into the garden, but there was no one in the music room to stop him. With a massive effort Lou pulled inward, thinking to write on the window behind the king's desk, but found instead that she could only scatter wider and thinner. She was losing herself at last.

"He's coming!"

Screaming the words as loudly as she could, though she had no lungs, no tongue, no mouth, Lou tried to tell them before she was gone completely. As nothingness overwhelmed her, she saw Theo leap to his feet and shout.

"It's Lou! They must be here!"

Gratified, Lou faded away.

17 June 1897

To Mrs. Ileana Vreeholt,

    I will most likely not be alive to send this letter in the morning, and even if I am, I doubt very much that I would have the courage. And so let me say here and now that I hate you. I hate you and blame you for everything that has befallen me, and I wish somehow for you to know that I reject you and the legacy you have given me: the dissatisfaction with life, the sense of superiority to everyone I meet, but most especially, the Claw. I reject you. I reject everything you have ever taught me. I reject this grotesque inheritance.

                        Nevermore your daughter,
                        Dacia

# PELES CASTELUL

Quite suddenly, the palace was swarming with Mihai's army.

There were shouting men and stamping feet, and howling that filled Dacia with a strange longing. She was on her feet, leaning toward the door of the king's study, before she came fully awake.

Something kept her from lunging forward, however. Someone was gripping her hand, pulling her back. She looked down, her gaze vague, and all at once the world came into sharper focus. Lord Johnny was holding her hand with both of his. She could feel the calluses on his hands, and see a small scar on the back of one, a little white parenthesis on the tanned skin. It was not the hand of a pampered society buck like Will Carver, she thought.

It made her wonder, abruptly, what had become of Will Carver. Was he still in Romania? Or had he fled, afraid of blood-sucking monsters stalking him in the night? A month ago she had hardly passed an hour without thinking of him; now she could hardly summon the interest to question whether he was safe.

"Dacia?"

She realized that she had lost focus again, and looked down at Johnny. His face was white and tense, his blue eyes fixed on her.

"I'm all right," she said.

"You looked like you might . . . like you might go to them . . ." Lord Johnny jerked his head toward the door, and the sound of the howling.

"No," Dacia said, her voice low. "No, I won't. I swear to you."

"John," said Mr. Arkady. "Here."

He was holding a freshly loaded pistol, and another was tucked into his belt. Johnny took the proffered gun and checked it before putting it into his own belt. He took up a rifle that one of the guards had brought and loaded it while Mr. Arkady loaded his own. Feeling useless, Dacia looked around and saw that the king was sitting at his desk still, only he had a brace of pistols on the blotter, and a rifle leaned against the bookcase just beside him. After making such a fuss about having a gun of her own, Dacia had left it in her room.

There was a knock at the door, and a guard announced himself.

"Enter," King Carol barked, and a young guard with a sheen of sweat on his forehead slipped into the room.

"Your Majesty, we're going to take you to the cellars. The queen is there already."

"We're to cower down there like rats? Ha!"

"It's for your own safety, Your Majesty," the guard said with a hint of pleading. There had been a great deal of discussion over this matter earlier in the day. "Since you won't leave altogether, you must go to the cellars!" He drew in a shaky breath, seemingly on the verge of babbling. "They came right in. The guards ran away. They ran away because . . . some of the intruders are . . ." His eyes darted to Dacia.

"Wolves?" She supplied the word with polite interest, even though what she really wanted to do was cry.

No. Not cry. Howl. What she really wanted to do was howl.

She could hear them coming closer and closer, the wolves. Her wolves. She was their leader, they needed her . . .

"Dacia?" Lord Johnny shook her shoulder.

With an effort, she looked at his face, concentrating on him and not the wolves.

"We have to get out of here," she said.

"If you'll come this way," the guard said, giving her a grateful look. He put one hand on the door.

"No!" Dacia startled them with her vehemence. "They're in the corridor already. We'll have to go out the window, into the gardens."

The guard leaned against the door, listening. A moment later he leaped back.

"They *are* in the corridor," he said in a hoarse whisper.

"We have to go," Dacia said, but she felt like her voice didn't have as much conviction as it had before. She was swaying toward the door to the corridor, and once again it was Johnny's hand on her arm that kept her from joining her family.

"There's a passage here," the king said. He got to his feet, weapons in hand, and crossed to one of the bookcases that lined the walls of the study.

"I thought those books looked fake," Dacia said to no one in particular.

She let Lord Johnny take her arm in a firmer grip. He was standing very close to her now, and she could smell his shaving lotion. It smelled like leather and spices. He was not exceptionally tall, and so they were much of a height, with the low heels that she wore. She had a sudden urge to press her cheek to his, and fought it back.

What was wrong with her? She wanted to join the wolves, she wanted to kiss Johnny, she wanted to run through the forest barefoot. It was as though a fog had completely covered her brain, and all she could do was feel these urges. She gripped Johnny's arm and clenched her teeth to keep from saying something inappropriate as the king lifted a hidden latch. A section of the bookcase swung inward to reveal a narrow passageway.

"We can go to my bedchamber, and from there to safety," the king said, leading the way down the way between the walls.

Dacia could still hear them, the Claw. She sensed other, higher voices, that she thought might be the Wing. And, too, the sound of heavy footsteps, of loud voices, carried through the wall. It seemed that Mihai had supporters of a more mundane nature as well.

"Vlad Tepes had thousands," she murmured to herself.

"What's that?" Lord Johnny leaned closer, and his breath brushed her cheek.

"If he means to follow Vlad Tepes," Dacia said as the king

stopped and fiddled with the latch of a door leading off the passage. "He will have *thousands* of soldiers—" Then something else occurred to her, and she put out a hand to stop the king. "Tepes wanted to kill the sultan himself. Mihai will come after the king himself—"

But it was too late. They stumbled into the king's bedchamber to see Mihai lounging at the foot of the bed, a pistol in his hand and a smile on his face.

"He came himself," Dacia said flatly.

Her stomach churned at the sight of Mihai there, on the king's bed. She thought of the bed in the hotel and sweat broke out on her forehead and down her back. No. She forced her mind away.

"Indeed I did come," Prince Mihai said, giving Dacia a look that made her aware that he was also thinking of the hotel and what had almost happened there. He turned his attention to the others. "Now, why don't you all make yourselves comfortable? Shut the door, please," he told the guard, looking over Dacia's shoulder.

Dacia turned to look at the man as well, and Theo . . . but he wasn't there. She clenched her teeth again to keep from making a noise. Theo had been last through the door. He must have seen Mihai and slipped back down the passage before he was spotted. Dacia gave a silent cheer and hoped that the resourceful young man would bring reinforcements.

She gave her attention back to Mihai, which was just what the prince wanted. He was still smiling at her. She clung all the tighter to Johnny's arm. She wondered how she could have ever been stupid enough to think Mihai so handsome and exciting.

Hadn't she seen the cruelty lurking in his eyes? Had he hidden it from her so well, or had she just made herself blind to it because she was so enthralled with being courted by a prince?

"You've come to me at last, whether you meant to or not," Mihai said to her. He held out his hand, the one that wasn't aiming a pistol at the king.

"I haven't come to you at all," Dacia said.

"But you have, and without your beloved aunt Kate lifting a finger." He clucked his tongue. "We shall have to punish her."

"She isn't yours to punish," Dacia said, doing her best to keep her voice low and commanding. She had a distressing tendency toward shrillness, if she lost control.

"Ah, but she is," Mihai said lightly. "And so are you. Now come here, like a good dog." He snapped his fingers and gave an ugly laugh at his own joke, while Lord Johnny made a sound that was rather like a growl.

"Here now," said the guard, indignant.

"Oh, so there's more than one dog in the room?" Mihai smirked. "Or should I say, more than two?" He looked past Dacia to the guard. "Far too many for my taste."

He shot the guard.

The bullet tore past Dacia, a streak of heat that made her shriek a little, and then the poor guard groaned and fell to the floor, a bullet through his chest. Blood began to gush out, and Lord Johnny pulled her away, putting an arm protectively around her, and moving her closer to King Carol, who hadn't said a word, or taken his eyes off Prince Mihai.

"Have done, Mihai," said King Carol. "Have done, before

more people must die. Your claim to my throne is the thinnest of excuses for your cruelty."

"Your claim to *my* throne is nonexistent, you Hungarian bastard!" Mihai leaped to his feet, baring his teeth at the king with his snarled words.

The curtains stirred, though there was no draft that Dacia could feel.

"You are a Hungarian bastard yourself," Dacia said coolly, causing both the king and Mihai to turn to her with expressions of equal parts astonishment and irritation. "His Majesty is not, in fact, a bastard, while your ancestors rather eschewed formal marriage, so you can hardly bandy that word about, Mihai." She released Lord Johnny's arm, and smoothed the front of her gown, doing her best not to look down at the guard's body as it bled onto the dark-colored rug. "Nor, as I've said, can you throw insults on the Hungarians. My understanding is that you are more Hungarian than Romanian yourself. Your family shouldn't have put mine in quite such a lowly role. Had we intermarried a bit more, you'd have real Romanian blood, and perhaps acquired some powers of your own."

"I don't need to have your monstrous powers," Mihai snapped. "I need only to command them. And even without your family, I have an army behind me, waiting for me to kill the usurper and take my rightful place as ruler."

"I am not a monster," Dacia said.

She knew then that she believed it: whatever she was, she was not a monster. Mihai was the monster. Something warm and soft, like the breath of a loved one, moved against her cheek. She smiled.

"I am a young lady of good family," she went on, "and I have suffered enough humiliation at your hands, Mihai. Put your weapon down at once, and stop all this foolishness."

"I think once we are wed, I will find a Gypsy sorcerer to take away your voice," Mihai said.

"I think if we were to wed, I would promptly tear your throat out," Dacia said in the same social tone he had used.

"You won't wed," Lord Johnny said tightly. "You won't ever see her again."

"Both of you step aside and let Mihai and me sort this out," King Carol demanded. "You can't possibly take the throne with only a handful of wolves to support you."

"So very true," Mihai agreed. "Which is why I have hired an entire army of mercenaries as well!" He cocked his pistol, aiming at Lord Johnny. "And there's no need for anyone to step aside. I'll just get rid of you all right now."

Dacia calmly moved in front of Lord Johnny.

"You aren't going to shoot anyone else," Dacia said.

She hoped that her fair skin didn't betray her by making her blush too obvious. She hoped, too, that Lord Johnny was standing too close to see what was happening to her gown. Slowly, so slowly, the buttons that ran down the back of her gown were undoing themselves. She put her hands, lightly clasped, to her waist, and tried to slip her hand into her reticule without drawing Mihai's attention to it.

"Step away from him, bitch," Mihai grated.

King Carol stepped forward, one hand raised as though to strike Mihai.

"You foul creature," the king began.

Mihai screamed with rage, spittle stringing from his chin. He leveled his gun at the king, and several things happened at once, creating a scene of madness that would haunt Dacia's dreams for years to come.

Mihai shot King Carol, but Lord Johnny shoved the older man down just in time, so the bullet tore through the king's shoulder, not his heart. Dacia's gown fell to the floor in a puddle of poplin and lace, and she was standing in her underthings when Theo burst into the room at the head of the royal guards. The window shattered and men with long mustaches and bared weapons leaped through: Mihai's mercenaries. Both groups opened fire, and Mihai grabbed Dacia's waist. She shook him off, snatching a knife from his belt and letting her reticule fall to the floor as well.

"Put the knife down," Mihai yelled, aiming the pistol at her now.

She smiled at him beatifically. "I won't stab you," she said. She slit her corset and the chemise beneath it with one long stroke of the blade, not caring that she nicked her skin twice. "I will prefer to use my teeth."

She cast one look toward Lord Johnny, on the floor covering the king with his own body. The young lord gazed back at her.

Dacia brought her arm up and flipped the heavy gold bracelet over her hand. It struck Mihai between the eyes and he clutched at his face, cursing. Freed of her Parisian finery, Dacia changed. When all four of her paws were rooted in the carpet, she stretched her neck up and howled. Mihai flung himself backward, scrambling across the bed toward the open window with his pistol pointing wildly around the room.

Dacia paused, taking just a moment to relish the power, the freedom of this form. Then she locked her gaze on Mihai, and growled low in her throat.

"So beautiful," Dacia heard Lord Johnny say as she leaped.

17 JUNE <stop>LOULOU I WILL ARRIVE IN BUCHAREST
WITH TWINS TOMORROW<stop> ARE YOU AND DACIA ALL
RIGHT <stop> WHERE IS YOUR MOTHER <stop> FROM
YOUR WORRIED FATHER

# PELES CASTELUL

Lou was herself again.

She was not corporeal by any means, which was fortunate, as she had no clothes. Instead she was a cloud of Smoke, hovering near the glass ceiling of the palace's central hall. She became aware of bats flying through her—an unpleasant sensation. The more so when she truly came to herself and realized that the bats were some of her aunts and cousins of the Wing.

Lou supposed that she could speak to them if they touched her, but she had no desire to. She knew why they were here, and she doubted very much that they would listen to her. She was glad she had no stomach to feel queasy, as she saw her cousins and aunt and uncles diving down at the servants and guards passing below. The servants were screaming and covering their heads with their hands, the guards cursing, and bats squealed with delight as red blood dripped from their claws.

Ignoring them, Lou gathered herself and soared through the palace, looking for Dacia.

She had barely started down the corridor toward the king's study when she found Theo tucked into the deep doorway of the music room. He was in whispered conversation with the captain of the palace guard, both their faces grim. She coiled herself down until she was level with Theo. The captain didn't notice her at first, but Theo immediately turned his head and looked at her gravely.

"Are you well, my dear Lou?"

She bobbed up and down in a kind of nod.

"I am glad. I worried when you disappeared that perhaps you were gone for good."

His dark brows were drawn together with concern. He had removed his tie and loosened his jacket, and Lou thought that it made him look very young.

She could not answer him, so she merely swished in the air, a kind of headshake and shrug at once. Then both of them noticed the captain, whose face was chalky as he stared at Lou.

"What is that thing?"

Theo drew himself up tall. "That *thing* is Miss Louisa Neulander, and you will address her with respect, sir! Now gather your men and let us proceed to the king!"

Lou followed, since Dacia was most likely with King Carol. But they were forced to stop just as they turned the corner. The corridor outside the royal bedchamber was completely blocked by wolves. The captain and his men froze, bulging eyes fixed on the wolves, who didn't stir, even when two of the soldiers swore and another loudly cocked his pistol.

"Stop," the captain said hoarsely. "Don't. Move."

"My dear Lou," Theo said softly. "The king, your Dacia, and John did not make it to the cellars as planned. We suspect the wolves are gathered here because—"

At last one of the wolves took notice, stepping toward them with a growl. It was an enormous wolf, mostly gray, and Lou looked into its eyes and recognized her uncle Horia. She made herself as dense as possible, shielding Theo. Uncle Horia fell silent, but he didn't back away.

"Could you look inside, Lou, and see if all is well?" Theo asked.

She knew that it was not all well, how could it possibly be? But she also understood what he meant: Was the king dead? Was it even worth their fighting through the roiling mass of wolves, their fangs bared and hackles raised to make them appear larger than they already were? As she slipped between them, she did not get a taste of Aunt Kate or Radu, and this cheered her immensely. Feeling hopeful, she swirled through the keyhole and into the royal bedchamber.

The situation within the bedchamber was very far from well.

Prince Mihai was pointing a pistol at King Carol, and although the king, his guard, and Lord Johnny were all armed, Lou knew it wouldn't matter. If Lord Johnny tried to shoot, Mihai would kill the king. Even if he himself died by Lord Johnny's hand, Mihai would still have succeeded in a part of his goal, at least. And Lou could sense more people . . . men . . . men with guns. But where were they?

She slipped across the floor toward the window, hoping that Mihai was too focused on the king to see her. Prince Mihai was saying awful things to Dacia, but Lou didn't let herself hear them. She needed to find those men . . .

There!

Outside the windows, which were open just a crack, there were more armed men. Mihai's men: they had guns trained on Dacia and Lord Johnny, and the blackness of night outside hid them from those inside the brightly lit room.

Everything, within the room and without, was balanced very delicately. Lou drifted about the hem of the heavy curtains, not sure what to do. Something needed to happen to upset the balance, and it needed to be tipped in the king's favor, but how? They were all armed, but Lou was the Smoke, which gave her little advantage here. If only Dacia—

Dacia! Dacia was the one who could change this. If Dacia were to transform, it would be a distraction. And as a wolf she would be better able to fight. And as the queen of the pack, perhaps she could persuade the other Florescu wolves to stand aside.

But how to tell her cousin? How to convince her to change?

Mihai shot the guard, and Dacia and Lord Johnny huddled closer together. Lou knew that they couldn't waste any more time, and stirred herself from the curtain fringe.

Lou slipped across the floor and glided up Dacia's skirts. Straining to make herself as invisible as possible, she tuned herself in to the conversation at last, so that she would know if anyone spotted her. Just as she did, she heard Dacia's cool words.

"I am not a monster."

And Lou knew that Dacia meant it, and that she was prepared to embrace her power. Lou pressed a ghostly kiss to her cousin's cheek and then she got to work. The back of Dacia's gown fastened with half a hundred tiny buttons. Lou gathered herself together as she did when she wrote on the mirror and undid the buttons as quickly as she could. It took all of her concentration, but once she got the hang of it the buttons popped easily out of their holes. The only thing holding Dacia's gown in place at this point was Dacia's own hands, pressed to her waist.

Then Dacia's gown was pooled on the floor, and she was grabbing a knife to slit her corset and underthings. A gun went off, and the king went down with a shout, while Lou arrowed through the keyhole, unlocking the door as she went so that Theo and his men could run into the room with pistols drawn. Within the room was chaos, outside in the corridor was . . . nothing.

The wolves had gone.

She followed their taste down the corridor and into a sitting room, where the entire pack was gathered, arrayed in eerie silence in front of Aunt Kate and Radu, who both stood, human and unclothed in the middle of the Turkish carpet. Aunt Kate's hair hung unbound down to her buttocks, and as Lou watched she shook it back and began to speak.

"My mother can rant all she likes about prophecies," Aunt Kate snarled. "But look at the hard truth in front of your eyes: the first Smoke in a hundred years refuses to follow Lady Ioana! The new queen of your pack refuses to follow her!" To Aunt Kate's further credit, she didn't choke at all on the words *new queen*. She went on. "I am tired of thinking of what is best for the Draculas. I want to do what is best for the Florescus!"

Several of the wolves yipped now, seeming to agree, but

others growled. Lou shaped herself into a column so that they could see her. Aunt Kate turned when she saw the attention of the pack shift to Lou and looked at her gravely, then she nodded once. It was almost a bow. The others followed suit, at least most of them did. And those who didn't found Radu snarling at them with a mouth that was more wolf than human until they, too, cowered on the palace carpet. Radu bowed to Lou, and she did her best to give him a regal nod.

Lou swirled back through the keyhole and out into the corridor. She wanted to make certain that Dacia and Theo were all right. But just outside the door to the king's bedchamber, she was stricken with the most horrifying pain she had ever endured. Each smoky particle of her body was on fire, and with a scream that was first silent, and then shockingly loud, she fell to the floor with a thud that was all too bruising, as she now found herself in human form again, in agony, and unable to move.

# GAZETA DE TRANSILVANIA

## 18 JUNE 1897

ALL ROMANIA is holding its breath, waiting for news from Peles Castle this morning after fighting broke out in the palace gardens at midnight last night. It seems that earlier in the day, King Carol had summoned the nearby regiment to patrol the gardens, but no official comment was made on the nature of the threat. There is no news as to who would dare to attack our beloved king and queen at their own home.

Two mortuary wagons were summoned in the early hours of the morning, and there is still no word on the safety of the royal family. *The Gazette* will post a special edition as soon as there is word.

# THE GARDENS AT PELES

Come, my darling," Mihai taunted. "Come here to me!"

He was standing behind a large urn in the palace gardens. Dacia had tracked him there after he'd jumped out the window of the king's bedchamber. She knew that he had a pistol in one hand, and a knife in the other. She could smell the steel of them both, along with the reek of fear and something else coming from the would-be king. It wasn't a bad thing, that other emotion he was feeling, and that's why it worried her. It was fear, mixed with . . . elation? Could that possibly be? Was he completely mad?

She slunk closer and got ready to pounce. And then she smelled the other scent, the one that was pure terror, and coming from a source far more familiar than Mihai.

The prince stepped out from behind the urn, holding Will Carver by that fashionable young man's shirt collar. The prince's smile was white and charming in the moonlight. Will Carver's teeth were just as white, but they were bared in a grimace of fear.

Mihai pushed Will to his knees and placed his pistol to Will's temple.

"Your dashing suitor came to my home to scold me," Mihai said. "Came into my very parlor to tell me that I—*I*—was an abomination! He said that he knew my secret and that I must leave Romania or he would call down the authorities on my head." Mihai laughed. "What a handsome fool! My uncle had him tied up and tossed in the back of a coach before he could straighten his tie!"

Will, for his part, seemed more frightened of Dacia than he was of the gun at his head.

"Call off your dog," he gasped to Prince Mihai as Dacia slowly advanced, her hackles raised.

"It isn't my dog, but it soon will be," Mihai said silkily. "Won't you, my love? You will be mine, and you will kill King Carol for me."

Dacia growled.

"Tell your dog to get back!" Will Carver cowered against Mihai's legs. "My father will pay whatever ransom you ask!"

If she hadn't been concentrating so fully on Mihai, trying to guess his next move, Dacia would have taken a moment to be utterly disgusted by her former beau's behavior.

"Don't worry about my dog," Mihai said, his eyes on Dacia and his voice still rich with self-satisfaction. "She won't hurt you, will you, my pet? You wouldn't do something like that; not to your beloved American dandy! No, it's the king you're going to tear with your fangs . . . or you'll watch Carver and everyone else you care about die."

The trouble with being a wolf was that Dacia could not tell Mihai that she would do no such thing, and that the only person in danger of being torn by her fangs was himself. She could not tell Will Carver to be a man and stop huddling there, staring at her with that horrified expression, either. But if she transformed so that she could speak with them, her nudity would probably shock Will into insensibility.

"You're a barbarian," Will Carver shrieked. "I'll have you arrested!"

Dacia and Mihai ignored him.

"Make your decision, Dacia," Mihai ordered. "Life with me, as my queen—my very biddable queen—or the deaths of everyone you love."

"Dacia? You named your dog Dacia?" Will Carver straightened in indignation

The wind had changed, bringing with it a potpourri of odors that lifted her spirits as they filtered through her nose. She knew these scents, and knew that they would change the tide of this battle. Dacia tensed and got ready to pounce, a surge of savage joy running through her. When she felt that all was ready, Dacia yipped.

At Dacia's signal, Radu leaped from one side, Aunt Kate from the other. Radu knocked Mihai down with the weight of his body, and his teeth fastened on the forearm that had held the pistol, forcing it down and away from Will and Dacia. Aunt Kate hit Will from the other side, bearing him to the ground and relative safety. The garden was filled with wolves, *her* wolves, but Dacia did not have time to revel in her power.

She ran for Mihai and Radu, struggling at the base of the urn. Radu move back, releasing the prince's arm so that Dacia could put her front paws on Mihai's chest. The prince looked around for his pistol, which Radu's teeth had convinced him to drop. It was almost within reach, but a little snarl from Dacia sent one of her cousins padding over to sweep it aside with a paw. Dacia looked at the little gray-and-black wolf—her cousin Stefan, she thought it was—and he lowered his head with a whine of subservience.

*As he should,* Dacia thought severely. She would have to think of a suitable punishment for them all, once this mess was over. The Florescus would be led from the darkness into the light by force if need be.

But first there was Mihai to deal with.

She looked down at the prince, and he stared up at her. He reeked of something Dacia could not place, some noxious scent that mingled with the blood seeping from the bite Radu had given him, but his face showed only triumph. He was clearly not going to surrender.

"You see?" he shouted. "You see what a great queen you will be? Together, we will expand Romania's borders across Europe! We will crush Hungary, take Paris as our new capital, build an empire the envy of Rome!"

The noxious odor oozing from Mihai had grown stronger, and Dacia knew it now. It was the stench of madness. And if she had any doubt as to her nose's abilities, it was swept away by his eyes. They were ablaze in the moonlight with the utter conviction that he would one day rule the world.

*I am already a queen,* Dacia told herself. *And it's time that I selected a new role for my people. They will be the protectors of the royal family, yes, but the real royal family.*

And as such, they must get rid of Mihai. His madness and his ambition would only continue to create strife. No, Mihai could not be suffered to live.

She looked at Radu, and expressed her conviction with a few low noises. Radu yipped, offering to do the job for her, but she curled her lip in refusal. A good queen would not hesitate to perform any duty she might ask of her people, she thought. She had read that somewhere, perhaps in a speech by Queen Elizabeth of England. One of her governesses had been quite obsessed with the ancient monarch.

Dacia realized that she was stalling, and that Mihai was starting to laugh, thinking that her continued hesitation meant that she was considering his words. She looked down at him, and whatever he saw in her eyes convinced him that she had rejected his suit once and for all. Mihai began to curse, but Dacia's teeth came down and silenced him. Forever.

And then the battle began.

Soldiers in nondescript coats—mercenaries, most likely—ran forward, shouting, and opened fire on Dacia and Radu. She leaped for cover, while Radu set up a howl that Aunt Kate joined, summoning the Claw to the fight.

Dacia, crouched behind an urn, waited for her cousins to take up the call, but the rest of the Claw were silent. Dacia knew that they waited for her, their queen. She leaped to the top of the urn, straddling it with her four strong legs, and howled to shatter the moon. From the gardens and within the palace the answer came immediately: howls, and the sound of gunfire.

A mercenary rose up in front of the urn and took aim at Dacia. She leaped off the urn, knocking him to the ground, and bit deep into his throat as wolves and men boiled out of the palace and into the gardens. The green coats of the royal guard mingled with the darker clothing of Mihai's hirelings. The Claw turned on the mercenaries at Dacia's order, but the royal guards, confused and frightened, fired on them all the same.

At last Dacia heard Radu shouting with his human throat, "Stop it, you fools! We fight for King Carol now!" She looked up from the man she had just killed to see her cousin standing naked in the moonlight, and then he shifted into wolf form once more.

Bullets sang in the night air, and Dacia twisted and danced, trying to avoid them. Around her were the bodies of wolves and men, some dead, some merely injured, and she was filled with rage at the losses her pack was suffering, and that rage allowed her to keep killing Mihai's men.

Their leader gone, surrounded by royal guards and wolves with blood-flecked muzzles, the mercenaries had finally broken and were fleeing into the forest when the Wing at last descended on the battle. Dacia hated Lady Ioana all the more for holding back.

Was she waiting to see if they were even needed, before she dirtied her claws? Dacia wondered. Or did she always prefer to hover above the fight and merely watch, like a voyeur? And the rest of the Wing . . . Would none of them defy Lady Ioana and join the Claw?

"Cowards!" Dacia howled at the bats that darted now among the Claw and the royal guards, gouging at their eyes with the sharpened claws at the top of their wings, squealing their nearly inaudible cries and biting at ears and noses with their needle-like teeth.

Dacia gave the order for her people to hide themselves. Mihai's men were gone, the royal guard was rounding up those left standing, and Radu led a pair of their cousins into the woods to herd those who had fled back to the garden. There was no sense in any of the wolves losing an eye to Lady Ioana. Dacia crouched under a stone bench, and watched as the Wing swirled overhead, looking for more victims.

"An excellent battle," yipped Aunt Kate, slipping beneath the bench as well. "You have proven yourself to be a powerful warrior."

"We shall not speak of it again," Dacia snarled.

Aunt Kate bowed her head in deference to her queen.

THE DIARY OF MISS MARIA LOUISA NEULANDER

*18 June 1897*

*From darkness, into light.*

# THE FOREST OF SINAIA

Be still, my houri."

Lou didn't know how she could be anything other than "still."
Her limbs were so heavy that she was afraid that she was now
permanently paralyzed. She also thought it more than a bit forward of Theo to call her a houri again, and more specifically, *his*
houri, but she couldn't speak, either.

But she did hate to split hairs over matters of decorum, since
she was currently wearing nothing but his coat. Whatever drug
Lou had been given had worn off at last, and she'd fallen heavily to the floor. Theo had found her and scooped her up, carrying her to the gardens, where there was a great deal of fuss and
bother going on.

The terrible urgency of before was fading now: the king was
injured, but it was not serious, and he had been taken to a safe
room to be tended by his physician. Mihai's men had been captured, and more loyal soldiers had arrived to search for any

hidden in the surrounding countryside. The Claw, too, had turned on Mihai's men, and were in the garden under Dacia's command, while the Wing had disappeared.

As they went out to join the wolves, Theo told Lou that the royal physician had deduced that she had been drugged but not poisoned . . . though it was nothing he had ever seen before. He assumed that she would recover, though he could not say exactly how long it would take.

The cool breeze on Lou's bare legs told her that they reached the gardens. She realized that her eyes were closed and opened them. She had that much control. Then she found that she could look around. The sky was beautiful, sprinkled with stars, and the breeze on her legs and cheeks carried a fresh scent of flowers . . . and a less welcome odor of blood.

Lou managed to turn her head, and then wished that she hadn't. Prince Mihai was lying at the base of a large decorative urn, and he was most certainly dead. Piled around him were soldiers in royal uniforms, and others in the dark coats of the prince's mercenary force. Wolves, too, lay in broken shapes among the statuary, and Uncle Horia, in human form and wearing only a pair of dark trousers, was directing the palace guard to gather their bodies.

Dacia stood beside Mihai's corpse in her wolf form, and blood was drying on her sleek fur.

"Oh, Dacia," Lou whispered, and it hurt to speak because her throat was so stiff still.

Dacia transformed, an unsettling sight rendered all the more unsettling by seeing her standing, proud and naked in the moonlight, the blood now smeared across her pale skin. Though she was no less magnificent, standing there like some ancient warrior queen. Some of the blood, Lou saw, was Dacia's own: a long gouge across one shoulder, and small, fine scratches on her pale face.

"LouLou, are you all right?" Dacia put out her hand, pushing back the sleeve of Theo's coat so that she could find Lou's cold fingers. Lou managed a faint pressure in reply.

"The drug seems to be wearing off," Theo told Dacia, with genuine relief in his voice.

Lord Johnny came up, a bruise on one cheekbone and his tie wrapped around one hand for a makeshift bandage. He took off his coat and laid it around Dacia's shoulders, and she gave him a look of gratitude through the mask of blood as she slipped her arms into the sleeves.

To avoid looking at the blood drying on her cousin's beautiful face, Lou tilted her head to look back at the sky. The stars were moving . . . no, something was moving across them.

"The Wing," she croaked.

"Let them go," Dacia said fiercely. "Let them hide in caves!"

Aunt Kate joined them, lithe and beautiful as a nymph in the moonlight, and as unconcerned about her state of undress.

"It's not as simple as that," she chided Dacia, her eyes on the sky. "Lady Ioana leads them, and she is not someone to be trifled with."

"I'll go," Lou mumbled. No one looked at her. She cleared her throat. "I'll go," she said, a bit louder this time. She could feel the Smoke beneath her skin, taste it on her tongue. Her power was returning to her as the paralysis faded.

"Lou, don't be silly," Dacia began.

But it was too late. Lou flowed out of Theo's coat and into the sky, arcing after the Wing like an arrow.

She soon caught up to them; the taste of them in the air guided Lou, and they were flying against the wind, which didn't bother Lou at all. She went straight for the front of the cluster of bats, where she knew she would find Lady Ioana. Her grandmother was distinctive in both her scent and the gray down her back, and in a heartbeat Lou surrounded her with Smoke and began to squeeze.

As much as she dared, Lou became dense. She tried to see how close she could come without actually reverting to her human shape, pinning Lady Ioana's wings to her side. The aging matriarch began to sink toward the earth, and Lou with her. She fought to hold herself together without becoming fully human and falling to her death. She concentrated so hard on this that she didn't notice how close they were getting to the trees below until they suddenly crashed through branches and landed in the crook of a beech's limbs.

Lady Ioana transformed to her human form, clinging precariously to the branches and forcing Lou's smoky hold to dissolve. Lou positioned herself on a branch a little ways away and changed as well. She had a thing or two to say to her grandmother, and she wanted a mouth to speak with, to make certain that the old woman understood her.

"You have betrayed a king, and forced our family to share your shame," Lou hissed, the hate in her voice surprising her, but not Lady Ioana, who merely gave her a haughty look. Before the old woman could say anything in her defense (or spread more poison, since Lou knew it was unlikely that her grandmother would see the need to defend herself), Lou continued on.

"You had me drugged! I could have died! And so could Dacia, fighting with Mihai! And now she's killed him—you made a murderer of your own granddaughter!"

"I did nothing of the sort," Lady Ioana snapped. "Dacia chose her own fate, just as you chose yours. We are Florescus, we have great power!"

"Which you have chosen to use for evil!"

"It is not evil to use one's power the way God intended it to be used!" The old woman clenched a gnarled fist in Lou's face, and Lou did her best not to flinch away. "Mihai could have made us great! Mihai would have risen to the highest heights, with our family surrounding him!"

"Well, he's dead now," Lou shot back, ignoring the sickening lurch she felt in her stomach at saying it again. She wondered if it would ever be easier to think about Mihai . . . and Dacia . . .

"You have destroyed the future of this family, and our country," Lady Ioana said. "If I could strip you of your powers, I would! You, Dacia, Radu, and all the Claw! They are traitors, and they will be made to pay!"

"You are an unnatural creature," Lou sputtered. Lady Ioana began to sneer, but Lou cut her off. "Not because of your powers, but because of the blackness of your heart! Murderer!"

"I am a murderer, Dacia is a murderer, in your eyes we are all murderers," Lady Ioana said in a taunting voice. "What does it matter anymore?"

"It matters," Lou said. "It matters that you killed your own granddaughters! Mihai deserved to die, but did they?"

"They would have taken my power from me," Lady Ioana said as though it were obvious. "They would have taken all that I have fought for! Katarina weakly let you live, and see how much destruction *you* have brought!"

"I haven't destroyed anything," Lou protested.

"That is because you don't understand what really matters. Family. Power."

"No, I—" Lou began to argue, but her grandmother cut her off.

"You little fool," said Lady Ioana with disgust. "I am done with you!"

And she flung herself backward out of the tree. Lou screamed and stretched out a hand reflexively, but her grandmother changed into her bat form before she could be hurt, and flapped off. The others of the Wing, who had been circling the tree in consternation, flew after her, chittering in relief.

Lou tried to go after her, but couldn't find the strength. Flying at Lady Ioana's left wing was a bat who used to be Lou's mother. Lou could not bring herself to face her mama, not tonight. And what would happen if Lou did capture Lady Ioana? Would her grandmother be imprisoned? Executed? She was evil, but she was also a very old woman.

Lou couldn't be responsible for that. She was not like her grandmother.

Well, not like her Florescu grandmother, anyway.

With the last of her strength she became Smoke and

slithered out of the tree. She oozed back to the palace grounds and into Theo's coat, which he still cradled in his arms like a baby.

"Are you well, my houri?" His voice was tender, and Lou blushed.

"Did you catch that old bat?" Dacia licked her lips in anticipation, then grimaced as she tasted some of the blood that was still smeared across her face.

"I did," Lou said. "She threatened us all, but there was nothing I could do . . ."

She felt foolish now, and weak. Lady Ioana was completely without scruples, and should have been stopped at all costs.

"Does she know that Mihai is dead?" Aunt Kate was wearing a soldier's coat with a darkly stained bullet hole in the left breast.

"Yes," Lou said shortly.

"Well, there's that at least," Kate said. "She'll want revenge for our betrayal, but at least she knows not to try and instigate another coup."

"What shall we do now?" Lord Johnny looked around, chewing his lower lip. "The king and queen are safe, I think all of Mihai's men have been captured. We need to see to the bodies, and Mr. Carver—"

"Must we?" Dacia hunched her shoulders. She raised her sleeve and scrubbed at the blood on her face, wavering a little where she stood as though her legs weren't very steady.

"I know what to do," Aunt Kate said, a touch ominously.

Dacia looked up. "No!"

"No, please!" Lou struggled down from Theo's arms, trying to make herself taller, but she'd been closer to her aunt's eye level when she was being carried. "Aunt Kate, I can't stand any more killing!"

"I am trying to show our family a better way," Dacia said at the same time.

Aunt Kate looked at them in great astonishment. "Dacia! My dear Lou! You don't think . . . Good heavens! I have no intention of *killing* William Carver! I've known him since he was in short pants! You and Dacia should go to bed at once, there has been entirely too much excitement this evening!"

Lou stared at her aunt for a moment, and then she started laughing. It wasn't her usual laugh; no, it was the laugh of a mad-woman. Staring at Aunt Kate, who was wearing a dead soldier's coat but still sounding exactly as she always did in the parlor at home in New York, Lou laughed and laughed.

She only got herself under control when Dacia started to sob.

24 June 1897

Dear Mr. Carver,

I am quite distressed at your accusations, and little know how to reply.

However, I must say that your ludicrous stories about my family are hurtful in the extreme, and your insistence that we were involved in the murder of a Romanian aristocrat has had me prostrate with horror these past two days.

I can only hope that you seek help for these delusions. It is shocking to find a gentleman of your tender years so indulging in drink, and I hope that you can find the strength to stop before you come to grief. Far be it from me to harm anyone's reputation through malicious gossip, but if you persist in spreading these lies about my family, I will be forced to counter your slander with the true tale of how you were found, drunk and raving, in the gardens of Peles Castle last week!

I think it best if you and I have no further contact, save that which polite society demands of us.

With best wishes for your recovery,
Dacia Vreeholt

# STRADA SILVESTRU

Give it to me! Give it to meeeee!"

"It's mine!"

A book sailed past Dacia's ear as she sat at the little writing desk in the corner of the sitting room. It hit the wall and fell, cover askew, beside the letter she was just finishing. Without looking around, she picked up the book, straightened the crumpled pages, and then put it down at the edge of the desk before blotting her letter. She calmly addressed an envelope while the whining behind her became screaming, put the letter inside, sealed it, and rang for a footman.

"Please deliver this by hand," she instructed the footman, raising her voice to be heard over the racket that her twin cousins were making. The footman took the envelope and fled with relief, and Dacia went to the doorway and called across the entrance hall to Radu, who was in the library with his father and Uncle Daniel.

"What is going on in here?" Radu said when he came in.

He looked in disbelief at Lou's younger brothers, who were scuffling on the floor for possession of a single, now very crushed and unappetizing, doughnut.

"Hold them down," Dacia said.

Radu reached down and grabbed each of the twins by his collar, picking them up and pinning them to the sofa with one movement. Dacia went to the writing desk and got the book they had thrown and came back to face them.

"Be quiet and listen to me, both of you," Dacia said, after getting their attention by smacking the book loudly into her palm.

"Why should we?" David looked at her sullenly.

"Because if you don't, I'll turn into a wolf and bite the both of you," Dacia said in a low voice.

That silenced both of them. They had heard some very strange things since arriving in Bucharest with their father a few days before. First from eavesdropping on Lou and Dacia as they told Uncle Cyrus their story, then from having a disheveled Will Carver, still unwashed and reeking of whiskey, arrive on the doorstep to accuse Lou and Dacia of being murderers.

"You can't really—" began Adam, but Dacia interrupted him.

"Oh, can't I? Are you really willing to risk testing me?" She leaned over them, and they shrank back. "Your mother is gone, and I am sorry. I do not know if you will ever see her again. If you wish to cry for her, by all means cry for her, but the rest of your bad behavior stops today.

"There will be no more fighting, whining, screaming,

stealing, lying, or arguing. You will do your lessons quietly and stop playing pranks on your tutors. You will speak with respect at all times, and above all you will be kind to your sister.

"You are Neulanders," Dacia reminded them, "from a very old New York family, and also Florescus, from an even older line. You will start acting like it. Today."

"What if we don't want to?" Adam had his lower lip out so far a raven could have perched on it.

"Radu," Dacia said.

Radu grinned. He leaned over the back of the sofa, so that the twins could see him grinning. As they watched in horror, his teeth became longer and longer, and his face stretched to accommodate them.

Dacia smiled. "Do I make my point?"

The twins looked back at Dacia, whose hands had shortened while her nails had grown increasingly long and hard. With apparent casualness, she scratched three long lines in the soft leather cover of the much-abused book. The boys nodded.

"Good. You may go."

The twins fled from the room, and Lord Johnny came in, chuckling. Dacia quickly returned her hands to normal.

"That was brilliant," he told her.

"Thank you," Dacia said, putting the book down in embarrassment.

"Nice to see you," Radu told the young lord. "I'll just be going . . . ?" He edged toward the door, shooting Dacia a wink.

"Actually, I need to speak to both of you. And to Lou," Lord Johnny said.

"She's gone to lunch somewhere with Theo," Dacia said, a little bubble of pleasure rising in her chest at the thought.

She was coming to terms a little more each day with her murder—execution—of Mihai and his men. Her nightmares did not cease, but she thought they might as time blurred the edges of the memory. She knew that it troubled Lou a great deal also, though her cousin seemed more concerned about the whereabouts of Lady Ioana, and her mother, of course. But Lou was blossoming under her newfound power, and also under the tender attentions of Theo Arkady, who had met with Lou's father's approval as well.

"Ah, he'll probably tell her, then," said Lord Johnny. At Dacia's gesture, he seated himself on the sofa so lately occupied by the terrified Terrible Twins.

"Tell her what?" Dacia sank down on a chair opposite, steeling herself for more bad news.

Radu hovered between sofa and chair, clearly torn as to what to do. Radu had done a lot of hovering lately. He seemed relieved that the Wing were gone, and that the Claw had sworn fealty to King Carol, promising to plot no more against the rightful king. But even though his part in the treasonous attack had been unwilling, he still smelled of guilt at times.

"I have an offer for you, from my employer," Lord Johnny said.

"Your . . . employer?"

"The head of our Society," Lord Johnny clarified. "He would like to invite you . . . that is, you, Dacia, Radu, Lou, Miss Katarina, and any other Florescu who might be interested, to join us in our battle against people such as Mihai."

There was a long silence.

"This represents a very bold move on the part of the Society," Lord Johnny said, somewhat awkwardly. "This is the first time that persons who are known to have . . . natural power . . . have been offered a position with us."

"Instead of just being hunted down?" Dacia said, but without any malice.

"Er, yes," Johnny said, sheepish.

"Well," Radu said finally. "I can speak only for myself, of course, but I'm certainly willing," he said with a faint grimace that was belied by his pleased smell.

"Capital!" Lord Johnny stood up and shook hands with Radu.

"I'll go tell Aunt Kate," Radu said, ducking out of the sitting room. "Maybe this will bring her out of her room."

Their aunt had retreated to her room the morning after the Night Attack.

Mattias Dracula, though he had quarreled with his nephew and fled rather than take part in the battle, had surprised them all by retreating to a monastery in Bucovina for a period of reflection, stopping only briefly to bid Aunt Kate farewell. Aunt Kate had said nothing, merely gone to her room and shut the door.

Dacia was staring down at the pattern in the rug. Finally she looked up at Lord Johnny.

"I know what I have to offer you—your Society, that is," she said bluntly. "But what do they offer me?"

"A good question," Johnny said.

But before he could continue, Dacia interrupted him.

"I have a reputation to maintain, you see," she said, her voice coming out a bit too high and fast. She thought again of her nightmares. In some of them, Lady Ioana and her mother watched her kill Mihai, and laughed. "I've managed, despite all this, to salvage that. My name remains untainted despite Will Carver's accusations and the Incident in London.

"My mother will not speak to me now, however, and my father might very well follow her example. My maternal grandmother is a fugitive, along with roughly half of my Romanian family. So I ask you, what can your Archangels do for me?"

She was panting slightly, and she realized with a start that she had twisted her fingers into the satin belt of her morning gown until the fabric had shredded.

But Lord Johnny's eager expression did not falter. He gazed at her from beneath his mop of hair—really, did he ever visit the barber?—and continued to smile. Then he reached out one hand and took her fingers out of the ruin of her belt.

"The Arc—the *Society* offers you the opportunity to go beyond balls and parties and worrying about your reputation, an opportunity to do what you know is right. But it also offers you a very interesting education in topics that would have given your governess the vapors . . . not to mention travel to exotic locales and exciting company." He smiled winningly at her.

"Exotic locales?"

"Morocco, Bombay, Australia . . ."

"Paris?"

"Naturally."

"Is that all?"

Lord Johnny laughed, and got to his feet. He held out a hand to Dacia, who took it, and he raised her up. Putting his other hand at her waist, he began to waltz her around the room.

"There's also adventure," he told her. "Not to mention romance!"

"Romance? Are you quite certain?"

"Oh, yes!" Lord Johnny bent his head and kissed her. "There must be romance!"

Dacia pulled back. "Your Society is very romantic, then? Lots of too-clever young lords who are going to write me sonnets and send me flowers?" She allowed herself to be kissed again.

"Well," Lord Johnny admitted, "mostly just *one* young lord who is planning to write you sonnets and send you flowers, but he's very, very dedicated to romancing you."

They heard the front door open, and Lou's excited voice calling out for her father.

"Papa! Dacia! Theo is taking me to Istanbul to meet his family!" Lou sang out. "We leave at once so that we have time to explore before I begin college!"

"Wonderful," Dacia shouted back. "Johnny is taking me to Paris!"

# AUTHOR'S NOTE

In the autumn of 2009 I had a fantastic idea for a story about two spoiled American cousins who travel to Bucharest and discover a Terrible Family Secret. The story would be set in the present day and be told through diaries, e-mails, and texts. I pitched the story to a good friend who is also a writer and she suggested that I set the book a hundred years (or more) earlier, which would make the Terrible Family Secret even more shocking, as young society ladies of the 1800s wouldn't even have words to describe things like shape-shifting. This suggestion really sparked my imagination, and I set to work researching Romania, about which I knew almost nothing.

My goodness! What a rich and fascinating history! I had no idea that Bucharest was one of the stops on the Orient Express, that it was called Little Paris, and was *the* vacation spot for wealthy Europeans in the late 1800s. But I soon realized that I could read about Romania all day for weeks, and still never really understand it or capture the feel of the country.

And so I suggested to my husband that we take a little trip . . .

In the spring of 2010 my husband and I took a private tour through Romania with our guide, Horia Matei of Adventure Transylvania. Horia took us to palaces and fortresses, cathedrals and graveyards, monasteries and museums and farmhouses. It was the trip of a lifetime! I wrote pages of notes and descriptions and took hundreds of pictures.

I started this book in Romania and finished it back home in Utah. I know it doesn't fully do justice to the rich culture and history of Romania, but I did the best I could, and I hope that you liked it. If you would like to see pictures and read more stories about our adventure in Romania, check out the *Silver in the Blood* page of my website, www.jessicadaygeorge.com.

# ACKNOWLEDGMENTS

This book needed a lot of help, and a lot of people deserve thanks, so bear with me!

First of all, a big thank-you to my husband, who wanted to go on a cruise, but didn't complain when I announced that our vacation that year would be a research trip to Romania. You, sir, are an excellent traveling companion! (I'm sorry about the food . . .) Thanks also to Amy Finnegan, who suggested that I set the book in the 1800s that fateful day as we rode the zoo carousel with our kids. Special thanks to my kids, too, who first put up with my leaving them for two weeks to travel to a place that probably seemed farther away than the moon, and then with my being gone every afternoon for months while I did the actual writing. I definitely need to give a shout-out to my awesome baby-sitters: Miranda, Ethan, Kelsea, Elisabeth, Emilie, and Sadie! And thanks, too, to the fantastic library staff at my local library, who make it such a delightful place to work and browse.

A great big thank-you hug goes to Mary Kate Castellani, my editor. This is the first book that Mary Kate and I did together from beginning to end, and it's been a joy. Many thanks also to Cindy, Cristina, Erica, Emily, Beth, Lizzy, Linette, Brett, and all my Bloomsbury friends. And to my editors who read the book but moved onward and upward before the work began, Michelle Nagler and Caroline Abbey, who both made me cry happy tears by immediately saying, "I just love Lou so much!"

Double and triple thanks served à la mode go to my agent, Amy Jameson, who not only encouraged me to write this book, but was so patient while I mulled and dithered and pondered over it for years.

And of course a big thank-you to all my family. My husband (again!), my parents and siblings, in-laws, and the kids (again!), who always remain so loving and supportive, no matter how crazy things get! I love you all!